Kidnap, or Murder?

A Story of Family Rivalries,

Diamonds, and Death in

the Vineyards ...

... as told by Richard Sibley

ISBN: 979-8-835205-05-9

In memory of Grandpa & Granny Sibley,
Grandpa & Granny Burnip,
Mum & Dad,
and Peter

This copy for Phil, Annie and family,
with thanks for permitting the
publication of your Grandad and
my Uncle Harold's exploits in
Algeria, November 1942. Perhaps
he's somewhere in the picture, holding
on to a plank, on page 42!
       Best wishes from

            Richard

PROLOGUE

REDMOND'S PAST

THE FOURTH GENERATION

EPILOGUE

PROLOGUE

"In Case of Death"

Jessica locked the steel security gate and strode briskly up the gravel path by a trim green lawn, her footsteps crunching on the tiny pebbles. It was her father's house. She had come out from Paris because of the message.

"Quite a mansion," she reflected, as her eyes scanned the white stairway leading up to the front door, the imposing brick and lime-stone frontage, the steeply sloped mansard roof with its dormer windows.

Slightly out of breath, she climbed the steps, turned her key in the lock and pushed the heavily reinforced door just half open. An ear cocked towards the staircase on her right, she looked across the oak-panelled hall and listened. It felt eerily quiet. She could *hear* the silence, but sensed that it might be broken at any moment. Stepping inside, she shut the door behind her, hung her coat on the rack and began a quick tour of the house to make quite sure she was alone.

She checked the kitchen, peered into the laundry and the adjoining garage, inspected the breakfast room and the patio, then the dining room and finally the lounge, leaving all the doors wide open so that she would pick up the slightest noise as she moved around the house. Not a sound. The ground floor seemed to be in order.

She hurried up the stairs onto the first-floor landing. Four of the five bedrooms looked as if they hadn't been slept in for months, but in his room a blue tee-shirt and a pair of jeans were strewn across the unmade bed. In his bathroom, a towel was draped over the side of the jacuzzi. A purple bathrobe lay on the floor by the door to the sauna. Not like him to be so untidy. Had he been disturbed? Had he left in a hurry?

She stepped warily back onto the landing, and tiptoed up a narrow staircase that clung to the walls, turning once before opening into a huge bright converted attic with dormer windows on all four sides. She sniffed—a faint smell of tobacco smoke... stale? fresh?—then she jumped as a startled face turned and looked at her.

4

She laughed at herself, for it was a mirror on the wall by her side. A mirror with the date and two little silver clock dials. Tuesday 28th September 1999. The hands pointed to 8 o'clock in front of a profile of the Eiffel Tower, and 7 o'clock in front of Big Ben.

Her father called this space his 'loft'. It was a cross between a study and a comfortable bed-sitter, occupying the whole of the top floor under the mansard roof. Bookshelves lined the walls. She made her way carefully between a black L-shaped sofa and a white coffee table with a round revolving top. Glancing across the room at his glass and steel computer desk, she noticed an open packet of Bristol Slims and an ash-tray with five thin cigarette stubs. He must be smoking again. He'd given up three years ago. But then, hadn't he always smoked *Gauloises* or *Gitanes*?

Redmond's 'mansion'

She hesitated, then headed downstairs and out through the kitchen to have a look round the garden. Nothing. No-one. Yet still that impression of an unseen presence. As she came back inside, she realized that *she hadn't switched off the alarm* when she'd opened the front door. But it hadn't gone off. If her father had left the house unoccupied, he would have set it before leaving.

She hastened up the two flights of stairs to the loft, sat on his swivel chair, spun it round to face the desk and switched on his computer. She clicked on the file-explorer icon, and scrolled down the list of names. What flashed up on the screen made her start with surprise—the last file was labelled "IN CASE OF DEATH".

*

On her train journey out from Paris to the suburbs, Jessica had wondered if all those overtime hours she was working in her barrister's office were the only reason she had seen so little of her father over the last two and a half years. Had she allowed her prosecution of a former government minister on corruption charges to take over her life? Or had her father deliberately cut himself off from her and her brothers?

When she was small he'd been a towering figure behind her push-chair, steering her cheerfully up and down the pavements, answering all her questions and commenting on the cafes, tourists and artists in the narrow streets of Montmartre. They'd lived in a top-floor flat with windows looking up to the Sacré Cœur. Illuminated at night, the white dome stood out high and bright against the dark sky as Jessica lay in bed. She'd always tried to stay awake and look out. She'd especially liked it when the silver moon moved across the deep blue behind the dome. She would call her father, and together they would look at that moon, and he would tell her that millions of people had wondered at it, just like them. He would tell her stories of those who lived in castles, or hovels, or caves, hundreds or thousands of years ago, staring at the same pockmarked crust that they could see. "We look up at our moon," he would say, "and the moon looks down on us, counting the months." Jessica would shiver a little as she imagined herself hundreds or thousands of years ago, living in a castle, or a hovel, or a cave, looking up at a moon that was watching her as it counted the months.

She remembered how when she was a teenager, he used to disappear two days a week to lecture at the Sorbonne, where he'd held a Chair in the History of Art. She knew that he'd moved to France in his early twenties to work at the prestigious School of Fine Arts in Paris, and that he had soon become the eminent Professor Redmond Wright, the Englishman who had written a controversial book on British and French orientalist painters. Since then he'd been much in demand as a consultant to art galleries, museums, auction houses and publishers all over the world. He'd been on a few television programmes, then a few more, and finally had his own prime-time series on 'Western Images of Islam'. Thereafter he appeared regularly, by now a celebrity, the expert on everything concerning the art world and the Muslim Mediterranean. His children had felt a little glow of pride every time their friends said they'd seen him on tv.

He'd later become some sort of advisor to the Minister of Culture, before doing a similar job at the Interior and Foreign Ministries. He was apparently one of a handful of experts consulted whenever there was suspicion of a terrorist attack or at times of tension between European governments and countries in the Middle East or North Africa.

He had been quite strict with Jessica and her two younger brothers, Adam and Jordan, but at the same time he'd played the modern father, organizing games and holidays with them and their friends, taking them to judo, football, fencing, to music lessons and on day trips to museums, theme parks or the seaside. Yet Jessica had noticed that outside the family he frequently got involved in petty disputes over trivia—he could never let a matter drop—or in highly charged confrontations with fellow intellectuals about the bigger issues of politics, history, religion, literature and art.

At times he'd been something of an embarrassment to his children. They all wished their father wouldn't draw attention to them as he got into arguments in restaurants and hotels, on the beach, in queues at the cinema or waiting to board the aircraft. Jessica recalled an incident when he had hit a man after an argument during a flight to New York. She couldn't remember what had been said, but there was a great commotion. She and her brothers were impressed that their father had knocked the man down with a single blow, but they had been mortified at the ensuing fuss. Immigration officials had blocked their entry at JFK. If a man from the French Embassy hadn't suddenly appeared, brandishing a security identity card and insisting that Redmond and family be allowed to proceed, they would have been put on a flight straight back to Paris.

Their parents had divorced ten years ago. At first the children had lived half and half, but now they all had their own flats in Paris. Adam had just joined a team of top advisers to the Minister of Foreign Affairs, and Jordan was fast working his way up the ladder at one of the big banks. Jessica saw very little of them, and for the last year or two she and her father had texted each other only occasional messages, meeting for lunch or dinner no more than two or three times every twelve months.

Last year in the summer, he had suddenly retired from the university and begun to work freelance. Jessica had noticed that he'd started spending considerable sums of money. First he'd bought this mansion with an enormous garden, eight miles north of Paris. The house was perched at the top of a wooded hillside. From the patio you could follow a panorama sweeping round from the distant Charles-de-Gaulle airport on the left, over Paris, the Sacré Coeur and the Eiffel Tower, to the skyscrapers in the business quarter of La Défense on the far right.

Soon cases of the finest wines were stacked high in his cellar. He sometimes ate in Michelin three-star restaurants, and he'd shown her a set of diamonds he said he'd bought at an auction. She had been amazed when, just before Christmas last year, he'd taken her for a drive in his brand-new red Ferrari.

She'd calculated that his spending over the last eighteen months must have been at least fifty million francs. How did he do it? Surely he couldn't be earning so much from his consultancies, lectures and tv programmes? She wondered if his absence from the house had anything to do with this recent prosperity. Had his new-found wealth made him a target for criminals? Or had he done something stupid? Could he have got involved in underhand dealings in the art market, making a small fortune but leaving himself vulnerable to blackmail or a feud between rival gangs?

Jessica had to admit that her father was now a closed book to her. He had been upset and depressed at the time of the divorce, but had re-emerged quite quickly, "wiser and stronger," he had said. She knew he'd had some tentative relationships that hadn't lasted, though lately he had seemed more settled. Had he found a new partner? And how on earth did he fund his increasingly lavish life-style? What did he really do?

Her blue eyes looking intensely into his, Jessica had quizzed him about the changes. She'd tried to press him on what she called his "new spending habits," but he hadn't fallen into her lawyer's traps. He'd looked away, laughed, and either changed the subject or given vague, unconvincing replies. "I've been saving for years, now I'm spending." "I made some investments and they've turned up trumps." "Don't worry about where it comes from, just help me enjoy it."

He'd been no more forthcoming when she'd asked if he was looking for, or had finally found, a new companion. He hadn't seemed to mind the questions, but he wouldn't give a straight "yes" or "no" answer. "Maybe, we'll have to give it time." "Not so easy at my age, you know."

She had concluded that although he'd played and joked with them when they were young and nowadays seemed to be quite enjoying life, it was all a cover for an oversensitive nature that showed itself in those flashes of temper. Perhaps he'd always kept his true thoughts and feelings well hidden. Sometimes he seemed to have become harder, and Jessica had been worried by a new glacial expression that she'd noticed the last time they met. As far back as she could remember, he'd kept himself fit with daily sessions at the gym, but recently the exercises had been supplemented by martial arts. And he'd joined a shooting club. Why? He'd told her that he'd bought firearms that he said were kept at his club, but on one of her rare visits to his house, she'd seen him hiding them away in a heavy strongbox under his bed.

Then last night, out of the blue, came a message from someone calling herself 'Leila': "URGENT. Redmond disappeared. Go to house and look on computer."

*

As Jessica scrolled down, her eye fixed on the file labelled "IN CASE OF DEATH". Her heart quickened. She double-clicked and the file opened without a password. It appeared to consist of a series of brief messages and a question:

"Disappearance = KIDNAP, death = MURDER
Beware enemies...
*   Meyers = rivals, danger*
*   Vincent kills*
*   MI6-Geoffrey, friend or foe?*
*   Watch for Stasi, Turks, Mourad*
* Ask Leila"*

Jessica froze when she saw the words 'kidnap' and 'murder'. She read slowly, then again, line by line: enemies... Meyers... rivals... danger. Vincent... she knew no-one of that name. MI6-Geoffrey? The Stasi? They no longer existed. Turks and Mourad?

She had always been good at puzzles and crosswords, and her father had encouraged the children to play word games and do quizzes with him and with each other. Yet now she was stumped by his notes.

"And Leila," she muttered to herself, "who the hell is Leila?"

"That's me," rasped a voice right behind her, "I'm Leila."

*

Jessica stiffened, her heart racing. It was a female voice, though husky and, she instinctively felt, quite sexy. She swung round and found herself looking up at a young woman with long frizzy black hair, dark sparkling eyes, and light brown skin. Stunningly beautiful?

She knew that for once the beauty *was* literally stunning, as it immobilized her for a few seconds. The woman was slim, with denim jeans, a light blue tee-shirt and a purple silk scarf. She looked about twenty-five, maybe younger with that girlish wavy hair.

So there had been someone in the house after all. Someone *living* in the house?

"Where did *you* spring from?" Jessica demanded. "Who *are* you?"

The woman ignored her questions.

"He's gone," she said. "He went away last Saturday, and he hasn't come back. We'll have to contact your brothers, in case I disappear too. And you," she added, almost as an afterthought.

"You scare me," said Jessica, trying to sound calm. "Have you been here since I came?"

"Right behind you," was the reply. "I was down in the cellar and followed you upstairs when you came back in from the garden."

Jessica shivered. She hadn't looked in the cellar.

"What does all this mean?" she asked.

"Patience, you'll find out!" barked Leila.

"Okay, keep cool," said Jessica, who was beginning to find the woman's attitude more than a little overbearing. "You could try to be more helpful. You could start by putting *me* fully in the picture, if I'm to tell my brothers. All these names, who are they? I've never heard my father talk about anyone called Geoffrey. And what has MI6 got to do with him? He hasn't worked for them. He was a university professor, not a spy."

She hesitated for a second, as images of a handful of diamonds

and a red Ferrari flashed across her mind. Then she continued:
"Who are the Meyers? Why are they dangerous rivals? Who is
Vincent? I've never heard of any of these people. The Stasi were
disbanded after the Berlin Wall fell, it doesn't make sense. Mourad
and Turks? What does he mean?"

She paused again, and then added, "Why hasn't he talked to me,
to us? In case of death? Kidnapped? Murdered? I don't believe it.
There's no reason why anything like that should happen to him.
He's playing some kind of game."

*

Leila assured Jessica that it wasn't a game. He really had disappeared, and by now she was convinced he'd been kidnapped. He
did indeed have rivals and enemies. There had already been several
attempts to intimidate him, to rob him, and to kill him.

"So you must have some idea where he is, who's responsible,
what's happened to him?" said Jessica.

Leila replied that before anything else, she wanted his children
to understand. Jessica was mystified. What could that mean? *Understand what?* She was beginning to feel oddly out of sorts, not
herself, as if she were watching a film where she was at the same
time a spectator and one of the characters. She listened carefully as
Leila spoke.

"We first met at the Magny-Cours racing circuit in central France
two and a half years ago. I was then thirty, he was fifty-two."

Jessica stifled an exclamation of surprise, for she could see that
Leila wouldn't welcome interruptions. She must be thirty-two or
thirty-three now, rather more than she looked. And Jessica's father
was over twenty years older than her. Weird!

Leila explained that the Magny-Cours event was organized by
wealthy businessmen, whose companies sponsored teams that
competed in old racing cars, four or five times a year.

"Redmond had come with Michel, a friend who owned an international brokerage company. I was with my boss, who'd been invited by his brother. My weekend got off to a bad start. On the Friday
afternoon during the drive down from Paris he was already making
pressing overtures, and in the evening I had to fight to keep his
filthy hands off me."

"What had you expected?" thought Jessica.

"By the end of that first evening, I'd already said goodbye to my job. I'd slapped my boss's face, and kneed his brother where it hurts, to keep them out of my room. I decided to cut short my weekend. I would find my way home the next morning.

"Perhaps I shook hands with Redmond during cocktails before dinner on the Friday evening. I can't say I remember. I first became aware of him when I went down to breakfast. I was relieved to see that my boss and his brother weren't in the dining room, but I felt awkward, not knowing anyone, so I sat at a large central table, more impersonal than the smaller tables with groups of four or six. As soon as I'd sat down, Redmond came and sat next to me. He started chatting, but I made it pretty obvious I wasn't interested. I wanted to get away, and I was wary of his attention. But he made me laugh, and I soon had to admit that I was enjoying my breakfast. I began to find him refreshing. He was relaxed."

Jessica was astounded. Her father... refreshing? relaxed? She listened as Leila continued.

"He was waiting for me in the hotel foyer where everyone congregated to be taken by coach to the race-track. I must admit I was surprised, and pleased, and... surprised that I was pleased."

During the day they kept drifting towards one another.

"I'd forgotten my intention to leave. We sat together at meals and talked and joked. We walked alongside the track and sat in the stands, and I realized that I scarcely noticed the cars that roared deafeningly round.

"We avoided the dark, noisy pits, full of fumes and the smell of engine-oil, which most of the guests felt privileged to visit. We preferred the sound-proofed bar overlooking the finishing line. Especially after a Mercedes-Benz Coupe shot out of a pit and would have knocked him flying if he hadn't jumped away."

Jessica frowned, but she still didn't interrupt.

"Soon we were both very bored with watching the cars going round and round, and listening to talk about gearboxes or profit margins, how to keep mistresses away from wives and who had the biggest bonuses. We just kept on chatting. In the end we drove back to Paris together."

Leila giggled as she described how irate her boss was at her behaviour—on the following Monday she resigned from the firm with immediate effect—whereas Michel, with an understanding smile, had lent Redmond and her his Range Rover and begged a lift home with his secretary.

"But that evening the secretary called from a hospital at Fontainebleau, and said they'd had an horrific accident. Michel had been in the front passenger seat and had been crushed. They got him out of the car but he died of head injuries in the ambulance. A Porsche with a German rear plate had forced them off the road at a roundabout. The police were trying to trace it. The secretary had severe cuts and bruises, and her husband a broken shoulder and arm. Redmond knew that he was the intended victim, and he felt responsible for his friend's death."

Two attempts on her father's life? German cars? *Two and a half years ago*, and he'd never told her? His friend killed, head crushed in a deliberate car crash meant for him? She frowned again and was about to butt in, but Leila held up her hand.

Jessica was astonished, and a little resentful, to discover that her father—with whom she herself had recently felt quite awkward—could have got on so well and so quickly with this striking young woman, whom she found all at once attractive, intimidating, and exasperating. She wondered about Leila. Was there a husband, a jealous husband, ex-husband or boyfriend somewhere in the background? Someone bearing a grudge? Someone who would have objected, who was looking for revenge, wanting to punish her father?

She hesitated, and then suddenly asked, "Are you in love with him?"

Leila burst out laughing.

"Come off it! He's old enough to be *my* father, I'm Algerian, I'm Muslim, and I'm married. At least, no longer really married, my husband and I separated two and a half years ago, a few days before the Magny-Cours weekend. When I discovered he'd slept with another woman, I left him within the hour. But we haven't divorced, and he hasn't accepted the separation. If he thought I was in a relationship, he would murder me. He'd probably kill your father, too..."

Was Leila joking? She smiled, and appeared to think hard for a moment.

"No, Redmond helped me out of a corner when we first met, and we get on fine together. That's all."

Jessica was not convinced. What if Leila was playing some kind of double game? That might explain the strange relationship. What if she was part of a plot? That sudden change of heart at Magny-Cours, staying on to spend the weekend with him when they'd never met before? He was a specialist in orientalism, a western school of art that Muslims might regard as insulting to their culture. He had also been party to sensitive discussions between Islamists and western governments. Leila had apparently been living with him for two and a half years. But was there some ulterior motive? Could she be trusted?

Jessica decided to probe carefully, to risk asking more questions despite Leila's prickly nature.

"He's an atheist. Don't you ever argue about religion? And you've obviously been sleeping in his bed. That's not just friendship."

Jessica was expecting Leila to explode. She didn't. She smiled rather sweetly, but spoke firmly.

"We never discuss religion. He has his beliefs, I have mine. You can't rationalize or argue about faith, it's a waste of time. As for what you really want to know, I might sleep in his bed when he's not here, and there are four other bedrooms in this house."

"They haven't been used for ages," Jessica retorted.

"There's a very comfortable sofa to sleep on up here," Leila continued, "and you can share a room, or a bed, without touching. You must realize there are many reasons why we can only be good friends. You know, I'd have preferred you to understand, but I don't really care what you or anybody else thinks."

Jessica couldn't figure out whether their relationship was physically intimate. Leila had seemed to imply not, but she hadn't explicitly denied it. Perhaps she was responsible for what Jessica was beginning to see as her father's re-birth, after he'd got over the divorce? Perhaps she was the source of his new wealth? Or perhaps she had played a part in his disappearance?

"It's an unusual friendship," she said casually.

"It's not just unusual, it's unique," Leila snapped back.

No, Jessica couldn't understand. She couldn't understand this attachment, whatever its true nature. But she knew she had to concentrate on her father's disappearance. Kidnap? Murder?

*

Leila sat back and put her feet up on the L-shaped sofa.

"Like I told you, he left last Saturday, three days ago. He said he'd had an urgent call and he quickly packed his bag. His mobile cut out two hours after he left. The problem is... I know he's more than just a professor."

"What d'you mean, 'more than just a professor'?"

"Well, his art research, his lectures and his trips abroad have sometimes been a cover for other activities. And you know that he found himself in the money almost overnight and immediately resigned from the university. Ever since then he's been preoccupied, very much on his guard. On Saturday he suddenly announced that he had to leave, something to do with security, he said. But he wouldn't tell me where he was going."

"What *has* he told you? What *do* you know?"

"I know there's a rivalry between a German family and yours, going back over three generations. I've been helping him to..."

"We should get a detective agency onto it, now," Jessica interrupted. "There's one I use regularly for work. They're very efficient."

For a few seconds, she wondered if her father's disappearance could have any connection with the special prosecution she was working on, but she soon dismissed the idea. She had been detached to a special court that dealt with serious charges of corruption against government ministers. In this case a notoriously violent criminal gang had been blackmailing the minister in question over his involvement in a financial scandal. But she could see no possible connection with her father.

"I think he's been very stupid," she continued. "He should have talked to us. Three generations of rivalry with a German family, and we've never heard about it? Look, right now there are four questions. Where is he? What has happened to him? Why? And who is responsible?"

Leila thought for a while, then looked fixedly at Jessica.

"It began with a diary written by his grandfather during the First World War, a diary that Redmond read only after his Aunt Caroline died a few years ago. It had taken nearly eighty years for the story to come out. Of course your father's never told you, and never told you he'd met me. Anyway, I've decided you ought to know what's going on."

"*You've* decided *what*?" Jessica protested. Who was this woman, whom her father had never mentioned, telling her what to do, taking decisions for him and for them? She struggled to appear outwardly calm.

"My father *is* working for MI6, or one of the French intelligence agencies, isn't he? Is *that* where his money's come from? It's not from his books, his consultancies and his tv work? And you, are you working with them? Or against him? Is it connected to the Islamists in Algeria or the Middle East?"

It was Leila's turn to frown. No, he hadn't worked for MI6, not as far as she knew, though he had done odd jobs for their French counterparts. And *she* was certainly *not* working against Redmond. His disappearance involved lots of stories within a story, "a bit like the Arabian Nights," she said, with what could only be described as a stern smile. She seemed full of contradictions. She was... 'vibrant' was the word that fitted, Jessica decided. Her feelings were deeply ambivalent. She was annoyed, yet intrigued. Wary, yet attracted. This girl... this woman, seemed bright, but she was hard, and could be very abrasive. She wasn't going to give much away.

"You know more than you're letting on," thought Jessica.

She who was usually perfectly clear-minded and sure of herself when pleading a case in court or cross-examining a witness, was now curiously unsure, in fact quite uncertain, about her father. She could think of nothing in his life that could have led to him being kidnapped, let alone murdered. But now she knew that he'd been keeping her in the dark about... about almost everything. Perhaps he really was in danger. And Jessica was beginning to be sure of just one thing. Despite the attempts to hide it, and whatever the motives, her father and Leila were living together. She did not approve.

REDMOND'S PAST

1. What Grandfather did in the Great War

My grandparents lived in Pitsmoor, two tram-rides away on the other side of town, the outer edge of my universe. We used to go for tea every Sunday, a fancy tea with pink icing and tiny sweet silver and coloured balls shining like diamonds and jewels on the cakes. Afterwards Grandfather would take me up to their attic, stand me on a stool by the window, and point out the steelworks where he'd been employed. We looked over Brightside and Grimesthorpe at the factories, chimneys and cooling towers stretching for miles along the valley bottom.

In winter when it was dark, I loved watching the flames and sparks shooting high into the sky, seeing the bright reds, yellows and whites of the furnaces and the molten metals mirrored in clouds of rising steam and smoke. When he opened the window, I could smell the burning coke and hear the thuds of the great hammers, the clankings and clashes of metal upon metal. In those days all the steel factories worked round the clock, seven days a week.

On the hillsides, row upon row of little black houses. I thought that bricks were made black, and I was a teenager before I realized that they were red underneath the coat of soot.

When Grandfather had left his job on a farm in rural Lincolnshire to start in the Sheffield steelworks in 1893, this was at the industrial heart of a great Empire.

*

They said I wasn't to go upstairs and disturb him. He was asleep. There were huddled conversations and whispers, so I knew something was wrong. I knew they were lying. I crept up to his bedroom. The curtains were drawn and he was on the bed, on his back, stiff and straight. Everything was still and silent. I felt his hand. It was cold. At the age of nine, my first awareness of the finality of death. I don't think I was unduly bothered by it.

Trying to act as if I hadn't looked in the bedroom, I went on up to the attic and was prying around as usual when I found a small silver key on the ledge behind the low, narrow door leading into a side-loft. I'd often crawled in there, imagining it was my den. It was scary in the dark. I took a torch and shone it around the enclosed space. In the far corner was a metal ammunition box with a padlock. I hadn't seen it before, and I clambered over to investigate. I couldn't open it, so I carried the box and the key downstairs and showed them to Aunt Caroline. She fiddled with the key and the padlock snapped open. She looked inside, took out an exercise book, then suddenly put it back and closed the box.

"Yes, well..." I can still hear her saying, "I'd better look after this. You shall have it one day."

In later years I only mentioned it to her once, and she was so sharp with me that I didn't dare mention it again. Aunt Caroline was a village schoolmistress who ran both school and village with the proverbial rod of iron. She was not the kind of aunt, or schoolmistress, whose decisions were to be questioned. She died in 1991, aged eighty-seven. At first I didn't think of Grandfather's ammunition box, and it was four years before a negligent solicitor wrote to me in France. He wondered if I wanted this box that had been overlooked when Caroline's affairs were distributed. It was another year before I went back to Sheffield to collect the box and the key, which still fitted the padlock perfectly.

Inside was a Bible inscribed "Presented to John Henry Wright by the teachers of All Saints Sunday School on leaving the same, Easter 1893. Prepare to meet thy God." Underneath the Bible was a stiff-backed exercise book. On the front cover he had penned "MY WAR-TIME DIARY", but the following words "for Margaret and the children, a record of what Father did in the War" had lines drawn through them. In the same, but rather shakier handwriting, had been added a dramatic "For Redmond. DO NOT OPEN UNTIL ALL ARE GONE."

All were now gone: my grandparents the diarist John Henry Wright (died 1953) and his wife Margaret (1978), their children, my aunts Lily (1977) and Edith (1982), my father William (1985), and finally eighty-seven-year-old Caroline (1991).

I do not know how Grandfather thought I might resist the temptation to read his secrets before all his family had died. Neither do I know whether Aunt Caroline had in fact perused the diary. I suspect that, severe and prim as she was, she might have looked at the first few pages, if not more, and then hidden it away until her promise that I should have it could be fulfilled.

There was some irony, as you will now see, in the fact that I opened the diary as the train pulled out of Sheffield's Midland Station on my way to London and back home to France. I began reading...

Tuesday 18th August 1914

I'm on the 9.15 express to London. I've bought this exercise book at the Midland Station. I'll keep a diary so that Margaret and the children will know where I've been and what I've done. It will be a few weeks at least. It's all happened very quickly.

On 5th August little Ernie Rookes the message-boy came running into the office, red-faced and excited and waving the Telegraph. *"By 'eck, it's true, it's true," he shouted. The news had been doing the rounds all night. We had declared war on Germany.*

We ran down to the works. Despite the heat and the din, all the men were jumping up and down and cheering and clapping. They sang that they would hammer the Hun and cosh the Kaiser. "Who's gonna fight?" a voice cried. Hundreds of hands shot up and there was a great roar as they all shouted "Meeee!" Many of them are only lads. That evening they all ran straight from work to the pubs to celebrate.

There were rumours that a Sheffield brigade was to be formed. I was ready to volunteer, but the boss said I was needed for planning the new schedules, and as a married man aged thirty-nine with four children I wouldn't be accepted for service. I was disappointed.

Tommy Harrison and Jim Heeley are married but have no children yet. They looked at each other, then shook hands and swore they would join up together. Young George Golding is engaged to be married. He turned pale and bit his lip, then smiled and said his wedding could wait a few weeks.

Olly Roberts and Jack Anderson, both twenty, took off their shirts and measured their chests with the office tape and started sparring. Jack laughed and punched Olly and said he was too puny to be taken. Olly nearly cried. Terry Knowles the office boy is only sixteen, but he's tall and he said he's going to pretend to be nineteen so they'll take him for service abroad.

Yesterday the boss called me in and said that the new Krupp guns and the Skoda howitzers had destroyed the forts defending

Liege in south-east Belgium. The British army has gone to help de-
fend France because the Germans are advancing fast. The boss
looked me in the eyes. "John," he said, "our commanders want a
manufacturer's view of the German guns. They urgently request to
know what material we can produce quickly, and what's in the pipe-
line. You've been chosen to go to France to pass on all we know."

A tall order. I'll miss home and the family but I feel proud and it
will be exciting. I've never been abroad. Now I'm on my way!

They say the fighting will be over by Christmas. I doubt that it
will last that long. The firepower on all sides is so massive that no
defences will be able to hold out for more than a few hours.

Two loose-leaf pages fell out of the diary. There were jottings about weapons and war materials that he'd scribbled down prior to meeting 'our commanders'. He had listed different firms, and alongside each name he had noted, together with the word 'secret', the goods that they were starting to manufacture: armour plating, gun barrels, torpedoes, shells, mines, grenades and a mysterious project for an armoured vehicle running on 'Holt's caterpillar tracks'. Grandfather had apparently been working for the previous three years with a research group preparing for war. Whilst trying to solve a problem of erosion in gun barrels, they had stumbled by accident upon what he called 'rustless steel'.

So he'd been involved in forward planning, in what his notes suggested was a network of rivalry among the Sheffield companies, as well as between English firms and the French and Germans. He mentioned a man called Godley from Essen, who had come on an exchange visit in the summer of 1913. Grandfather didn't like him. "The young German from Krupp's is clever, but too cocksure to my taste. He talks all the time, as if he knows everything, and he tries to make friends with everyone." He added that nothing Godley had told them was news, for they'd sent their own 'exchange spies' to Essen. They knew all about the latest siege gun Gamma, developed under a shroud of secrecy, that had now proved so effective in flattening the fortifications of Liège. "An irritating young man," Grandfather had concluded, "I was glad to see the back of him."

*

Wednesday 19ᵗʰ August 1914
On the train to Southampton. I'm in a first-class carriage, with

soft velvet seats and a white linen cover on the head-rest. All the men are officers. They have top class accents. There is also a well-dressed posh lady in my compartment. She makes polite conversation about holidays in France and Germany. She keeps eyeing me when she thinks I'm not looking at her. I suppose she considers I don't belong here. But what is she doing on this train going to war?

(Same day, later) On the boat to France. It's a passenger ship, which is luxury compared to the big battleships and merchant ships that are taking the troops over. I've had a four-course meal in a first-class restaurant. White table cloth and napkin, silver knives and forks, fish in sauce, then roast lamb and two veg, sponge pudding, cheese and a glass of red wine. Cost five shillings. I've never spent so much money on a meal, half my weekly wage a few years back.

The posh lady and an officer are sat at a table opposite mine. She keeps glancing my way. Is this how these folk behave? Is this war? Through the windows a thin line on the horizon. The coast of France, I heard her say. My first sight of abroad.

Thursday 20th August 1914

Arrived in Le Havre yesterday, then on to Maubeuge in the north. Not able to write on the train in France. It was very cramped with hard wooden seats and no compartments. The British Expeditionary Force has arrived in the town. There are thousands of troops in the square and they are sleeping outside. Cobbled streets, a few fine buildings in the town centre. All the houses have wooden shutters on the windows. The air smells different, like dank stagnant water.

That lady was on the train again. From a few seats away down the carriage she looked at me. I hardly slept but kept seeing her in my mind. This diary is not a good idea. Anyhow the censors won't let me do it. Unless I can keep it hidden.

Wednesday 26th August 1914

No, the diary is not for Margaret and the children. This morning I was driven in a big open car to a manor house in the country. My first ride in a car. It was noisy and shaky on the cobbles but I felt very grand going past all those men marching. The French have been into Belgium but they are now retreating as the Germans are sweeping all before them.

The house had a huge hall and big rooms with lots of uncomfort-

able old furniture and creaking polished floorboards. It smelt of wax, leather, and wood fires. After the meeting, on the way back the driver said I'd been with what he laughingly called "French and the French," Sir John French our commander and the French chief called Joffer.

They questioned me on our production of mortars, field guns and machine guns. Sir John doesn't speak much French! Joffer is very jolly and fat round the middle. He talked fast and an officer was translating.

Then we all went into a large dining room with chandeliers and we had the biggest dinner I've ever seen. They called it 'lanch'. It went on for hours and there were several wines and lots of different glasses. I said to the captain sitting next to me that I was surprised they could make a meal last so long. "Yes," he whispered to me, "an' yer know, Joffer NIVAR allows ANYTHIN' t'interrapt 'is lanch."

The commanders then withdrew and here I had another surprise. I was shown into a glass conservatory with big green plants and sat in a wicker chair overlooking neat flower-beds. The lady from the trains and the boat came up and sat down right next to me.

She is much younger than me and really very beautiful. Under a black cape she wore a maroon dress. It shaped tight round her bosom and waist and hips and I suppose it was the wines but I felt quite giddy. She talked French to a soldier who served us coffee in tiny cups. It was horrid, black and bitter. I put in a lump of sugar and I quite liked the second sip. To me she spoke English with no accent but I've never met an English woman like her.

Well she's called Suzanne and said I should call her Suzy. She said her father was English and her mother French and she spoke both languages, and German as well. And yes she knew I'd guessed she was following me but she was there to intercept anyone who tried to talk to me for more than two minutes. She was shielding me not following me.

I couldn't think of anything to say. Why did a woman have to do that? She smiled, then said we would meet often and she kept touching my arm and her fingers set me alight. It was like electricity. I can't get her eyes and lips and hands and the rest out of my mind. She talked about Oxford and London and Paris and asked me about home. I felt uncomfortable, really very awkward.

Then she got up and we went into the hall. She disappeared up the big staircase. I'm afraid I was really stiff as I watched her walking upstairs. My driver came in and he drove me back to Maubeuge. He didn't know who Suzanne was.

Friday 4th September 1914

Madness. The whole world has gone crazy. The French attacked at Charleroi in Belgium but they lost thousands of men. Joffre (that's how it's spelt) ordered a general retreat. All our men marching, 20 miles some days. Horses everywhere. They are pulling more loads of fodder for themselves than artillery.

On Tuesday morning I was caught in a terrible battle. We had been through the town of Compiegne and we stopped at a village just south called Nery. We were to leave early morning but a mist held us up and everyone was having breakfast, all very cheerful. They watered the horses and were getting ready to move on when a blaze of fire and shells came out of the mist.

The horses bolted and it was bedlam in the streets. I thought my ears were going to burst with the noise, it never stopped. After some hours the cavalry came to relieve us and the battering halted. But there were bodies all over, men and horses, and many of the most gallant had not survived.

My first witness of battle at close quarters. Dead bodies with bits missing. Arms and legs and heads lying in the road. The wounded with grey faces and open, bloody holes in their chests, stomachs, thighs and heads. Flesh or brains hanging out and white bones showing. They screamed as they were lifted up to be carted off on the long road back home.

I'd never imagined it would be like this. These were professional soldiers, Britain's finest. I remembered the untrained lads back home, celebrating the chance to join up and 'hammer the Hun'.

A big motor car with a staff officer came for me and I was taken away. I was dropped at a hotel called 'Le Grand Cerf' in the centre of Senlis. Suzanne was sitting outside at a table drinking coffee.

She took my arm and I melted. The rest of the day and the night was like they write in books. Walking on air, on a cloud, like a dream. When she touched me I came alive.

We had a splendid supper at the 'Grand Cerf'. She looked after everything. I couldn't believe it, she led me upstairs and we did things I had no knowledge of before. She took me in so many ways *and I slipped in along with her. It all just happened, I don't really know how. It lasted all night and I was quite giddy but in the end I just kept going over and round the delicious parts of her body. It is crazy all this slaughter and blood and death and yet I am delirious with happiness. My mind is overflowing and my body too, it feels strong. I was so full of her but I have just realized, I left her behind and the Germans arrived in Senlis two days ago. She seems to move magically so I'm sure she's safe.*

Here glued into the diary was a small square piece of faded brownish paper. It was headed in italics *Le Grand Cerf* and there was a stag's head in a rectangle at the top. It was stamped in green ink "1er septembre 1914". Below, in neat handwriting:

Consommé de volailles 2   Asperges 2   Soles St-Germain 2
Côtes d'agneau 1, Rôti boeuf bien cuit 1, haricots, pommes rissolées
Plateau fromages
Glaces vanille 2   Cafés 2
1 Montrachet 1911, 1 Chambolle-Musigny 1906
Armagnac 2

What a souvenir! In my hand was a piece of paper that Grandfather and Suzy had touched, and that he'd put in his pocket a few minutes before going upstairs and 'slipping in' with her. If they ate and drank all that, they were pretty well fuelled to keep going right through the night. But his delight was to be short-lived...

Sunday 13th September 1914
I feel terrible and confused, while everyone around me is so cheerful and pleased. Our troops have advanced a lot in the last week. The papers are talking about 'The Battle of the Marne'. The front line is now miles beyond Rheims. I am billeted at Chantilly in the magnificent Grand Condé Hotel, in a small room at the top. Joffre's headquarters are just down the road.

On Thursday last we were moving forward quickly and I stopped in Senlis. I wanted to find Suzy. The whole town had been occupied and much damaged by the Germans, who had left the previous day. The Grand Cerf hotel was still there with its metal 'stag' signboard, but the houses opposite had all been burnt out, mere shells now with most of the inner walls gone, the floors collapsed, bricks and plaster all over the place. I went inside the hotel and everything looked normal, a great contrast to all around.

A young woman called Josette was behind the bar. She told me in English that the hotel had been the headquarters of the German staff officers. That explained why it hadn't been destroyed. The proprietor had left before the Germans arrived and a cook had been brought in from a nearby restaurant to make lavish meals. They had drunk all the hotel's supply of champagne and the best wines.

I went upstairs. I wanted to see the room again, where I'd spent those hours with Suzy. And there she was, sitting in an armchair staring out of the window into the courtyard. She seemed dazed and very sad. She said the hotel had been commandeered, and so had she. To avoid being forced to serve all the officers she had accepted the advances of a handsome German civilian. She told me how she'd spent days and nights doing as he wished and I gathered it had been much as with me.

I began to understand what she was doing in this war and why she had been detailed to shadow me. And perhaps why she had spent that delicious night with me. It was a terrible shock. Then suddenly I imagined I saw his face. "What did he look like?" I asked her. She took a photograph from her purse and said "Gottlieb". There he was, staring at me, smiling and arrogant as ever. Godley Meyer, our young German guest from pre-war research meetings in Sheffield.

I couldn't touch her and felt broken right through my whole body. I couldn't even find words to speak to her, I was paralyzed. An officer arrived to interrogate her. I showed him my pass and he said I must go to Chantilly. I left her without another word and walked the rest of the day and the night and arrived this morning. It was only a few miles but I must have wandered around in circles in the fields and woods. All the time I was walking I could see Godley's smooth handsome face and he was kissing Suzy. All over her body, and she let him do what he wanted. I found myself shouting and crying in the dark and the rain. I want her, and I hate him. I've never before felt hatred like this.

*

By November 1914, battles were being fought from lines of trenches. The front didn't move over the next few months (years, as it turned out). How wrong Grandfather, consultant to the Allied High Command, had been about defences being overwhelmed!

Most of his 'war' diary entries were now about his meals and his walks with Suzy. She was also in Chantilly much of the time though he was very bitter when she disappeared, sometimes for days and even weeks. He was ferociously jealous of Gottlieb, and wondered if she had other young lovers. But he evidently found great happiness when they were able to see each other.

Wednesday March 24th 1915

A beautiful sunny Spring day. We walked in the woods and although it's only March it was really warm. No-one was there and we bathed naked in a stream, then lay in the sun side by side. Several times she took me and I let it all happen. I have found a real life here—the food and the wines and love and the sun on my body and even just looking and walking around is so intoxicating. She calls me her fair Viking and I call her my little filly.

All this delight while men are being maimed and shot to pieces. I still think of those horses at Nery running amok and getting shredded by shells and the filth and the foul smells and the noise.

When she's not here I dream about her. I fear when she goes away she's on what she calls her mission, but I'm sure she's behind German lines and doing it in his arms to get information. Is she HIS French filly? I feel so lonely every time she goes away.

Caught between two passions, his love and his jealousy, he never mentioned his wife and family. He seemed quite unaware of any consequences for his life at home, until suddenly one day in April.

Monday 19th April 1915

On the train from St Pancras to Sheffield. I was told only yesterday morning that I was to have a week's leave, and that I am to get a ticket for the Cup Final. United will be playing Chelsea. It's in Manchester because the Crystal Palace where they usually play the final is being used to train recruits for the Navy. This train is full of men who are on leave for the week.

Well I'm not thinking about the football, it's next Saturday but I am very worried about seeing Margaret and the children. Was France real? I've been away eight months but I'll be home in two hours and it's like waking up, as if it was all just a dream lasting only a few seconds. Suzy, her presence, her body, her voice, she's sliding away. Margaret is moving into my mind now. I've been living some-

body else's life, not my own. I'll have to tell her what has happened.

Monday 26th April 1915

Waiting at the Southern Railway Station for a train to Southampton and then on to Paris and Chantilly. The children were fine. William will be six next week and he wants to know all about the war. The girls are growing up. Lily is fourteen and quite a young lady. Edith and Caroline were a bit shy with me. I think I've been too severe with them.

I went to the office but there was hardly anyone left that I knew. They've all enrolled except for the oldest ones. Little Ernie Rookes was still there, too, all gung-ho for the war. It will be his turn soon. He told me that Tommy Harrison and Jim Heeley and George Golding have all joined the Sheffield battalion, and the lads Olly and Jack. Even Terry the office boy fooled them about his age and got in.

It was quite a relief to go to the Cup Final. Several thousand at Sheffield Victoria Station for the trains to Manchester. All very excited you wouldn't know there was a war, except that many were in uniform, some with bandaged heads and arms in slings and on crutches. An enormous crowd. In the end an easy win 3 goals to nil. It rained throughout and was very dark and by the second half we couldn't see much. We'd won the Cup again, but there wasn't a lot of celebration.

I was happy being surrounded on the train and in the football ground by all the men in uniform. I saw Jim, Tommy and George and we chatted about the war. It took me back to France and closer to Suzy. Should I feel ashamed that when I was with my wife and children, I was missing a love that I pined for? I felt so desolate and empty at home. I just wanted to be in Chantilly.

Margaret talked endlessly about the children, about food shortages and how expensive everything was. I couldn't tell her, and I couldn't find things to say. We were very awkward. I don't know what I'd expected. We'd become like strangers to each other. She complained that I had hardly ever written to her, and said she had given up writing because I didn't respond. I had not realized but it is true, I haven't written very often.

I'm returning to the front but I feel excited and alive again after a week when I've mostly felt depressed in spite of seeing the family and Sheffield United winning the Cup.

So Grandfather had had his family and his friends and his football—the game that became known as 'the Khaki Final'—and all he wanted was to return abroad to an horrific war in which men and horses were mutilated, for he'd found another world where family and football and friends were forgotten, a world where he'd discovered more than he'd ever dreamt of at home.

He was informed that his secondment as advisor to the general staffs had been prolonged indefinitely. Although he was hardly ever consulted now and his posting abroad was no longer justified, he didn't seem to wonder why he was kept on, and he never thought about what would happen when the war ended.

He never asked for leave, and he was to remain in France for the next three years. He seemed totally dominated, as if Suzy's beauty and her sensuality were blinding him to the consequences of what he was doing. Once, he asked her if she did the same things with other men as she did with him. She said she would stop seeing him if he asked such questions, so he never again spoke to her about his fears, which made them even more painful.

After a meeting of the top military and political brass at Chantilly on December 6th 1915, he attended two meetings between the British and French commanders. Haig had replaced Sir John French. By June 1916 Grandfather knew there was to be an offensive on the Somme. Suzy was away and he wanted to see 'his' artillery and machine guns in battle so he asked to be posted with the Sheffield men who had joined up in September 1914.

Friday 23rd June 1916

For two days I've been with the Sheffield City Battalion. I've been chatting with Tommy and Jim and the others.

Last night we were sitting in bright moonlight round a table made of empty ammunition boxes, drinking tea and talking about home. Tommy Harrison and Jim Heeley had just had letters from their wives. Jim's wife is expecting, and George Golding has had leave to marry his fiancée. Suddenly the lads, Olly and Jack and Terry, started whispering, and then Jack said, "Hah! We mustn't forget to empty our pockets before we go into action. All those postcards of naked French girls. Wouldn't do to have them sent home in the parcel if Jerry cops us. They send back everything they find on you, you know."

Olly and Terry laughed, Tommy and Jim coughed, and George went very quiet. Well, it turned out they all had them. Then Jim looked at me. "Johnny," he said, "we're only human. I know you would never let Margaret and your kids down, but we might die at any moment. We can't behave as we would at home. And we have all day and all night to think, to imagine. We miss our women folk, terribly. But sometimes we need a bit of relief."

"Yes," said Terry, now eighteen, "at Colincamps the only people left in the village are a few peasant girls. They sell eggs and chickens to the soldiers. And," he winked, "if yer pays a bit more, yer gets a bit more." George looked very uncomfortable.

Saturday 1st July 1916

6.30 a.m. The Big Push at last. The battalion is to take the village of Serre up on the hill in front of us. I'm at HQ in John Copse. The gradient is not steep but we cannot see the village from down here, only the first couple of hundred yards up to a slight hump. All is quiet and I'm surprised to be able to write. There are hundreds of red poppies, marigolds and blue cornflowers in the fields behind us. The larks are singing. Bees, grasshoppers and beetles and other insects and small animals, voles and mice and the occasional rabbit or hare. I wonder what they make of it all. They somehow survive. Suddenly fearful noise from the guns again. There's been a tremendous battering now for a week. They say the gunners are bleeding from their ears.

Tuesday 4th July afternoon

I couldn't write until today. In twenty minutes they'd gone, half the battalion killed or maimed.

The first wave went forward at 7.20 as our guns lifted. There was a terrific explosion about a mile to our right. A few minutes later the second row of men went out. At 7.30 the whistles blew and the rest went forward, but the last two waves didn't even get to no-man's-land. They walked in line and were cut down by the machine guns that ripped fire from the German trenches on the hump. We had been told that their front lines would be flattened, all weapons destroyed, all troops dead or withdrawn. For more than a week they must have dug in deep under the barrage of our guns. They'd kept quiet, waited, then massacred our men in less than two minutes.

George Golding got back, covered in dirty white chalk mud and dust but only scratched. He said men were lying horribly maimed in pools of water calling for their mothers, sisters, wives and, he said, staring hard at me, "a few seemed to be mouthing 'Fifi' or 'Mimi'...". Some had begged to be helped, others had pleaded to be shot, but the men had orders to walk on.

Tommy Harrison lay for over two days in a shell-hole with Jim Heeley whose face had been blasted off in the first minutes—he died in Tommy's arms after a couple of hours in agony. His poor wife, and the unborn baby! Tommy's leg was amputated yesterday. It had been severed by shrapnel. The dead have been piling up in the rear as they evacuate the wounded. I saw Olly and Jack lying side by side. Jack's face was grinning but his legs had gone. Olly looked scared stiff and he had a hole in his forehead. They were both crawling with maggots. There were not enough sheets to cover them, so I pulled their bloodied coats over their heads.

Monday morning a ragged group of three came back. One of them was Terry Knowles the office boy, only eighteen though now he looks nearer thirty. He said they'd got through the wires on the right and up to Serre. It was only a few flattened farms and houses on either side of the road. They were surrounded by fortifications and were isolated and could do nothing so they turned round at dark but got stuck and had to wait another day.

There were long gaps in the diary now. Grandfather went back to Chantilly and he described bitter arguments between Haig and Joffre, with the latter insisting that the 'offensive' was to be continued. Haig's subordinates were not convinced. Then one day, he listened as Haig criticized the 31st Division for their 'lack of resolve' on the 1st of July.

Haig said he thought a lot of the men had never left their trenches. He claimed that the 31st Division in particular, on the left wing, had been slow to advance. He said he believed many men in the 94th Brigade at Serre hadn't moved.

I didn't think what I was doing. I found myself standing up and shouting at Haig about men who had volunteered, been kept idle for two years without proper training, and were mown down by machine guns after walking a few yards in the first seconds of a battle that had been disastrously planned.

Two sergeants grabbed me by the elbows and pulled me out of the room. I was still shouting. They took me back to the Grand Condé, said I was to pack my bags and wait in the hall. After a couple of hours Suzy came and told me that Haig wanted me put before a firing squad for insubordination.

He wasn't shot at dawn. As a civilian adviser, he wasn't subject to the full code of military discipline but he was evicted from his quarters in the big hotel at Chantilly. Two days later he was let off with a severe reprimand. Suzy arranged for him to have a room in the Hôtel d'Angleterre in the town centre. He didn't seem to have wondered how she had such influence.

He had lost any remaining interest in the war since the Somme massacre. He thought only of Suzy, of their love and the betrayals that he imagined in the arms of a young German lover whose smiling face became an obsession. She had told him that Gottlieb was two years younger than her. Grandfather himself was thirteen years older than Suzy, and he seems to have become haunted by the idea that the age difference gave some advantage to his rival.

In fact he was able to stay in Chantilly only because she was much more important than he had realized. She had somehow got him seconded to the French General Staff. When they moved to Beauvais in December 1916, she had him transferred to a small hotel there. For the next year and a half he took part in no more high-level discussions.

The allied forces counter-attacked in August 1918 after the German spring offensive, but victory still seemed a long way off. Not until September did it look as if the war was coming to an end. Only then did Suzy tell Grandfather the truth.

She said that from the beginning she'd arranged for me to be posted close to French HQ. She'd worked things through their Military Intelligence and our Secret Service Bureau. She said she had been responsible to both British and French espionage. One of her jobs had been to shadow me on my first mission to France. But she had allowed her personal feelings to influence her. She said that for our four years, she'd had my mission extended and had me billetted near to her so that we could continue seeing each other as often as possible. She put her arms round me and said she loved me, that she'd loved me since she first set eyes on me as I sat nervously in that railway carriage going to Southampton.

She asked if I was ready to give up my family life in Sheffield and live with her. I'd never thought about what would happen after the war. I didn't know what to say. She suddenly stood back and looked away as she told me that she was now a very wealthy woman with a hoard of treasure hidden in several secure places. She'd been well rewarded by the allies, and by the Germans too, by Gottlieb, for she had passed him documents and information which the British wanted her to plant.

She then looked me straight in the eyes and announced that she had a daughter aged eight. She'd never told me. She said that after the war she would have fun with this girl she'd hardly seen since she was a baby. Their future together was now secured, and they would at last be able to collect and enjoy the fruits of her work, of the risks she had taken.

She knew that the Secret Service Bureau had tried to follow her, to find out where she was hiding her treasures. But she considered that it was none of their business. She was very angry. She knew that a couple of their agents who had been sent out to keep track of her movements had been killed. One had been shot by a stray sniper's bullet at Ypres. The other was in a trench that had taken a direct hit from a shell near Thiepval Ridge on the Somme. Such a waste, each and every death was one too many, she said. In any case, she'd always managed to give them the slip. They were amateurs compared with herself.

I was lost for words. She said something about the games she would be playing with Delphine after the war. She talked about Champagne and Burgundy, about "diamonds and gemstones, my presents from the allies." She grasped my arm and declared, "No-one can find them, unless they can solve my riddles. No-one." I think she spoke of "the paintings and the little ballet-dancers safe in Constantinople, my gifts from the Germans." That doesn't sound right, but I wasn't really listening to her any more.

Grandfather panicked. Now he had to make up his mind. What was he to do? He was caught, caught between his family and his mistress. The first time he had faced up to this dilemma. He didn't seem to know who he was any more.

Suzy told him they could live together, a life of luxury and love. They could live in London, or Oxford, or Paris, or anywhere he chose. New York if he liked. She knew not why, but it was him she wanted, this serious tall Englishman with blue eyes, and it didn't matter where. Once they had secured her treasures, they would be wealthy for the rest of their lives.

In his diary on the evening of September 30th 1918 he wrote just one word.

Paris.

*

Saturday 9th November 1918

I hadn't seen Suzy for a few weeks and was very dejected. As so often, my mood is the opposite of those around me.

Nothing to do here now the war is going to be over and all the action is miles away. I was sure I would see her soon but I was detailed to visit a field camp near Senlis where they had some special German prisoners. I was told to interrogate about a dozen of them. If I suspected they had been spying I was to get the guards to arrest them. Not my job really but it gave me something to do. They were tired and dirty and smelled of tobacco and schnapps and had very bad breath. I had an interpreter but they all spoke good enough English, so I sent him away. The last one I saw was... Godley, Gottlieb Meyer.

He smiled and looked very satisfied. Still arrogant in spite of being a prisoner, he smoked and instead of me interrogating him, he talked slowly about the war. He said the most important thing for him had not been the fighting or the strategy talks or the comradeship, but his French mistress he'd met here at Senlis in 1914. I wanted to throttle him but I let him talk. I wanted to know and I didn't want to know.

He described their furtive meetings and how she disappeared sometimes for weeks on end. He believed she was with the French officers, "spying and spooning," he said, staring me in the face. He talked about their own love-making and he leered at me, all the while making lewd remarks about French women. He said Suzy had taught him a lot. I wondered if she'd told him about me. He didn't seem to know who I was, to have recognized me from our research group discussions before the war.

He then announced that he had been in the village of Serre on July 1st 1916. He said he'd particularly wanted to watch the battle there, and at the beginning of June he had asked to be sent as a special advisor to the artillery on that part of the front. He was sure that among those who set off towards the German lines on that clear blue morning, there must have been men he had met when he was in England before the war. He had himself been responsible for the plan to dissemble the machine guns that had ripped through the Sheffield battalion.

I thought of Jim with his face shot off and his widow back home with a small child. Of the young lads Jack and Olly who'd sparred in the office and whom I'd found lying dead, side by side. Tommy with his missing leg. These boys and men, my workmates and friends, had been cut down in just a few minutes. I wanted to hit out at the man facing me, the one who'd set the trap for them.

Had he learnt from German intelligence, or worse, from Suzy, that I was down the slope facing him, watching from the other side? I thought of him making love with her. The war was won and I was going to live with her, but I felt as if Gottlieb had beaten me in a series of hostilities over the last five years.

He suddenly started sweating and became agitated. He said his commandant had informed him last month that Suzy was an English spy who had been with him throughout the war to get information about German weapons and movements. She had deliberately mis-informed them about the allies' aims, and had got detailed plans from him that she had passed on to the French and the British. He could have one last visit.

He met her a few miles behind their lines. She refused to make love with him. He accused her of betrayal. She had at once under-stood. She got close to him as if to kiss him but he saw a knife which she took from a girdle round her waist. He had cried out, pushed her back, snatched his pistol from its holster and shot her, right in the middle of her forehead.

He didn't seem to be sorry. In fact he looked very pleased with himself. He said that after a lot of argument the Germans sent her body to some French villagers to be buried. He also said that since she had betrayed him, he was glad he had shot her and that he would reclaim the rewards that he had set aside for her, "the pic-tures and the statuettes." By now I was burning with hate and was barely listening. I called two guards and told them to handcuff him and put him in a cell. He turned and winked twice at me as he was led away. I knew then that he had indeed recognized me and had enjoyed torturing me about Suzy and about the battle at Serre. They were going to lose the war, but he'd had his victories.

Sunday 10th November 1918
Last night I couldn't sleep. I went to the tents and got the guard to fetch Gottlieb and take him behind the wall at the far end of the field. He stared at me and seemed puzzled. He started up, and grabbed my arm. Then he tried to hit me.

I ducked away from his blows and knocked him down, then took my Webley and fired it for the first time in this war. I shot him in the middle of his forehead and then I fired into his privates. I opened his shirt and using the barrel of the pistol as a pen, I carefully traced with his blood on his stomach, "For Suzy, JHW."

The guard came running and I told him the prisoner had tried to overpower me and I had had no option but to shoot. He laughed and went to fetch a wooden coffin. We lifted Gottlieb and put him inside. I looked at the body and saw that my inscription was still there. His blood had dried quickly.

"One Hun less," said the guard, shrugging his shoulders and smiling. We agreed to say that he'd been shot when trying to escape. I didn't care that he was a Hun. He was my enemy. I was pleased that he was dead, that I'd shot him, and that I'd inscribed her name and my initials on his belly.

A few minutes later I went back to the coffin and went through his pockets. I felt ashamed doing that, but I thought there might be something belonging to Suzy. There was nothing, only a crumpled packet of cigarettes, a lighter and a scrap of paper. Not even a wallet with a photo or anything that might have reminded me of her. I looked at the piece of paper and I was sure it had her tiny, neat handwriting on it, so I took it.

Monday 11th November 1918
11 a.m. Bells are ringing everywhere and it's all over. Everyone is singing and laughing. I feel lower than ever. What is going to happen now? What am I to do?

Here endeth my War Diary.

*

It wasn't quite the end of the diary. On the next two pages there was a postscript.

Friday 9th November 1928

This is the first time I've opened my diary since the end of the war. I used to shed tears for her, and I still think about her every day. Perhaps I should have told Margaret, but Suzy was part of a world so different from home that I wasn't able to open up about it. Now I believe that it wouldn't have been right. Two worlds and two different selves. After ten years, for a few minutes each day one of those selves dreams about what might have been. I then have to come back to the self that everyone here knows.

I've often wondered about Suzy's daughter. She will be nineteen now, the same age as William.

I suppose I've been one of the lucky ones. Olly and Jack didn't come back. Jim Heeley didn't make it either. He never knew he was father to Eileen, now a girl aged twelve. Tommy Harrison, who'd lost a leg, found it difficult to get work after he had to leave his job in 1920. Later I saw him selling newspapers on Fargate. He died a couple of years ago, a broken and bitter man. George Golding got home like me, unscathed. Except that the scars are in his mind. He says he still wakes up screaming sometimes.

His scars are from the dreadful things he lived. Mine are from the most wonderful moments any man could wish for.

The saddest was the other two.

Terry Knowles, the lad who volunteered when he was sixteen, pretending to be three years older. He went through the whole war with the Sheffield battalion, what was left of it. He survived the battles at Serre then Neuve Chapelle then back on the Somme and then Arras and Vimy Ridge. He came through it all, such a cheerful lad. He was only twenty when he got home in December 1918. He died of the Spanish flu the next February. I went to the funeral. His mother said he was gone in a day and a night. Bright as a button one minute, struggling for breath the next, dead before the morning. He was a real hero.

And Ernie Rookes, the office boy who was all for the war. He was so looking forward to it. His turn came when he was eighteen. We knew he'd died in his first battle, Vimy Ridge in October 1917. Some years later I bumped into his younger brother Fred on Brightside Lane and he told me what had happened. He said they'd found Ernie in a barn half a mile behind the front line. They claimed he was hiding, that he'd run away. He was arrested and court-martialled for desertion. *Three officers found him guilty and condemned him to death. Haig confirmed the sentence the same evening, and Ernie was shot before sunrise. He refused to be blindfolded. He wanted to show a defiant face to every man in that firing squad.*

There were only blank pages after that last diary entry. But as I flicked through them, trapped between the last two pages I found a sheet of paper, creased and soiled. I flattened it with my palm. At the top was a stag's head in a rectangle, the stamp of the *Grand Cerf* hotel, like the bill for their meal. Below I could just make out the small letters in neat handwriting. "For my little daughter, we'll have fun with these clues one day... But you'll have to work on your English!" Then, a set of what seemed to be rather childish rhymes, under the heading *Champagne*.

The other side was headed *Burgundy*, with a clearly inscribed "Now, let's be serious. These are more difficult. My darling, when you are grown up?" followed by what looked like more clues. At the bottom of the page were the initials "S.B-C."

I looked at the first rhyme on the 'Champagne' side. Four short lines.

> *Once we were five,*
> *Now we are two,*
> *The upstart is vulgar*
> *But my red's still true.*

On the other side, under 'Burgundy', the rhymes seemed to be more sophisticated. They began:

> *Visit ye brothers, who live with five sisters.*
> *On finding the chapter and verse,*
> *Give to each in his language, his colour that glisters,*
> *And he will then give you the purse.*

This was the paper that Grandfather had taken from Gottlieb's pocket. The German must have stolen it from Suzy after he'd shot her. In my hand were her riddles, the clues to where she had hidden her rewards from the allies! Had Grandfather gone back to France to look for the 'hoard of treasure hidden in several secure places'?

I have a childhood memory of talk about his 'holiday abroad' in the 1930s. If he did go to look for the treasure he cannot have found any, for there were no signs of fine living in our family. The only diamonds and gemstones I ever saw were the sparkling decorations on the cakes of a Sunday afternoon in Pitsmoor.

*

The day after I'd finished reading the diary, I went to Senlis and looked up *Le Grand Cerf*. It was there, still a hotel with its metal stag sign, though from the outside it looked a bit scruffy. Should I step in and go upstairs? I hesitated, then decided against. I felt it would have been intruding on their intimacy. But as I was about to walk on, I changed my mind.

There was no-one at reception. I stepped up a narrow, creaking staircase. A dark corridor, faded flowery wallpaper, threadbare carpets. I half-opened four doors. Musty smells, drab fittings, old brown and white photos over each bed. In the fifth room, an open window looked out onto a courtyard. The room was bright, embalmed with the fragrance of a white lilac tree in the yard. There was an armchair, red velvet, where I believe Suzy must have sat one morning, head bowed in silence. An iron bedstead, with encrusted flowered medallions in porcelain above the bolster pillows. I knew this was it. On the wall behind the bed, a framed black and white photograph, 'Rue de la République, Senlis, 10 septembre 1914'.

The metal stag head and 'Hôtel Gd Cerf' signs are just visible on the right. Opposite, the still smoking shells of houses.

September 10th 1914. A Thursday. The day after the Germans had left the town. The day Grandfather found her sitting in that room. The day she first told him about Gottlieb.

Sober and somber, I left the hotel and walked across the town to the military cemetery. I strolled down the *Allée des Soupirs* looking at the tombs and headstones. I stopped in front of a neat grave with fresh flowers, a marble headstone and a glazed oval image of a pretty young woman. For a moment, her face with its hint of a smile seemed familiar, but I didn't yet realize why. Below her portrait, the inscription was in both English and French.

SUZANNE BURRIDGE-CARNOT

30 SEPTEMBER 1888 —30 SEPTEMBER 1918
SHOT BY THE ENEMY ON HER THIRTIETH BIRTHDAY
SHE SERVED BOTH HER COUNTRIES

*

30 SEPTEMBRE 1888 - 30 SEPTEMBRE 1918
FUSILLÉE PAR L'ENNEMI LE JOUR DE SES TRENTE ANS
ELLE A SERVI SES DEUX PATRIES

She had once again slipped through the lines, and been brought back to Senlis to be re-buried. I saw that I was born on the same September date that she was born and had been shot by Gottlieb Meyer on her thirtieth birthday. The very day that Grandfather was choosing 'Paris'.

2. William's Puzzle

My father William Wright was a rather shy man who never claimed to be anything other than 'ordinary', a word he often attributed to himself as a kind of safe haven. He didn't want to stand out from the crowd. Yet he was to play his part in an extraordinary puzzle whose pieces did not at first seem to fit together.

He was aged nine when 'JHW' came back from the Great War. He had for four years been used to living with his mother and his three elder sisters. I once heard him recall the 'trauma' he had felt as their home suddenly resounded to the heavy-booted tramping of a man about the house. He confessed that in his teens and even in his twenties he had sometimes been scared of his father, who was prone to occasional angry emotional outbursts.

In the 1930s, during the Depression, he was an elementary school teacher in Brightside, a tough district in the east end of Sheffield. Drunkenness, violence and crime were rife. Each year he had charge of forty ten-year-old boys. One of his former pupils told me that they all wanted to be in his class because they knew he wouldn't bully them, that he would treat them with a kindness they rarely found, inside or outside school.

He continued to live with his parents until 1938, when he married and moved to the other side of the city. On the outbreak of war a few months later, he enrolled in the Royal Signals, and for the next six years he was moved around from service to service and unit to unit. I knew he'd been attached to the Navy and was on a ship escorting the disastrous attempt to land Canadian troops and British and American commandos at Dieppe in August 1942. Two years later he was with a Canadian battalion landing at Courseulles-sur-Mer on Juno Beach in Normandy on the morning of D-Day. He said he'd been lucky because there was heavy fighting and a lot of casualties among the first to go ashore. He somehow landed unharmed, soaked and weighed down with his kit, rations and rifle, his morse code key and a drum of cable.

He later wrote an account of the latter part of his war. I still have it. He drew neat maps with dotted lines, dates and arrows tracing his movements, from the landing at Courseulles on June 6th, the first month and a half in Normandy while Caen was being taken, the sweep across northern France into Belgium and Holland, the failure there and the hard time in the Ardennes either side of Christmas. He described his advance towards and into Germany, the horrors of entering Belsen concentration camp, and finally in October 1945 handing in his kit at Thirsk in Yorkshire.

He occasionally talked to my elder brother James and me about the war. I can hear him now, speaking in a slow monotone, sitting at the dining-room table, his eyes shut. We listened eagerly as he described the liberation of Europe.

"In France, Belgium and Holland we were cheered and mobbed, embraced and kissed, especially by the larger and plainer women who plastered lipstick all over our faces and necks." He once added, perhaps forgetting that we were listening, "We soon started avoiding them and seeking out the prettier girls." I was astonished, it didn't sound like him. But my brother grinned, so I smiled too.

His last diary entry, after over two hundred pages of relentless movement and incident, was a stark "16 November 1945, back to Brightside School."

*

Only the year before he died, he showed me a script he'd typed out recounting what happened to him during the 1942 Anglo-American landings in North Africa. I didn't know he had taken part in this episode, he'd never mentioned it before. When I asked him why, he simply said that it was time to set the record straight.

On the afternoon of November 10th 1942 I was with the Navy and taking part in the Allied Landings on North Africa. Having made a successful landing just west of Algiers the previous Sunday, together with eight other ships, ours was detailed to proceed some 120 miles along the coast and make a further landing at a port named Bougie.

On the evening of the 11th, we were heavily attacked by German aircraft flying from the island of Sardinia. Several of our ships were hit by bombs. Everyone was busy picking up survivors from neighbouring ships, and the gunners were firing at the enemy planes in an effort to defend ourselves. Our upper deck was loaded with tins of petrol. The army had captured the local aerodrome, but the allied planes couldn't fly to our defence, as we hadn't been able to unload the fuel.

The following dawn, November 12th, we were again attacked and almost immediately three bombs straddled our top deck and our ship the KARANJA was in flames from end to end with blazing petrol. Fortunately the Captain had ordered all the landing craft onshore with their crews as soon as the raid started, and when the order to abandon ship was given they raced to pick us up out of the water, where we all were keeping afloat with planks or lifebelts. During the two raids we lost eight ships out of nine, and some 30 of our ship's company, including one of my own section, were killed or lost.

The burning *Karanja* off Bougie, 12 November 1942

It was about 9 a.m., some 3 hours after the raid started, when we got ashore. Our signals section, without any gear and with only the clothes we happened to be wearing when we were bombed, were without a job and nobody had any time to attend to us. Our Lieutenant in charge decided we should take steps to get home.

After marching west for several days we caught the Constantine-Algiers express, where we travelled in a first-class carriage with an Arab and his wife and their two little girls. We tried to teach them the English values and a few words, without any encouragement *from the father who was rather hostile in his attitude.*

On arrival at Algiers we were given a Naval overcoat to cover our semi-nakedness. We embarked on a liner (the ORSINA) which was on its way from Australia to Liverpool via Gibraltar. At about 5 o'clock on a Sunday morning, my wife was awakened by an unshaven, unkempt individual dressed in shorts and a heavy coat and not much else. However, survivor's leave which extended over Christmas did a lot to repair the damage.

The day after he died I found the typescript in a drawer in his flat. I had just learnt that he had in fact omitted the most important part of this Algerian adventure.

*

When I called the hospital from France, the nurse told me his condition had suddenly deteriorated. I packed a few things and set off on the road to Calais. This was in March 1985, nine years before the Channel Tunnel opened.

Ten and a half hours later I walked into the ward at the Hallamshire Hospital. There were three beds on either side. I was almost blinded by the white sheets and the bright red blankets. Two old men were lying motionless. Two others were propped up against their pillows, with eyes closed and loud, irregular croaking emerging from half-open mouths. The last bed in the far corner was empty. Had I arrived too late?

In the opposite corner, a man was wriggling about in his bed, arms and legs all over the place. I didn't recognize him at first, his face was so grey. But it was him. He saw me and shouted "Over here." He suddenly calmed down, and motioned me to pull up a chair. He smiled. I hadn't expected that. His speech was slow but distinct, and he appeared perfectly lucid.

"You're here," he said. "Now listen. And don't interrupt me."

I was taken aback by the firm, determined tone as he continued.

"D'you remember? What I wrote about HMS *Karanja* and Bougie?"

I nodded. He was having difficulty breathing. So I spoke.

"Yes, it was fascinating. But I don't understand why you never told us the story before."

He grabbed my arm and squeezed hard.

"I said don't interrupt." A brief pause. "I didn't tell the whole truth. Now just listen."

Whatever he wanted to tell me, he was trying to get it out as fast as he could.

"After Bougie, I didn't go straight home to England. On the train to Algiers, I was trying to communicate with the two little Arab girls sitting opposite me, between their father and mother. I tried speaking English words. I made gestures. The girls laughed. They made hand signals and spoke Arab words that I tried to repeat.

"Their mother was covered from head to toe. Her eyes looked nervous at first, but I'm sure she started smiling. It was only a game, but the father took it badly. He spoke gruffly to his wife. She said a word to the two girls, who stopped playing. I looked out of the window. I didn't want to get them, or myself, into trouble."

It had been a big effort for him, just talking. He began to cough, and motioned me to pass a glass of water that was on his bedside table. He took a few sips, waited, then a few more, and handed the glass back to me.

"When the train stopped in Algiers the woman climbed down to the platform after me. There was a big gap between the steps and it was a long way down, so I turned round to help the two little girls. Then the father began shouting and he pushed past them. He knocked one of the girls down the last two steps. But the mother had gone. The man turned angrily to face me. I lifted his daughters and put them down in front of him, then I turned and fled."

He was speaking quickly now, but he paused again. Another sip of water.

"By now my unit had gone on ahead, so once I was outside the station I headed towards the harbour. I remember a wide avenue and a pavement lined with trees. I'd crossed a couple of roads, when the Arab woman appeared out of a doorway. She motioned me to follow her, but I hesitated. She'd gone a few steps when she turned round. I could see her bright blue eyes fixing me, shining at me, glistening. I can't explain why, or what I was thinking. I had to follow her. I couldn't help it."

He was talking much faster, a faint blush of red in his cheeks.

"I found myself walking up a narrow street, between overhanging houses. It was a steep climb. We'd left the wide avenues behind, and were going up to the Casbah, the old Arab town. As we got to the top of the hill, she turned into a courtyard. She held a finger tight against her veil where her lips were. Then she sat on a bench and motioned me to sit beside her.

"I was amazed when she started speaking a few words in English. 'Me never let out. Me slave. Him cruel. I scared. You good. You kind.' She removed the veil covering her face. She was younger than I'd thought. Eighteen, maybe nineteen? All I could see was a glowing face and those sparkling steel-blue eyes."

My father, here on his deathbed, was no longer the timid and doubting man he had often been. But I was sure he was hallucinating. An Arab woman with blue eyes? An eighteen-year-old with two daughters?

"She took me into the house and said that she had a message for me. She had chosen me because I looked more sensible than the others. I was to take a boat called the *Orsina* two days later. A man would board the ship at Gibraltar and he would make contact with me. For two days she kept repeating a few words and letters that didn't make sense. I wasn't allowed to write it all down but had to memorize it.

"In fact I did something I shouldn't have. The message wasn't very long but I noted it down in morse code in case I forgot a word or a letter. I've never told anyone since I delivered that message, but I can show you now."

He held out his hand with a small card he'd been hiding under the blankets. I hesitated.

"Go on, take it," he ordered, "and then you must destroy it since it's not legal by military rules and we could both be in trouble if they find out."

I took the card and saw the dots and dashes of the morse code followed by a handwritten translation that he had presumably added later: 'Stmo Cacor. Meso ABBnrIfset. Shan Edmo riedbu.' He didn't give me time to ask what it meant.

"She said I mustn't forget a single letter, capital, full stop or space. Every hour or so, she made me repeat the message until I was able to do it several times without a single mistake. For two days and two nights we spent our time together in a dark room. There was a window looking onto a balcony, but it was covered by a wooden trellis with tiny holes. I wasn't allowed to look out or to go outside. She told me it was *harim*, forbidden for men. We lay on couches covered in cushions. She said her name was Fatima, and that this was Delloula's house. Delloula was her cousin."

He paused once more, but he was no longer struggling to speak. His eyes were alive and he was excited and strong.

"We lay together, looking at each other, talking and dozing. I'd known nothing but war rations for three years, and Delloula brought in great silver trays of food. Whole roast chickens, shoulders of lamb, beef stews with mountains of semolina, chopped cubes of tomato and beetroot and cucumber... vegetables that I'd never seen but later learnt were aubergines and courgettes, artichokes, pumpkins... carrots sweeter than I'd ever imagined. There were salads, tasty yellow rice, stewed apples with cinnamon, lots of spices and sauces that I'd not tasted before. Delloula served hot mint tea poured in a long thin stream from the spout of a silver teapot.

"We slept side by side, in each other's arms." He looked sternly at me. "I told your mother long ago and she never held it against me. Strange things happen in wartime."

Then he began to struggle again, but managed to continue.

"I was tempted to stay on, but on the third morning Delloula came in and said I must leave. She said Fatima lived a hundred miles away in the hills, that her husband Mohamed was coming to fetch her, that I would never see her again. Delloula was nervous and anxious to get me out of her house. Had she betrayed us? I feared very much for Fatima. We embraced, and I hurried away through the courtyard and down the hill.

"I found the ship bound for Liverpool, and as it chugged away I stayed on deck looking at the bright white terraces of houses, Algiers framed by the green hills and the blue sea and skies. Delloula had dressed me in an Arab coat and I must have been a real sight. But on the boat there were lots more like me in all kinds of strange garbs. Anyway, I delivered the message when a young man who'd boarded the ship at Gibraltar approached me and mentioned 'Fatima' and 'Delloula' as if they were code words. He said 'message' and I spelt it out for him twice. I asked him why I should be the one to act as go-between. He replied that their agents were trailed by both allied and enemy services so they frequently used random soldiers and citizens. Then he just nodded to me and walked away."

So he was wearing not a Naval overcoat, but an Arab's *burnous*, on his early morning return home.

The colouring had drained from his face, as the effort of talking had exhausted him. He dozed off and there were long gaps between each breath. A white-coated doctor appeared, looked at him, and reprimanded me.

"Don't let him talk. He'll be gone in five minutes if you let him say any more."

Two nurses came to change his bed, so I went to the cafeteria. What my father had said was so out of character that I decided it was some kind of long-suppressed desire, perhaps triggered by a memory of the woman on the train, her eyes peeping out from her niqab. In his last moments, he was getting delirious and had imagined it all. I thought again, an Arab woman with *blue* eyes? An eighteen or nineteen year old with two daughters old enough to talk and to play games on the train? It couldn't be true. And yet... I had his little card with the morse code and its message.

When I returned to the ward I found they'd pulled the curtain round his bed. He was lying with his eyes closed and I couldn't see if he was breathing. As I pulled up a chair, he opened one eye a little, then asked for his glass of water. This seemed to revive him.

"There's something else," he suddenly said, both eyes now wide open and staring at me.

He began mumbling about someone called Manfritt. It seemed to be some kind of inspector who had visited his school, discovered he was retired, and visited him at home.

"Be careful, if Manfritt finds you," he said. "I didn't like Manfritt. He came to see me two weeks ago. At first he was charming. He talked about schools. And about the wars. He asked if I could show him my war diary. I did. Then he asked a lot of questions. He started shouting about my father and about another man called... I can't remember. He was very angry and he scared me, but after a few minutes he calmed down. He said he was sorry. He said I was like his father used to be. Then he asked about you. He asked where you lived, what you did. He said he would find you. You must beware. Beware of Manfritt!"

The memory seemed to have upset him. He became agitated again, and caught a flailing foot in the metal rail at the side of his bed. He started struggling. I tried to free his foot, and to calm him.

"It's alright," I said. "Just keep still." He reacted aggressively.

"Oh for Christ's sake, leave me alone!"

I had never before heard him blaspheme or swear. He had always been so puritanical about foul language.

Five minutes later he was dead.

*

Fast forward ten years, a whole decade after my father's death and half a century after the end of the war.

The month after Leila and I had met at Magny-Cours, we went to Senlis one Saturday morning to put flowers on Suzy's grave. Afterwards I showed her an odd little museum, a couple of hundred yards from the cemetery. It occupied the ground and first floors of a house on the corner opposite the cathedral. Five tiny rooms with low ceilings, stacked with souvenirs of the Spahis.

I thought she would be interested, but she said she'd never heard of the Spahis. I explained that they were cavalry regiments of Algerians and Moroccans who had fought for France in the 1870-71 Franco-Prussian war, in 1914-18 and again in 1940. The museum was a memorial to these colonial troops who had been garrisoned at Senlis from 1927 to 1962. I had visions of Arab horsemen charging into battle in colourful costumes, but she wasn't at all happy at the idea of Algerians fighting for the French army.

We paid five francs each to a friendly woman at the entrance, and went inside. We wandered past uniforms of scarlet and white cloaks, bright red and green pennants, flags with stars and crescents, exhibits of swords, daggers, saddles and stirrups. I was stooping over some coins and medals in a glass cabinet, very much absorbed in what I was looking at, whilst Leila must have been getting bored. She said she was feeling in her bag for her mobile when she suddenly noticed me pointing excitedly at the faded pages of an open notebook in the cabinet. It was written in an old-fashioned handwriting that reminded me of the Gothic scripts my German master had shown us at school. And it *was* written in German.

I had seen a paragraph where 'Gottlieb', 'For Suzy, JHW' and 'Josette' could be made out among the German words. True, we were in Senlis, where Gottlieb and Suzy and Grandfather JHW had stayed, and where Josette had worked at the *Grand Cerf* hotel. But a German notebook in a Spahi museum? With these names and initials?

I asked the friendly woman if she could open the cabinet. No, security did not permit. Leila explained that her great-grandfather had been a Spahi stationed at Senlis during the war—a story she'd invented on the spur of the moment, though it subsequently turned out to be true. The cabinet was unlocked, and we were able to leaf through the booklet. I took photos of all nineteen pages.

We noted the name and dates on the inside cover: *Hauptsturmführer Hans Meyer, 1940-1942.* I said I thought the rank of Hauptsturmführer was the equivalent of Captain in the Waffen-SS, the military wing of Hitler's storm troopers.

We asked the attendant how the notebook had come to be here. She traced the reference number in a manuscript catalogue, and suddenly became very talkative. It had been posted to the museum from a small town near Sétif in Algeria by an old Spahi called Mohamed. Leila pricked up her ears at that, because her family lived not far from Sétif and her great-grandfather's name was Mohamed. But it was a very common name.

Apparently when the Germans invaded and occupied northern France in May 1940, Hauptsturmführer Meyer was put in charge of the Spahi barracks. The Germans had taken over the stables for their own cavalry, keeping on a few Spahis to do the menial jobs. Mohamed, who was stationed at Senlis, worked for Meyer for almost two years, and in the spring of 1942 they were transferred together to Algeria. In December Meyer was invalided back home to Germany, leaving his notebook in North Africa. After the war, as a wounded veteran he was given a job at the Pergamon Museum in Berlin.

The Spahi museum's records stated that Mohamed had found the notebook in 1976, and sent it to Senlis hoping they could locate Meyer. They traced him to West Berlin: *1 BERLIN 33 (Dahlem), Lentzealle 129*, and put his document in the post. A month later it was returned by his wife, and they kept it in the museum as a record of life in the barracks during the first two years of the Nazi occupation.

When we got home we transferred my photos onto the computer and tried to decipher the handwriting. With the aid of a dictionary and my schoolboy German, I discovered that Waffen-SS Captain Hans Meyer had pulled strings to get the post in Senlis because he wanted to shed light on a story his mother had told him many times when he was a child. His father Gottlieb had been shot whilst trying to escape from a camp near Senlis. The body had been transported home to Berlin with that bizarre inscription, 'For Suzy, JHW', written in thick black dried blood on his abdomen.

I told Leila I'd been to the Pergamon Museum in the early 1970s, and suggested going there to see what we could discover. A week later we took a plane to Berlin, not quite knowing what we were looking for or where to start, but hoping to unearth some more facts about Hans Meyer.

*

At half past ten on our first morning in the German capital, we were sitting in a cafe on the corner where Unter den Linden meets the pedestrian area leading down to the Pergamon.

Unter den Linden had been spruced up and was brighter than what I remembered from the 1970s, when it was in the communist zone of East Berlin, but I was disappointed that it hadn't been re-furbished to resemble what I'd seen in old photographs of pre-First World War days. An avenue with smart restaurants and cafes, ladies in fur coats and gentlemen in bowler hats discussing important business and their love affairs over coffee and cakes, bow-tied waiters serving from silver trays under the lime trees, fine buildings with Doric and Ionic columns and sculpted friezes.

Now it lacked grandeur. With few exceptions the buildings were rather plain. There were hardly any restaurants and no cafes under the lime trees. I sighed when I saw a poster in the boarded-up window of a building near the Brandenburg Gate announcing that it was to become Berlin's Madame Tussaud's.

"At least there's not a MacDonald's. Not yet," I said.

"Don't be such a snob," was the instant retort. "You like going to MacDonald's with me!"

As we drank our coffee, we began putting together what we'd discovered so far, and were working out our next moves. We'd started the morning by taking a taxi to Lentzealle. It was in Dahlem, a residential suburb which had been in the West Berlin zone before the wall fell. There were blocks of red-roofed post-war flats, clean and tidy but all monotonously alike. The taxi dropped us off at number 129, and Leila exclaimed "Yes!" as she saw a 'Dr. Barbara Meyer' nameplate on one of the mailboxes in the hall.

The flat was on the ground floor. We rang the bell, and a blonde thirty-something woman opened the door very slightly. I said in my hesitant German that we were looking for a Hans Meyer. The woman opened the door a little more and answered in almost perfect English. Yes, Hans was her grandfather, but he'd died when she was a little girl and she couldn't remember much about him.

"So you are Gottlieb's great-granddaughter," Leila said. The woman paled and snarled "Go away, leave me alone," then tried to shut the door. I blocked it with my foot, pushed it open and declared, "You can close the door, but you won't stop us making enquiries. You'll be hearing from us!" As we turned away she slammed and bolted the door.

We took a taxi to the Pergamon, and tried to find out more about Hans Meyer. We asked at reception but no-one had heard of him. We asked a guide, who shook her head and turned away. We approached the oldest attendant we could find, who said he'd never heard the name and asked us to move on. As we walked out onto the pavement, an old man caught hold of my arm.

He whispered that he'd known Hans, who'd been given a job for life at the museum because he was wounded in the war. Later it emerged that in the early 1950s Hans had been recruited by the Stasi, the communist Secret Police. In those days half the museum employees were agents. Since the reunification of Germany, the Stasi files had been opened, and you had to be very careful because so many friends, neighbours and colleagues were out for revenge against those who had spied on them.

The man gave us a slip of paper on which he'd written 'Heinrich Keller'. He told us to go to the Stasi museum on Ruschestrasse and ask to see this employee who might be able to help us. After stopping for our coffee, we took a clanking yellow U-Bahn train to Magdalenenstrasse, then walked round to the museum, the building that had been the Stasi headquarters. I shivered when I saw the stark grey-brown eight-storey block lined with dozens of identical windows.

Heinrich Keller was the first person we met just inside the entrance. He had a name-badge on his lapel, a wizened old man watching everyone coming in through the swing doors. When I told him we'd come from the Pergamon where we'd been given his name, and that we were looking for information about Hans Meyer, he smiled politely, pressed the lift button and took us up to an office on the top floor.

He seemed surprisingly willing to help, and nodded as we explained that we were journalists doing a series on the lives of French, British and German soldiers and that Hans was one of five Germans who had been selected as an example of what happened to the war-wounded. Keller kept on nodding.

Then he put on his coat and took us outside and back on U-Bahn line 5 to Alexanderplatz and on to another grey and brown building only a few yards round the corner from where, half an hour earlier, we'd been having our coffee. He took us up the stairs to the third floor and into a room looking onto a dark courtyard. Five minutes later he appeared with a box of index cards and said we were welcome to look through the documents but that the office would be closing for lunch in just under an hour.

The cards had mostly typed information, which was much easier to read than the manuscript in Hans's notebook, and I quickly picked out the ones that seemed to have a chronological summary of his record, covering the war and immediate post-war years. Leila photographed all the cards that I selected.

We found Keller downstairs and thanked him, saying we had some useful information and that we would try to visit Meyer's family in Lentzealle. Keller hesitated slightly, smiled politely again, then suddenly said, "My father Gustav worked with Hans. And Herr Geoffrey, you must know Herr Geoffrey?" He stared at us as we shook our heads, then he showed us outside, bowed, and went on his way. We went to the Pergamon cafeteria for lunch.

We felt uneasy about having been to the Stasi buildings. It was obvious that Keller had been warned to expect us. He seemed to already know that we'd been to the flat in Dahlem, and our meeting had most likely been deliberately set up. Why had he been so willing to let us see the information on Hans Meyer?

Over lunch we pieced together Meyer's life and movements from what I had understood in the Stasi files. Suddenly Leila leaned over and whispered in my ear that she'd noticed a woman she'd seen earlier in the Stasi building, sitting at the table just behind us, listening to every word we spoke. So we left the rest of our lunch and went to our hotel. We discovered everything in turmoil—all our things strewn around the floor and over the furniture.

I looked out of the window and spotted two broad-shouldered young men in dark glasses looking up from the street. We decided to leave at once since we weren't equipped to cope if they were carrying handguns. We hastily packed our bags and paid the bill. I went outside to hail a taxi.

Leila said that as she was walking out through the hotel foyer, the two heavies came in. She grinned at them and tried to walk past, but one of them grabbed her arm. They had her cornered, so she kicked the first one. He yelped, and the hotel receptionist started screaming. The second one caught hold of her and held her round the neck from behind. Hearing the scream, I ran back in, pulled him off, and hit him a clean uppercut, leaving him stretched out on the floor beside his pal, blood streaming from his mouth. Without looking back we ran out to the pavement, jumped into the taxi, changed our reservation at the airport and took the first plane back to Paris.

When we got home and looked at the photos of the files, we found that the Stasi had combed through Meyer's military record and reconstructed vast chunks of his past.

He had joined the Waffen-SS in 1938 and quickly risen through the ranks. As a captain in this elite force he had indeed been able to choose his post in Senlis, where he had searched the town-hall archives and found the *Grand Cerf* hotel register for 1914. He discovered the name of the mysterious 'JHW'. He then went to the hotel and met Josette, who was still working there. She told him about "beautiful Suzy," "handsome John Wright the Englishman," and "the good-looking Gottlieb Meyer."

In 1940, however, what with Panzers and Messerschmitts, Hans hadn't a lot of use for the horses and cavalrymen of the Spahi barracks. In reality he had been handling a treasure-trove of antiques, paintings and personal valuables that the Nazis were stealing from art galleries and Jewish families in France. The Algerian called Mohamed had helped him hide the loot in the stables whilst he arranged shipment to a Herr Gustav Keller at the Pergamon Museum.

In April 1942 Hans was transferred to Bougie in North Africa, where he was to take delivery of part of a consignment of gold bullion and jewellery that the SS had seized in Tunisia. He had Mohamed recalled from Senlis, and together they hid a portion of the bullion that Hans was setting aside for himself. They buried it for safety outside Mohamed's village near Sétif, until such time as Hans could secrete it back home. The Stasi files suggested that this was part of the so-called 'Rommel's gold'. They noted that Rommel himself had taken some of the treasure to France, officially to finance his defence of the Atlantic Wall, but also perhaps to swell his carefully accumulated personal fortune.

Soon after the allies landed in North Africa, Hans was assigned to take a special plane to Berlin with works of art looted from Tunisia and Algeria. His 'invalid' status was a pretext to cover this secret mission. He stayed in Germany for the next two years, working with Gustav Keller, collecting goods requisitioned by the Nazis in Amsterdam, Paris, Warsaw, Budapest and Prague.

Because of the shortage of able-bodied men, in late 1944 he was transferred to the retreating German army and spent Christmas in the Ardennes. At the end of December he was seriously wounded, shot in the stomach, and was invalided home.

Much enfeebled by his war wounds, he was reportedly 'a mere shadow of his former self'. It was to his poor mental and physical health that he owed his undemanding post-war job as an attendant at the Pergamon museum. After the war he married Monika, and a son called Manfred was born three years later.

Like many former SS officers, he settled into a protected post-war existence which, for those who found themselves in the Soviet zone, would later include working for the Stasi. A sick man, he never followed up his discovery of the identity of the 'JHW' who had shot his father Gottlieb, whilst the bullion he had stolen and buried in Algeria also seemed to have been forgotten, until the Stasi interest was awakened.

Hans died in 1977. We noticed a handwritten addition to the last file card. It showed that his son Manfred and his granddaughter Barbara had recently taken his records out of the archives and examined them. A rubber stamp mark revealed that Manfred too worked for the Stasi. He and his daughter must have known everything that Leila and I had just discovered, including the references to JHW, Suzy and Gottlieb, and to the story of the hidden gold.

*

"I have to know. I have to go and question my aunts and my grandmother," she announced.

On the plane back from Berlin I'd told Leila my father's story about Fatima, Delloula and the coded message.

"My mother says my great-grandmother's name was Fatima,"

she explained. "Fatima's husband was called Mohamed, and there is an old aunt Delloula still alive and living in Algiers. There must be hundreds of Mohameds, Fatimas and Delloulas around Stif and in Algiers. But I have to know."

The next day she took the first available flight from Orly airport to Algiers. One of her cousins drove her on the narrow road winding through the hills to Bordj-Bou-Arreridj, where her parents had lived before coming to France. It was a growing town on a plateau west of Sétif, which she pronounced as a single syllable, 'Stif'.

She spent a week questioning her relatives. Grandmother Kahina had at first refused to talk about her parents. She seemed afraid, and wanted to hide whatever was disturbing her. Then she began to reminisce.

Apparently Mohamed had left Fatima and gone to serve in France with a Spahi regiment. When he returned, Kahina was aged five. She remembered that her father came back with a tall soldier in a light green uniform. Or was it grey? With Mohamed he spoke a language that they told her was German. That didn't mean much to her, but he'd been very kind to her and her sister, giving them sweets and chocolate. There had been a lot of noise and fuss about some big boxes that were brought in an army lorry to the house, and then taken away by her father and the soldier.

Kahina said she remembered bitter disputes afterwards between her parents. She then recalled how Fatima had left them on the station platform in Algiers. She and her sister Nora had been scared, living at home without their mother. Leila asked her if she had any recollection of an Englishman. "Don't you remember an English soldier on the train and at the station in Algiers, when your mother disappeared?" She hesitated. No, she could only remember falling down onto the platform, and her father being angry. After a few days their mother had come back, and they soon moved into a much bigger house, where Kahina and Nora still lived today.

They said Leila couldn't talk with Nora, who was suffering from some kind of dementia. So she went to see her great-uncle Idir. He seemed embarrassed at first, when she asked about Mohamed and Fatima. But he'd always been very open with her, and soon he told her a secret he said he'd kept for more than fifty years.

When he was a boy aged ten, his uncle Mohamed had made him help load some very heavy boxes onto the backs of four mules, and take them up into the hills where they'd buried them on land owned by the family. When they'd finished, Mohamed clipped Idir hard around the ear so that he wouldn't forget, and as a warning never to reveal the hiding-place.

Idir too remembered the soldier. He recalled one day when his uncle had become very angry. The two men had shouted at each other in a language Idir didn't understand. Then Mohamed shouted in Kabyle, making accusations about the soldier and Fatima. When Idir was a bit older he realized that his uncle had been so angry because he'd suspected Fatima had been unfaithful.

In the fifties during the war between the Algerian FLN and France, Mohamed and Idir had dug up some of the gold ingots to fund their armed militia. As well as financing the FLN, thanks to those ingots all the family had fine clothes, beautiful homes, and big cars. When Leila asked Idir if there was any treasure left, he said yes, some of it was still buried where he and Mohammed had hidden it. But he didn't need it now. As far as he was concerned it could stay up in the hills for ever, *inch Allah*.

Leila thought that she herself might have a claim on some of this treasure. After all, she was Mohammed's great-grand-daughter.

She had returned to Algiers, where she climbed up to the old town to visit Great-Aunt Delloula, now in her nineties. Delloula wasn't always coherent, but after talking in Kabyle, pressing for news of all the family in France, when asked about Fatima she began speaking a curious kind of old-fashioned French.

She shut her eyes and recounted the story of Fatima and the English soldier William. There was Leila, sitting at her great-aunt's knee, holding the hand of the old lady who had met my father! Delloula said she was tired and asked Leila to come back the following morning, when she would explain about Fatima and what had happened during the 'European' war.

When Leila returned the next day she found the house in mourning. Delloula had died during the night. Leila was distraught. Had the strain of being about to reveal Fatima's secrets been too much? Then one of her cousins took her aside and told her that Delloula had spoken a few words just before she died, saying "Tell Leila that Fatima was not Fatima." It didn't make sense.

I was mystified by these discoveries. Both of our families, Leila's and mine, involved with the Meyers from Germany? And with each other? Our meeting by chance in France half a century later? It didn't seem possible. There were too many coincidences to be mere coincidence. Had our meeting been pre-arranged? Had she herself been complicit in setting up what was becoming more than a short-term friendship? If so, why?

I could not believe that she was knowingly part of some plot or conspiracy, although she could certainly seem intimidating, hostile even, with her cutting remarks and her pugnacity. Perhaps the recent threats to my life and safety, to *our* safety, had begun to induce in me a state of paranoia?

What Leila had learnt suggested there was some substance to my father's story. She explained that Fatima could have had two small daughters by the time she was eighteen because in those days it was quite common for Algerian girls to be married at fourteen. And she reminded me that Bordj is in Kabyle country. I knew that the Kabyles were Germanic nomads who settled right across North Africa long before the Arabs, indeed before the Romans. Leila's father was Arab, but all her mother's family are Kabyle, and some of them have blue eyes and fairish hair. There was no reason why Fatima shouldn't have had 'steel-blue' eyes.

*

I had wondered about the possibility of some curious trick of fate when I learned that during the war both Hans and my father had been to Bougie in Algeria, and later to the Ardennes region of Belgium and France. Hans must have left Algeria at the time the *Karanja* was sunk in November 1942. I did not see how their paths could have crossed. But I had to reconsider the evidence about the Ardennes. My father had noted in his diary that he spent Christmas Day 1944 on a farm in southern Belgium.

25 Dec. Passed through Quatre-Bras, Charleroi, Philippeville, Ro-sée, Anthée and to the village of Serville. A glorious ride in beautiful weather, with roads dipping and climbing. Christmas dinner of cheese and bully-beef sandwiches. At the end of the day we found a good billet on a farm.

We sang Christmas carols and didn't get to bed before midnight. The farmer's little daughter Denise played with us. I drew pictures for her and wrote out a poem and a message on a card, with my address so that she could write to me after the war.

On the afternoon of Boxing Day, his unit had to move on, and he mentioned a battle a few miles east, at a village called Celles-sur-Lesse. The Germans had counter-attacked and the battle raged for three days.

28 Dec. We had to clear out the village in the morning. We crept down the sides of the main street, throwing grenades into each house as we advanced. I was loaded down with my wireless equipment, and my rifle which I'd rarely had to load and had never fired.

On this occasion, a group of German soldiers came out of a house with their hands up. I was detailed to watch over them while the others cleared the street. I lined them up along the side of a house. We had been told to beware of Germans who surrendered, since they often turned on their captors. I trained my loaded rifle on them in case they tried anything.

Suddenly, to my left in an outhouse window, I saw a German soldier preparing to fire at me. I aimed and shot twice. He shook violently, then crumpled and fell out of sight. Hearing the firing, my platoon rushed back and I was moved along the street out of danger.

I'd killed a man with the only two shots I ever fired in my life.

Those extraordinarily detailed Stasi files recorded that when the Germans counter-attacked in the Ardennes just after Christmas 1944, Stormtrooper Hans Meyer was with a group that occupied a Belgian farm at Serville. He claimed that the farmer's ten-year-old daughter had shown him a card with a drawing, a poem and the signature, name and address in Sheffield of William Wright. There it was in their files, the address of 'William, son of JHW', they noted. The address where Manfred was to visit my father forty years later.

Of course, the two soldiers were on opposite sides of a moving front line, and there was no way Hans could have found my father on that war front. But the day after they left the farm, Hans's battalion retreated further east, where they were cornered in Celles-sur-Lesse after some fierce fighting. Most of his comrades were captured, and he was shot in the shoulder and stomach when trying to free a group being held prisoner.

The Stasi had taken these details from the full report they had found in the reconstructed archives of the regiment to which Hans had been attached. They noted that the British did not want to be burdened with wounded prisoners, and he was handed over to the German Red Cross. He was very weak after losing a lot of blood, and was transported to Berlin in an ambulance.

*

Back at Brightside School in November 1945, my father was quite unaware of the rivalry between himself and Hans Meyer. Their affairs with the same young Algerian woman. The identity of the soldier he believed he'd killed in a hamlet in the Belgian Ardennes. A hoard of gold at the heart of the coded message he'd carried from Algiers to Gibraltar.[1] He also died in ignorance of his father's romance with Suzy, of her treasures and the shots that had killed Gottlieb.

He'd had a visit from 'Manfritt', the Stasi agent who had learnt of those hidden treasures and the gold bullion, who knew about the rivalries between the two earlier generations. But *why had Manfred Meyer spurned his opportunity for revenge*, sparing my father and thereby allowing me to hear at first hand, two weeks later, some curious wartime secrets? Why had he and his daughter not found me, as he'd promised my father they would?

---

[1] The 'code' was easily unlocked. When Leila returned from the visit to her family, we had soon deciphered it. Could British Intelligence really have been so unprofessional? Or had Fatima herself composed the message? We reversed the order of the syllables and added obviously missing words. 'Stmo Cacor. Meso ABBnrlfset. Shan Edmo riedbu.' 'Most in Corsica. Some in Bordj Bou Arreridj near Sétif. Hans and Mohamed have buried it.'

3. The Girl in the *Jeu de Paume*

I was walking through the Tuileries Gardens in central Paris. To my left was the Orangerie art gallery, to the right its twin the Jeu de Paume. I found myself thinking of that day almost thirty years earlier. In the Orangerie, Monet's 'Water-Lilies' paintings were exhibited in a spacious circular hall where you can still see them today. But back then the Jeu de Paume displayed a hundred or more of the most famous Impressionists, before they were removed to be swallowed up in a mammoth collection at the Musée d'Orsay.

Those paintings were reproduced in countless books and on posters and postcards, where they always seemed familiar yet somehow unattainable. Back then in the Jeu de Paume, they hit you directly. As you entered the building, at the end of a short corridor you were met by the gaze of a strangely naked girl. She was sitting on the grass and turning to look you straight in the eye. Manet's *Déjeuner sur l'herbe*.

In the collection were several other Manet paintings with equally striking characters. The lady in white sitting by the green railing in *Le Balcon*, the colourful *Lola de Valence*, the defiant little tart *Olympia*, naked and unashamed on her bed.

It was while looking at *Le Balcon* that I became aware of a dark-haired girl standing alongside me. There was an uncanny likeness to the seated lady in that painting. Black shoulder-length wavy hair with two curls on her forehead. A mysterious and rather sad oval face. Dark eyes. We seemed to be moving through the rooms at the same pace. I could feel her looking at me quite insistently. Our gazes met once or twice, but my stomach tightened at the prospect of starting a conversation.

I wandered slowly downstairs and outside where I crossed over to the Orangerie. I wanted to see the 'Water-Lilies'. I soon realized that I wasn't alone. She had followed me, and was looking at me far more intently than at Monet's paintings. After shifting several times round the room, I looked straight at her. Her eyes brightened, and she smiled just slightly as her gaze fixed mine. She was trying to

61

encourage me, but I froze.

A brief pause, then I made my way downstairs to the exit, and hurried the few yards to a circular pond where I'd earlier seen some small boys playing with their model boats. I sat on one of the chairs, iron-framed and with hard green wooden slats. The boys and their boats had gone. I'd been there barely thirty seconds when she appeared. She sat on a chair opposite mine, on the other side of the pool. She looked at me and smiled again faintly, her reflection showing upside down in the water. I was quite paralyzed.

Edouard Manet, *Le Balcon*

Suddenly another girl appeared and sat beside her. They started talking. My Manet girl seemed to be telling her companion about me. She relaxed, turning to her friend then looking at me. They both stared at me and laughed. I stood up, turned, and walked away.

I didn't go to the library that afternoon. I must have sat on park benches and in cafes, brooding and hopeless, I can't remember.

When you lose a girl because you haven't dared, haven't even tried, nothing else matters. Iron in the soul.

That evening I was walking up the Rue de l'École de Médecine in the Latin Quarter, looking for a place to eat. I noticed the signboard of a cafe, *Le Coup de Coeur*. I turned to look at the menu and bumped into her, right in the middle of the narrow street.

She looked at me defiantly. I put my hands on her shoulders, then kissed the two curls on her forehead. She took my arm. We walked on together, and stopped to dance in a little square where a man was playing an accordion. Then we embraced long and tight, before she guided me along the pavements until we came to a doorway in the Rue de Vaugirard, opposite the Senate.

She pushed me into a courtyard and then to a winding stairway, up five flights and onto the top landing. She took out her keys and opened a door. The flat, two converted maids' rooms under the attic roof, smelled of wooden floorboards and coffee and warm books because the sun had been shining on the roof-slates and skylight windows all day.

We lay on the bed and quickly undressed each other. We caressed and kissed and made love. It wasn't so difficult, after all. For some time we just lay there, side by side. Darkness fell and our bodies were lit up on the bed by a big round moon shining through the two skylights. I don't remember when we spoke for the first time. We rarely said much. We were so absorbed in each other for what seemed an age but was only a few days.

One afternoon, after I'd climbed the stairs and knocked gently on the door, she didn't half-open it and greet me with her usual conspiratorial smile. I knocked louder. No answer. Not a sound.

I pushed hard and the door burst open. The sunlit flat was empty, with bare floorboards, just a bookcase and the bed with a mattress. I sensed someone behind me, and turned to see the girl she'd met in the Tuileries.

"Her father came and took her away," she said. "He didn't approve of your romance. He's counting on her marrying Gilles. He's afraid you'll ruin everything. He forced her to take her things and go home with him."

"Where do they live?" I asked.

"Laurence won't be able to see you any more. He's taken her away to the country. I think they have a *château* in Picardy but I don't know where."

*

That was in 1968. As I crossed the Tuileries Gardens now, twenty-eight years later, I knew that I hadn't forgotten her. At first I'd tried to find her, but had had to give up. We'd never really spoken and she'd disappeared without a trace. The concierge, the other girl, and everyone else in the building obviously had orders not to talk to me. Ever since those few days, I'd avoided walking past her flat.

Looking now at the Jeu de Paume, I regretted that all the paintings had been moved to the Musée d'Orsay. The intimacy has gone. The new museum is always packed and you can't see much of the paintings on account of the crowds. Then I thought of the 'Water-Lilies', and decided I would go and look at the real thing at Giverny, where Monet's house is now a museum. It too is always packed with tourists, but at least you can walk in the gardens.

The following day I drove across the gently rolling countryside of fields and woods full of pheasants, deer and wild boar, part of that noble old French landscape of nature fashioned by many generations of careful management. The main street at Giverny was crowded with pedestrians, mostly Japanese and American. I took the last free space in the car-park.

Monet's house is a maze of bright colours. The reds and oranges of the bedrooms, the yellows of the dining room, a blue-tiled kitchen with a huge wooden table, earthen sinks and bronze taps. Outside, the green miniature Japanese bridge in the garden is cute, and if the water-lilies are crisper than on his canvas, that is not so much on account of his impressionist technique as because he was going blind when he painted them. I walked onto the bridge and stopped in the middle, leaning on the railings, looking at the pond. As I turned to walk back to the house I bumped into her. Again!

The dark eyes, the seriousness with a curious touch of warmth, the hint of a smile and the two curls. She looked me straight in the eyes, just like the first time. We were in Monet's garden, but she was a Manet figure, the lady sitting by the balcony rail. She addressed me in French.

"Ça ne m'étonne pas du tout. Je savais qu'on se reverrait un jour!" I'm not at all surprised. I knew we'd meet again one day!

"Moi non plus! Moi aussi!" I said. Me neither! Me too!

She said that she'd often come here recently because she knew we'd find each other, and it seemed one of only two or three obvious places. We walked together through the gardens and out to the road. We held hands, strolled into the village, and took a table for lunch in a secluded and expensive restaurant that had opened recently to cater for the Japanese and Americans. We ate caviar and shared a rib of beef and a bottle of Pétrus. We talked. More than we'd ever talked before. She told me her story.

Her father had kept a tight rein on her. He had brought forward her marriage to Gilles, who was a student at the École Nationale d'Administration where the top civil servants of the future are trained. He graduated a brilliant first on the list. For a few years, he was a high-ranking civil servant in the Finance Ministry. Then they'd spent some time in West Africa. They had a grown-up daughter, Delcia, born in 1976.

Now they were back in Paris, where Gilles was on the board of several big companies. They had a luxury flat in the Boulevard Saint-Germain. Only the previous year, she had discovered that throughout their marriage and before, Gilles had been two-timing her. Well, three or four-timing would be more appropriate, for he'd always had a string of mistresses, long-term and short-term. Laurence had never suspected.

All those late nights at the ministry, the telephone calls summoning him to a sudden crisis meeting on a Sunday morning, the trips on government business abroad. Never once had she suspected, until the morning when a big van had arrived and an enraged Mistress Number One had dumped piles of furniture in the street, complaining that he'd gone off for a holiday with Mistress Number Two and that Mistress Number Three was pregnant again.

Laurence looked fresh and alive, not at all frayed or distressed by her discoveries. She and Gilles had separated and were coming to an arrangement over the property. She was to keep the Saint-Germain flat. Her father was wealthy, and was giving her a substantial monthly allowance. Her mother had died some years ago.

She said she had always known but never admitted that she had unfinished business with me. Then I told her *my* story. What had seemed a happy marriage and family life in France, with a sudden and, for me, unexpected divorce seven years ago.

Laurence said she wasn't free that evening or the next day, but we could meet two days later. Why not at the Musée d'Orsay, where all the Impressionists had been taken from the Jeu de Paume? I wasn't happy about the delay, but said okay, 10.30 the day after tomorrow in front of *Le Déjeuner sur l'herbe*.

*

I was at the Musée d'Orsay half an hour before it opened. In with the first batch at ten o'clock, and straight to the *Déjeuner sur l'herbe*.

I sat on a bench opposite Manet's painting, but barely glanced at it as I looked eagerly at every person who came into the alcove where the painting was hung. I looked at my watch. 10.15... 10.20... 10.23... 10.26... Two minutes later I stood up.

A party of schoolchildren were squatting in a semi-circle in front of the painting. Their teacher was explaining how it had shocked art critics at the *Salon des Refusés* in 1863. An old man was standing in a corner. He was looking at me and seemed quite agitated. He glanced at the painting, then again at me. 10.32... 10.34...

Where was she? Why was she late? *Parisiennes* are always late, I thought, though I hadn't imagined she would be, after all these years. 10.40... 10.50... The old man was still staring at me. He was tall, upright, straight-backed. Suddenly his fists were clenched and he started swinging his arms back and forth. He looked menacing and slightly mad, but at 11 o'clock, he turned and strode away.

I waited until two in the afternoon, then gave up. I had her phone number at the flat in the Boulevard Saint-Germain. She didn't have a mobile, but she had my numbers, home and mobile. I decided to wait until she called me.

She didn't. Not that afternoon, nor evening. I wondered, had I got the wrong day? So I went back to the Musée d'Orsay at ten o'clock the next morning. No Laurence. I waited until one o'clock. Now there could be no doubt.

Should I call her? If she didn't want to meet again, there wasn't much point. But I had to know. I called.

"Allo, Delcia à l'appareil." Her daughter. I asked to speak to Laurence. She hesitated. I heard a muffled sound and then, "Oui, bonjour. Laurence est... Laurence n'est pas... elle n'est pas là." Laurence is... Laurence isn't... she isn't here.

I explained that we'd had an appointment at the Musée d'Orsay the day before, but her mother hadn't turned up. She interrupted me at once, and spoke in English.

"You are Redmond. My mother mentioned you, before she... You'd better come immediately. Do you have the address? ... Good. Fourth floor, left."

I took a taxi and was there within five minutes. I didn't have the code to open the door into the entrance hall, so I called again. The door clicked open as Delcia repeated, "Fourth floor, left."

I was vaguely aware of the opulence of the surroundings. Thick red and black carpets, wrought-iron banisters with a gilded rail, polished parquet flooring, stained-glass windows, and mirrors everywhere. That was just the entrance hall and the staircase.

I didn't take the lift, but ran up the wide stairs two at a time. She was waiting for me, the door open. She reminded me of Laurence, the oval face and the way she stood with hands clasped, and... where else had I seen that face before?

"Come in, please."

She sounded very grave. She had been crying.

"What's the matter? Something's wrong. Where's Laurence?"

Delcia showed me into a small *salon*. We sat opposite each other on stiff-backed sofas. She looked straight at me.

"My mother was found yesterday morning at La Châtaigneraie, our home in Picardy. She'd gone there with her father. He found her floating in the swimming pool. He called Doctor Moreau, an old friend of his. A first examination showed no reason why she should have drowned. No heart attack, no stroke. But it seems she had swallowed a whole bottle of sleeping pills. After he'd examined her, Moreau found the empty bottle by her bed. He was so distressed. He'd known her since she was a baby."

What could I say? I was struggling to take it all in. I looked round the room. There was a photograph on the mantelpiece. I looked again. It was the old man I'd seen in the Musée d'Orsay, in front of *Le Déjeuner sur l'herbe*, the old man who had stared angrily at me.

"Who's that?" I asked.

"That's Mother's father, my Grandfather Vincent," she said. "He's seventy-nine, but still very active. He's kept remarkably fit and strong for his age."

"Where is he?"

"In Picardy. He wants her to be buried there, in the chapel

graveyard at La Châtaigneraie. The funeral is on Monday."

"I saw him yesterday, in the museum," I protested.

"It can't have been him," she spluttered through tears. "He was at La Châtaigneraie all day yesterday. He'd found her in the pool early that morning."

"I must come to the funeral," I began, "we'd only just..."

"I don't think you should," she interrupted, suddenly looking quite angry. "Grandfather wouldn't want that. They had a terrible row after you'd met her at Giverny, because she was so keen to see you again, 'to make up for the lost years,' she'd said. He went berserk. He told me you'd tried to stop her marrying my father, all those years ago. You do realize," she added, looking quite sinister, "that if you *had* married her, I wouldn't exist."

The atmosphere had become very hostile. Delcia was spitting out the words now.

"Grandfather thinks, and I agree with him, that she killed herself in despair, because she'd seen you again. I think she'd forgotten you, but meeting you like that brought back all the memories. It was too much for her. Grandfather blames you for her killing herself. If you hadn't met again, it would never have happened. He says she was so fragile, like her mother had been. Now, I think you'd better leave."

I didn't remind her that Laurence hadn't forgotten me, that on the contrary, she'd been to Giverny as one of two or three places where she hoped she might find me. I shook hands with Delcia and withdrew. The encounter had lasted barely ten minutes. I decided that she had inherited some of her grandfather's unpleasant character. Although she had cried into a handkerchief and was looking a little bedraggled, I was struck by how remarkably beautiful she was, though rather skinny. I later learnt that she had been a teenage model and had recently appeared on two magazine covers. Perhaps that was where I'd seen that face.

*

Almost eight months later, it was May 1997, my mobile rang just as we were sitting down to a late breakfast. I'd met Leila a few weeks earlier.

"Hello, is that Redmond? This is Delcia."

"Who?"

"Delcia, Laurence's daughter."

It was a few seconds before I focussed on her.

"What do you want?"

I must have sounded very abrupt, but the name had triggered a memory of her hostility when she had more or less ejected me from her *salon*.

"I'm sorry," she said, "I'm so sorry, really. I owe you an apology. If you can, if you will, I would like to see you here. Can you come to the flat?"

I hesitated.

"You must come." Her voice sounded very plaintive. "We've discovered that Mother didn't commit suicide. She was murdered."

I went cold, very cold. I was overwhelmed by two clear images of Laurence. Her face at Giverny, and her young body in 1968. As I looked at that face and that body, I could see them both quite lifeless.

"Are you still there?" It was Delcia. I'd forgotten her.

"Yes," I mumbled, "I'm here. Where's her father?"

"That's just it," she said, "that's why I'm calling you. He's in prison. He killed her. He and his friend Doctor Moreau, the one who did the autopsy. He's been arrested too. Please come!"

*

"Palatial", Leila said, as we walked through the hallway and up the carpeted stairs to the flat in the Boulevard Saint-Germain. "Your girlfriend, womanfriend I should say, must have been wealthy. Was she *very* posh?"

Jealousy? I don't think so. A sort of wariness, perhaps, with just a hint of rivalry. My memory of Laurence hadn't faded when I met Leila. In fact it had become stronger, because I was better able to confront it. I believe that had Laurence lived, we would have spent the rest of our time together. But my relationship with Leila could end at short notice, so for the moment I was living with the memory of the one and the daily reality of the other. I didn't have to choose between them.

Delcia opened the door. We were shown into the small *salon*, and sat on the stiff-backed sofas. Coffee was served by a maid. I introduced Leila, and explained that I'd told her about Laurence. As soon as the maid had retired, Delcia started talking.

"I never really believed that Mother had committed suicide," she began, looking at Leila. "She said she wanted to see Redmond as soon as possible, but had had to put the meeting off for two days since she had urgent business with Grandfather. She was impatient to get back to Paris."

Delcia explained how the truth had emerged.

"The locals trusted Doctor Moreau. They'd all been his patients for years. He'd delivered more than half the village, two or three generations in some families. But recently, he'd discovered he had cancer of the pancreas. He knew he hadn't long to live, and he'd confessed to his wife, telling her what they'd done with Mother. Madame Moreau had never liked Grandfather. She claimed he'd raped her at La Châtaigneraie. She was fourteen at the time. When her husband told her that Mother was already dead when they'd put her in the swimming pool, she went straight to the local *gendarmerie*. The judge authorized them to disinter the body. They took it to Amiens for further examination and concluded that she'd been strangled."

Delcia said she'd wanted to know *exactly* what had happened when her mother had died, so she'd been to see Vincent in prison. He had a soft spot for his granddaughter, and she could always get him talking.

"Apparently they were driving from Paris to La Châtaigneraie where they were to spend a couple of days sorting out all the clothes that had lain untouched ever since the death of my grandmother. On the way Mother told him that she'd seen you at Giverny, and that you were to meet up two days later at the Musée d'Orsay, 10.30 a.m., in front of *Le Déjeuner sur l'herbe*. He was furious. He drank two bottles of wine with his dinner, and after the meal he began drunkenly reminiscing about the 1930s when he'd studied at the College of the famous Oxford linguist, Professor Burridge. He said that whilst in Oxford, at the age of twenty he had seduced a wealthy French widow. A marriage was quickly arranged, but she died of cancer two months after the wedding. He inherited her property at La Châtaigneraie and this building of six floors and thirty apartments at the smarter end of the Boulevard Saint-Germain."

We listened as Delcia explained that Vincent had also admitted to Laurence that soon after he'd returned to France he had married again, a young girl who would become her mother. There were rumours that she had inherited a fortune, but he soon discovered the rumours to be unfounded. Thirty-five years later, his wife discovered all his secrets. She overheard him talking with Doctor Moreau about his past: Oxford, the widow and her death, the rumours of an inheritance, this motive for their hasty marriage and his disappointment.

She had confronted him. That evening, he fed her a soup of death-cap mushrooms. Tasty, and as deadly as the name suggests. She died three days later, a seizure and finally a day-long coma after much bowel pain and vomiting. Moreau did the post mortem, recording that she had died of a heart attack.

"After a drunken Vincent had confessed all this to Mother, he heard her saying she would tell his story to me and to the police. He grabbed hold of her and tried to make her promise not to say anything.

"The next morning he woke up to find he was on the floor, and she was lying lifeless beside him. He had killed his wife, and now he'd strangled their daughter. He called Moreau, and together they put her in the swimming pool and arranged the suicide scene. The *gendarmerie* accepted their story. After all, Moreau was a widely respected local doctor."

By now Delcia was sobbing into her handkerchief. There was an awkward silence, and I was avoiding her gaze. I saw that Grandfather Vincent's photo was no longer on the mantelpiece. In his place were identically framed photos of four young women. I recognized Laurence, with Delcia on her right. But who were the two to her left? All four faces had a number of common features. That oval face, the restrained smile. I looked again at the photo on the left. It was the same one I had seen on the headstone in the Senlis cemetery. Suzy, Suzanne Burridge-Carnot. That was where I had seen those faces. The photo between Suzy and Laurence must be Delphine. I recalled the words Delcia had spoken a few minutes earlier, "the famous Oxford linguist, Professor Burridge." In front of me were four generations of women from the same family, the Burridge-Carnots. Suzy, Delphine, Laurence, and Delcia.

*

We said nothing to Delcia about Grandfather and Suzy, about her treasures and the fact that I had a copy of the riddles. How much did she already know? I decided that for the moment it was best to keep quiet and that if she had heard of Suzy's English lover and had made the connection with me, I would feign ignorance.

We left her and went for lunch at 'Les Deux Magots', the famous *brasserie* on the Boulevard Saint-Germain. Once the waiter had taken our order, I took a piece of paper that I kept in my wallet. It was a copy I'd typed out of the clues for Champagne and Burgundy.

"If Delphine had her mother's riddles and clues, then someone in their family must have seen them and worked out what they meant," I said. "Since I found the paper in Grandfather's diary, I've always believed there must be another copy somewhere. Maybe it was lost, but perhaps Delphine had it. Vincent married her because of the rumour about inherited treasure. In spite of his claim that there was no fortune, he could have been lying. Maybe he *has* seen Suzy's riddles. Perhaps Delcia has. They can't know that I've got a copy. They're obviously exceptionally wealthy. The treasure must have been collected years ago."

An old man sitting at the next table turned, looked directly at me, and spoke in a slightly diffident tone.

"Excuse me, it's very rude I know, but I couldn't help hearing you talking about riddles and clues and treasure. Perhaps I can help you." He was English. "I may be getting on in years, but I'm still pretty bright. During the war I worked at Bletchley Park, you know, where we deciphered the Germans' Enigma messages. After the War I graduated to MI6. And you, aren't you the professor who did that television series on Art and the Islamic World?"

"That's right," I said. "It's very good of you to offer to help us."

I thought for a moment, then asked the old man if 'five sisters' might mean anything in Burgundy. I noticed that he was squinting down at my paper, his eyes quickly scanning the riddles. He looked disappointed.

"Oh, that's not so much in my line. More mathematics, or letter puzzles. I'll have to think about it. By the way, I saw you coming out of that smart building on the corner of Saint-Germain and Raspail," he said, with a querying look.

"We were visiting friends," I replied. "And what are you doing here?"

"Oh, I've been looking up old contacts from the days when I liaised with the French services."

There was a long pause. He stood up and took a card from his pocket.

"If you need support," he announced, "just call one of these numbers. We could have helped you in Berlin, you know, if you'd stayed. Manfred and Barbara, the Meyers, they've traced you, they're following you, and *they* have support. In fact we did help you in Berlin. When she told her father you were in town we stopped him going after you, the day you knocked out the two Stasi hard boys at your hotel.

"There are some very unsavoury characters who remain loyal to the old Stasi organization, the network and their chiefs. They're not always efficient. They missed you twice at that Magny-Cours weekend. But they are sadistic, they enjoy meting out punishment, and they will do that as soon as they get their orders. Manfred Meyer is one of their top men. Like us, he and his daughter are aware of your interest in Suzy's treasures, the artworks in Istanbul and Hans's gold bullion. They obviously have a claim on all that."

"They won't get near the Nazi loot," I said, "and what Suzy hid away must have been recovered years ago. Do you think there's any of it left?"

"You must also beware of Vincent and Delcia," he replied, ignoring my question. "After all, their claim would be stronger than yours. The doctor too, what's his name? Morin? He's dangerous. And you cannot ignore the gangs of criminals who are implicated in the case your daughter is trying. They will do anything to put pressure on her."

I looked at his card, which had no name but two telephone numbers, one with a central London code, and one in Paris.

"Who do we ask for?" I said.

He hesitated, then smiled.

"Geoffrey," he said, "just ask for Geoffrey." He paused again, then added, "Actually, you needn't say anything. Calling either of the numbers will trigger the alarm and we won't be far away. You," he said, looking at me, "you are the grandson of Suzanne Burridge-Carnot's English lover, John Henry Wright. And you my dear," he turned to Leila, "you are Leila."

Before we could reply, he smiled again, shook my hand, bowed to Leila, and walked away. I wondered how old he was. He looked about sixty-five, surely not in his seventies. They wouldn't have employed ten-year-olds at Bletchley Park during the war. Did he really work for Britain's Secret Intelligence Service? He had apparently been having us closely followed and he appeared to know everything about us and our rivals. He must have had extraordinary resources at his disposal, but there was something about him that didn't seem quite right.

*

A week later, the phone rang and Leila answered it. I watched her face as she scowled, then reached for her cigarettes.

"Are you sure?" she asked. I waited as she listened intently, slowly blowing out two perfect rings of smoke.

"How does he do it?" she said as she rang off. "That was Delcia. Vincent and Moreau were let out of gaol yesterday. Pending an appeal, they're out on bail. Only eight months after strangling his daughter! She says he's still very angry that you and Laurence had planned to meet again, and he's found your address here. That man is clever, he's a double murderer, and he's getting away with it. Again!"

4. Turkish Delights

I first went to Istanbul in the early 1980s with my wife, my brother James and my sister-in-law. We found the city hot, dusty, unfriendly, and irritating. We were constantly pestered for worthless souvenirs, and began to feel what we imagined to be an underlying hostility. Soon we were anticipating danger round every corner, swarthy men with moustaches and knives waiting to pounce, to kidnap our women. We left two days earlier than planned. Communist Bulgaria, field after trim field of fruit trees in straight irrigated lines, was reassuringly spruce and ordered after Istanbul.

When I returned over a decade later at the invitation of a Turkish friend, I was bowled over and was soon making frequent visits. I discovered that I felt more at home in Istanbul, particularly over the Bosphorous in the Asian districts, than in any other city I knew. Baghdad Avenue was bright and colourful, with its wide flagged pavements, its cafes, sandwich bars, fashionable clothes shops and dozens of tall dark-haired long-legged mini-skirted girls with sunglasses turned up on top of their heads. The Fenerbahçe district had parks, tennis and volley-ball courts, beaches looking onto the Sea of Marmara, a marina and dozens of restaurants serving an extraordinary variety of foods. It was so easy to relax, to sit around and get fine cheap meals at all times, literally any hour of the day or night. The waiters took pride in giving us the best service, an attitude that was apparently lost in Britain some time after the Great War.

I had been invited for a holiday by Ebru, a student whose doctoral thesis I was supervising. For a few years thereafter, I visited her family regularly. Her father and aunt were the children of a former military governor of Istanbul who had been imprisoned whenever he found himself in opposition to the government, and who imprisoned the previous governor each time he was back in office. I asked her if they made some kind of agreement between adversaries, like keeping each other imprisoned in relative comfort. Turkey's prisons were notoriously foul.

"Oh no," she replied, "Grandfather was fed on bread and water, and left in a filthy hole. He did the same to them. But they always made sure they stopped just short of letting each other die."

The family was resolutely secular and republican, in the revered Ataturk tradition. They had a comfortable villa with a luxuriant garden, balconies and turrets looking onto the pleasure boats and the Sea of Marmara. In summer, like many residents of Istanbul, they left the stiflingly hot city and retreated to a house by the Aegean Sea. After an early-morning swim we would have a leisurely Turkish breakfast—three kinds of goat's cheese, celery, cucumber, tasty tomatoes, olives, peppers, smoked ham, fruit juice and coffee. The days passed with more swimming, relaxing on the beach, visits to museums and nearby archaeological jewels. Troy, Ephesus, Pergamon, and lesser known yet almost equally awesome sites. In the evenings we always went for another swim, then back home to the summer house—a fifty-yard walk from the beach—for a shower and dinner. Afterwards we would spend hours chatting on the patio under a canopy of vines.

This was paradise.

*

After Ebru married and moved to northern Cyprus, my visits to her family stopped. I didn't return to Istanbul until August 1997. I was to give a lecture at Boğaziçi University, splendidly situated on an American-style campus in the hills overlooking the Bosphorous a few miles north of the old city. Leila accompanied me for what we planned to be a week's holiday. After my lecture a distinguished lady in her fifties introduced herself as a professor of fine art. She said her husband was the curator of a museum with quite a few orientalist paintings and others by some relatively unknown Turkish artists. Would I like to see these pictures? Her husband would also show us some unusual paintings and small sculptures that were in his reserve store, most of which had never been seen by outsiders.

I said we'd be delighted. The professor called her husband on her mobile, and fixed an appointment for ten o'clock the following morning.

The museum was a large building on the waterfront on the European side of the Bosphorous. There were two security guards at the narrow entrance, and four armed policemen in a cramped office a few yards further on. They searched our bags and frisked me. They telephoned to get a woman to check Leila, and we were still waiting when the curator appeared. He waved aside the policemen and took us through a garden to the main building.

It was an eighteenth-century palace, ornate on the outside but very cold and bare inside, with whitewashed walls, high clear-glass windows which let in too much light, and no furniture beyond the odd chair or bench. There were magnificent views over the Bosphorous, whose waters lapped up against a balustrade. We saw no guides or attendants, and we were the only visitors. It was ghostly, a great contrast with old Istanbul's crowded monuments, and chillingly unlike any other museum or art gallery I had ever seen.

The curator showed us round the galleries—his wife had lectures that morning and had said she would join us later for lunch. He pointed out this or that western orientalist, a few French Impressionists, and many works by Turkish artists, all of whom seemed to be imitating western styles of art.

By twelve o'clock we'd seen only half of the main rooms. Was the curator deliberately slowing us down? He carefully steered us this way or that, smiling only when something was 'not possible' or 'not worth seeing'. He reminded me of East-European guides back in the nineteen sixties and seventies.

At twelve he took us into his office, a grand room on the first floor with carpets, a modern desk, and a battery of telephones and computers. I noticed rows of security screens in an adjoining room. Coffee was brought in by an intimidating waitress. She also reminded me of Eastern Europe in the sixties and seventies, with her hair severely tied back, her high-heeled canvas shoes, and the grimaces as she served us.

The curator's wife was to join us at half past twelve. She arrived twenty minutes late, smiling and chatty. Throughout the lunch—water and no wine, no aperitif or starters, tasteless fish with chips, ice-cream... a very measly and unturkish affair—the professor talked, carefully ensuring that Leila was included in the conversation. Her husband seemed to sulk and hardly spoke. Over coffee she suddenly turned to him.

"Now Yavuz, have they seen the store-room paintings?" I tried not to laugh. His name means 'grim' or 'stern' in Turkish.

"No," he growled, "we didn't have time."

"Well," she said, looking at her watch, "I don't have to be back at the university until half past three, so we can have a look."

"But I have an appointment at two," he said, shaking his head.

"Then I'll show them," she replied brightly.

"I'll cancel my appointment," he scowled, and took out his mobile. He stood up and walked to the far end of the dining-room to talk on his phone. He made two calls.

"Sending warnings ahead?" murmured Leila.

"It'll be alright," said the professor, looking at me very deliberately eye to eye. The curator insisted on us having more coffee. I imagined attendants hastily hiding paintings. At last he guided us down the stairs into a cold, wide corridor. There we saw, in the dim light, rows of paintings on easels covered by blankets, which our lady professor pulled away, revealing reclining odalisks with Pashas and eunuchs, naked girls in baths and pools, groups of women in richly decorated courtyards and on terraces overlooking the Mediterranean. Harem images.

I felt an instant shock of surprise and excitement. Some of the paintings resembled works by Jean-Léon Gérôme, the French artist who had painted hundreds of voyeuristic images of naked 'oriental' women. Others were in the style of the Englishman John Frederick Lewis, whose female figures were never naked. His wife had been his model, but these women were different, more genuinely eastern. A few paintings looked like the work of the American Frederick Arthur Bridgman, who hadn't been to Constantinople, or so I believed, and whose odalisks were always lightly veiled, in tantalisingly transparent garments. Had these famous artists actually seen inside a harem?

If so, this would bring a fundamentally new angle to interpretations of orientalist paintings, for of course men were not allowed inside the 'forbidden space'. With the exception of a handful by women artists, all western paintings of harems were purely imaginary male fantasies. Or could these be Turkish painters, imitating western styles, as they did so well in the collections upstairs?

Leila was beginning to fidget and shiver. It was cold in this dark corridor and she was visibly bored. She'd never liked orientalist images of harem women.

"Ah!" said the professor to her husband, "You haven't shown them the Green Gallery."

"Closed for repairs," he barked, with a face like thunder.

"This way," she said firmly, leading us upstairs into a green-tiled hall. The curator fumbled with some keys, which she snatched from him to open a door leading into a long gallery that looked onto the Bosphorous. I gasped out loud. Leila looked at me anxiously.

"Impossible," I said, for hanging on the walls were dozens of paintings by French artists of the nineteenth and early twentieth century. There were Manets and Monets, Pissarros and Sisleys, paintings by Renoir, Cézanne, Van Gogh, a few early Picassos and some Cubists, works by Matisse, a series of bronze Degas ballet dancers, and a collection of surprisingly small bronze Rodin statues, erotic poses of men, women, and couples.

"Remarkable copies," said the curator, "Osman Hamdi Bey held schools here where he instructed budding Turkish talents in western techniques. This is a sample of their work, which Ataturk insisted should be kept here."

I looked at the professor. She was, again, looking me direct in the eye, with a slight shake of the head. I now understood why the curator had been so unhelpful. These paintings and sculptures, all pre-1914, dating from before the fall of the Ottoman Empire, were genuine. Were they catalogued anywhere? Listed as 'stolen' or 'missing'? They were worth billions of pounds, francs, dollars... billions of whatever currency. Anyone who could get their hands on just two or three of these artworks would become a multi-millionaire overnight.

"Very good imitations of styles," I said to Yavuz, "and a choice of subjects in complete harmony with the French painters, though not, I think, copies of any existing known works."

"That's right," he said, "we're very proud of this Turkish talent." Anticipating further questions, he added hastily, "We've kept this collection hidden for almost a century now, because there might be suspicions and the art market could be thrown off keel for several years. We want to avoid any controversy. We must keep our paintings and sculptures here in Istanbul."

"Quite," I said, looking at my watch. "Well, we've taken up more than enough of your time. Thank you for your generosity. We must let you get on with your work."

Ballerinas and erotica by Degas and Rodin? All those pre-First-World-War French artists? And the odalisks? An amazing collection, among which must be Suzy's 'paintings and little ballet-dancers in Constantinople', her 'gifts from the Germans'.

Someone had wanted to make sure that I would see them.

That evening the professor called to invite us to join her on a trip to Ankara. She said she would show us some of the sights there and some places on the way back. Above all it would be an opportunity to have a serious talk.

"Tomorrow morning. Early start. We'll meet up at 7 a.m. in front of the club shop at the Fenerbahçe football stadium. We'll be well out of the city before eight."

*

She arrived at seven fifteen, driving an old Peugeot 504 estate. She jumped out, put our bags in the back, instructed me to take the wheel and Leila to sit in the front while she sat behind. She said we were to call her by her first name, Aysun, which, she told us proudly, means 'as beautiful as the moon'.

She soon explained that the 'green-gallery' paintings and statues came from various municipal collections in Alsace. They'd been taken by the Orient Express to Constantinople in July 1914, after the Sarajevo assassination of Archduke Franz Ferdinand. The Germans feared that if there was a war, the French would invade Alsace—a province formerly in eastern France that Bismarck had annexed in 1871. They wanted to keep their artworks. They believed they would be safer in Constantinople, protected by the might of their Ottoman ally.

They were too right. The Turks had hidden them away and never returned them. And Aysun said that the harem paintings *were* painted by the western artists, who were sworn to secrecy, never to admit they had been allowed inside the women's quarters of the Sultan's palaces. Originally the paintings were to be seen only by the Sultan himself.

"All those Impressionists and Post-impressionists must be available for everyone," she insisted. "Of course my husband is mad with me for letting you see them. The Turkish government will be too. They want to keep these works of art hidden away. So do the Islamists, whose ideology is opposed to all figurative art, never mind anything so degenerate. In fact they want to destroy the whole collection.

"Yavuz only let you see it because I said your reactions, as an expert from France, would show whether there was any danger that the French were still looking for the paintings. I had to promise you would never speak about them."

I was surprised at what looked like a betrayal of Turkish secrets on Aysun's part. Most unlikely behaviour. But could those western artists really have been inside the Sultan's harem, and no-one ever know about it? Paintings from collections in Alsace? They would have been catalogued, and we would know they were missing. On the other hand, Alsace had moved backwards and forwards between France and Germany four times between 1871 and 1945. Artworks might not have been high on the list of priorities, and catalogues could have been destroyed or hidden away in archives.

In Ankara Aysun took us to a comfortable hotel where she'd booked rooms, and we had a late lunch in the hotel garden.

That afternoon she took us to the Museum of Anatolian Civilizations, a brilliantly presented exhibition of antiquities. Aysun was the best guide I'd ever had. Apart, that is, from her pronunciation of the 'Hittites' whom she called what sounded like the 'High Tits', at which Leila collapsed into a fit of uncontrolled giggling. I remained more or less composed, and discretely told Aysun the correct pronunciation.

When we'd finished, we had a look inside the museum shop. On the way out Aysun suddenly pulled us aside and ushered us through an emergency exit into a garden. She hurried us down some steep steps and into a taxi.

"Well, that's got rid of them for the rest of the afternoon," she announced. "We've been followed since we left Istanbul. They watch me like hawks. And now you've seen all those paintings and little sculptures, they won't let you out of their sight for long. They'll follow us all the way on the road back. You're going to have to be very careful from now on."

We visited the Ataturk Mausoleum, and then relaxed on the terrace of a rather grand café in the centre of Ankara.

Leila said she was getting a bit fed up with men ogling her all the time. The professor instantly retorted, "My dear, it's when they stop ogling that you have to start worrying."

At the hotel that evening, she smiled cheerfully and waved at two rather miserable-looking men who were sitting in the foyer. They didn't smile or wave back.

*

The return journey to Istanbul took three days, as we stopped to visit the many sites of cultural interest that Aysun wanted to show us. On the second afternoon we arrived at the historic site of Ephesus, as large and as well preserved as Pompeii. We walked around from district to district in what had been a bustling Greek and then Roman city over two thousand years ago.

Suddenly I heard a cry, "Redmond! Redmond! Hey, Redmond!" It was Patrick and Nicolas, two of Adam's friends from home, with their girlfriends. We laughed at the coincidence, took photos, exchanged news, and agreed to meet for dinner.

Aysun found us a hotel, and at eight we met our friends in a cafe for an aperitif. An hour later we moved on to a restaurant. Afterwards they accompanied us to our hotel, and one of the girls remarked to me as they were leaving, "That girlfriend of yours certainly attracts men. Our two are very much in awe, and did you notice those guys who were everywhere we went, cafeteria, bar, restaurant, hotel... They never seemed to take their eyes off her."

"No," I said, "what did they look like?"

"Oh, you needn't worry," she smiled, "they're not much competition. Two rather heavy guys in their mid-thirties, and a group of three men with a muscular blond woman. And there was a German couple too, an older man with a young lady. He looked at Leila all the time. And the girl looked at you. Maybe it's just that everyone thinks you're a strange couple to be together. At first we thought you were with the Turkish lady, more your age and style, you know. It took us a while to see that you were with the younger one. Patrick said 'How does Adam's father do it?' "

"Look," I said, "you can tell him that I haven't had to *do* anything. I wish people would mind their own business."

"Okay, okay," she said, "I'm sorry I mentioned it. I seem to have touched a sensitive point..."

At breakfast I saw two of the groups that were following us, but there was no sign of a German couple.

That morning we visited Pergamon, an ancient citadel perched at the top of a hill. More magnificent temples and amphitheatres, with views for miles around. Then we drove to the nearby site of a Roman villa that was being excavated before the valley was flooded for a new reservoir. It was a site I'd visited with Ebru. It will soon be under water.

There was no-one about. I showed Leila and Aysun to the steps leading down to some underground baths I remembered, with spectacular mosaics and pools. Aysun said the steps were too steep for her, so she stayed outside while we went down to what must have been one of the best preserved Roman indoor baths anywhere in the world.

There was a pool protected by a large glass dome. The water, however, was murky and covered in green moss, which I didn't recall from my previous visit. Leila and I crouched by the edge of the bath, imagining ourselves to be the Roman proprietors of the villa.

Our Roman Pool

As we stood up I heard a scream and I felt someone grasp hold of my neck from behind. My throat was pressed very hard and I was suddenly very cold as I was shoved into the water and my head held down. I remember panicking as I was sure I was about to drown.

When I came round I was lying face down on what turned out to be some hard Roman flagstones. Leila was massaging my back and legs. I moved my shoulders, turned over, and saw Aysun talking into a mobile phone. She looked at me.

"We have to get out," she said.

My head and neck were aching, and I felt very weak. My mouth tasted as if I'd been eating a mixture of water cress, spinach and raw frog.

"What happened?" I muttered.

"Two men were hiding in an alcove, waiting for us. One of them pushed you in and held your head under the water. The other pinned me down and I couldn't move or shout. Then I heard two cracks. The grip on me was released. Aysun was standing there with a revolver. We pulled you from the pool, shoved them in, and managed to carry you upstairs. We'd better go. Can you stand up?"

I was trying to take everything in, still wet and dazed as I walked to the car-park. The Meyers were on our trail. Two men? Their Stasi thugs?

A silver-grey Nissan drew up. Out jumped a blond girl and three men. The ones who had been watching us at Ephesus?

"I do wish you wouldn't keep changing your plans. You'll have to keep us better informed than this," said the girl.

"Who are you?" asked Leila.

"Geoffrey's Turkish team. He's told us to look out for you. You must go back to Istanbul tonight."

"We will," I replied, "but before *you* set off you'd better check in the baths over there, down the steps and under that glass dome. And," I added, "I hope you make a better job of clearing up the mess down there than you have of 'looking out' for us since we've been in Turkey."

Geoffrey's Turkish team? He was having us followed again. To protect us? Our security urgently needed organizing. I was angry with myself for not being more alert.

*

Leila took the wheel and drove off, muttering that we'd have to sort things out with Geoffrey. Meanwhile, there was some sorting out to do with Aysun.

"Explanation, please!" I said, turning round and staring hard at her.

"Quickly. And the truth, this time," barked Leila.

"I'm sorry," came the reply, "I'm really sorry." Aysun hesitated, and I saw that she was crying.

"Quickly," Leila repeated.

"My sole concern has always been the paintings," Aysun began, "and the sculptures. But I soon discovered that it was much more complicated than I'd ever imagined. There have been threats to my life, and to my daughter. I now know—as you do—that their intention is to get rid of you. It's because I've let you see the art collection. Ever since we've been away from Istanbul, I've had to keep our pursuers informed as to our movements. But I've tried to protect you. I shot the two gorillas who were holding your head under water, Redmond, and who would have raped you, Leila, before they threw you in the pool too.

"It's the first time I've used that gun, which I've kept in my bag for four years. They'll kill me now if I stay in Istanbul. They will certainly try again to get you. You must go home to France immediately and forget about everything you've seen. You won't be safe anywhere. You'll have to get some kind of protection, the police or private security. They won't leave you alone. *Both* of you are now in danger.

"I'm going to go with my daughter to the village where my grandparents brought me up. It's in the far east of the country, an area controlled by the Kurdish separatists. I'll be safe there. I'm Kurdish, not Turkish.

"And by the way," she added, seemingly on the spur of the moment, "that German couple who've been following us. I've met the man before. He came to my office a year ago. He was very polite. He said he represented the German government, and that the paintings and statuettes belonged to them. He recalled that our countries were allies in the First World War, and that the artworks had been sent to Constantinople for safety. He claimed that Germany should now recover them, and that he had been mandated to negotiate on behalf of his government. I told him I had no idea what he was talking about, and that he should enquire at the Ministry of Culture."

Leila drove fast on the highway. Twice the police stopped us for speeding. Each time Aysun suggested a reduction in the on-the-spot fine, paid in cash and with no written record, all of which seemed to meet expectations. We were back late in our hotel at Fenerbahçe. A message was waiting for me, from an American colleague. He was a specialist in orientalism and was in Istanbul with his wife. It was an invitation for dinner the following evening. I rang his mobile and accepted. I called Aysun to invite her and the curator to join us, but she said they weren't free. She was doubly sorry, she said, because my American colleague was an art critic of international repute, and the restaurant that he'd booked was one of Istanbul's finest.

It turned out, indeed, to be very smart, and expensive. It was on the European side, at the far end of the big Hippodrome Square beyond Santa Sophia. We relaxed at tables which seemed to have been specially laid out for us in a rear courtyard. It was warm and the atmosphere was convivial. I talked orientalism with my colleague and his wife. Leila chatted with two students who had also been invited—an American called Jennifer, and Estêr, a tall girl with dark skin, black hair and eyes, and very thick blood-red lips. She was from Van in eastern Turkey, near the borders with Armenia, Iran and Iraq.

While we were having coffee Leila and Estêr went inside to the toilets. Ten minutes later I realized they hadn't returned. I suggested that Jennifer should go and see if they were alright. Perhaps one of the girls wasn't well. She came rushing back screaming.

"They've gone, they've been kidnapped!"

Estêr's bag lay open on the toilet floor, its contents spread about, and there were spatterings of blood on the walls. A window had been smashed—there was blood there too—and the waiters who had served us were tied up and gagged. We followed a trail of spots of blood down a narrow corridor and out into a back street.

I rang the emergency numbers for Geoffrey.

*

Cyprus. Gazimağüza, the city known more familiarly in English as Famagusta. Part of it is in the Turkish Republic of Northern Cyprus. There is a thriving community with Turkish cafes and shops in narrow streets. In the main square, a bright yellow British pillar-box with an embossed Crown, 'GR' and 'Post Office'. The faithful are called to prayer from a minaret built onto the Gothic façade of the Cathedral of Saint Nicholas, converted into the Lala Mustafa Pasha Mosque.

I'd been here for two days. Blazing sun. Unbearable humid heat indoors and out, day and night. Two days waiting for news. Geoffrey had phoned me in Istanbul, about an hour after I'd called his numbers. He said their Turkish team had let us down. He apologized, and added that he'd sent two of his best operatives to free Leila. I said I hoped they wouldn't arrive too late.

He apologized again, then told me to go to Ataturk airport where a ticket for Cyprus would be waiting for me at the Turkish Airlines desk.

"Cyprus? Now?" I asked.

"Yes, straight away. Leave your stuff in the hotel at Fenerbahçe. We'll collect your things and get them sent on."

He said a taxi would pick me up at Ercan airport and drive me to a hotel in Gazimagüza where he would contact me. They'd identified Leila and Estêr's captors and located a possible hiding-place, in the deserted buffer zone between Turkish and Greek Cyprus. They were ready to move in and free the girls. I said again that I hoped they wouldn't be too late. He said I wasn't to worry.

I was to call him only in an emergency, if I was in danger. Never simply to get an update. But I'd now spent two days and two nights in Cyprus without news, and with Leila kidnapped by a gang that was evidently not too gentle.

Suddenly I thought of Ebru. I called her mobile, and she answered immediately.

"Where are you?" she asked.

"Sitting outside a cafe opposite Lala Mustafa Pasha Mosque in Fama... in Gazimagüza," I replied. She exploded.

"What? Where? You're kidding. I'll be over in five minutes."

She emerged from her car, leaving it in a 'no parking' zone in front of the café. She grinned and gave me a big hug, lit up a cigarette, and said she was now teaching at a school in Turkish Cyprus. She asked what I was doing here.

I told her, omitting most of the details: I was here because my friend Leila had been kidnapped two days before in Istanbul, and was apparently somewhere in Cyprus. She was, I said, with a girl from Van, called Estêr.

Ebru gasped. Then she motioned me to be quiet and picked up her mobile. She talked in Turkish, with great urgency, too fast for me to understand. After two or three minutes she rang off and put her phone on the table. I asked her what she was doing.

"Calling my aunt," she half-smiled. "She was for many years the mistress of one of Turkey's top generals, and our family is very well connected with the military. In less than half an hour the Turkish army will be looking for Leila and Estêr. They will find them, if they are anywhere on this part of the island."

She sat back and lit another cigarette. I said nothing about Yavuz's museum and the art collections, but told her about our meeting with Aysun. I said we'd been on a trip to Ankara with her, and that she was Kurdish. Ebru stiffened, picked up her mobile and called her aunt again.

"We'll soon know," she said. "The army controls everything here. And they know everything. About everybody. Especially Kurds. Have you had dinner?"

We ordered *mezeler*, steak, salad and chips, and a bottle of *rakı*. As we ate, and I was all the while thinking about Leila, Ebru told me how she'd left Istanbul and found a post teaching English here in Cyprus. She'd married a university lecturer. She chatted and tried to make me laugh, but I was exhausted and dispirited. A police siren sounded from a neighbouring street. It became louder and then wailed full blast as the vehicle entered the square to our left and stopped in front of us. I thought they were going to put a parking ticket on Ebru's car, but it wasn't a police vehicle. It was a Turkish army van.

Two young soldiers leapt down from the front and opened the side door. Out stepped Leila, her face bewildered and, so it seemed in the bright street lighting, bruised down one side. She looked around, blinking. One of the soldiers pointed to Ebru and me. Leila shrieked and ran forward, arms outstretched. But no Estêr.

*

Leila recounted how she'd been drying her hands in the washroom at the restaurant in Istanbul, when she saw Estêr drop her bag. Half the contents fell out all over the floor, so she bent down to help collect everything. Someone came up behind her and pinned her to the floor, face down.

"I couldn't breathe, let alone cry out. I tried to struggle free, but someone grabbed my hair and knocked my head on the tiles. Blood dripped from my forehead as I was yanked up and marched out into the street. When I resisted, I was kneed hard in the back. It hurt. I was then shoved into a van, through the side door and onto the floor. I was hoping that Estêr had been able to warn you, but then I heard her talking. She obviously knew our captors. I couldn't make out what she was saying. It was a language I didn't know, but it didn't sound like the Turkish I'd been hearing over the previous few days."

When the van stopped a man's voice had ordered her to get out. She stepped into the courtyard of a ramshackle house, surrounded by a high wall. She was taken downstairs into a basement. Two young men pushed her into a room with a marble table and bright lighting. There were wires and various tools on a workbench. They had untied her hands, pulled her clothes off and sat her on the cold marble table top.

"If I'd seen them on the beach I might have found them cute," said Leila, "but I've never known such fiery hatred as what I felt when they touched me. One of them stroked my thighs and smiled as he moved his face close to mine. I was cold, in pain, and *humiliated*. I knew he was going to violate me. In faltering English, he asked why we'd gone to Ankara, what we were looking for in Ephesus, why we'd rushed back to Istanbul."

He was soon forgetting to interrogate her as he started to make suggestive remarks. He undid his belt and lowered his jeans, while the other one whistled and clicked his tongue noisily.

"I couldn't think of any way out. I couldn't hope to hold off the two of them, but I decided I might be able to cope with one at a time. In two quick movements I had stabbed my heel into the one who had lowered his jeans, and I kneed his jaw with the other leg as his head came down towards me.

"He grunted and crumpled, but he wouldn't be out for long. The other one shouted as I turned to face him. I was wondering what lay beyond the door and if I could get out, when he shouted again. The first boy was groaning but was struggling to his feet. I heard footsteps and realized that the shouting had attracted the attention of others upstairs. Now I would have no chance of getting out. In any case I hadn't thought it through… I was stark naked."

Estêr had come running downstairs. She began screaming at them. "Give her her clothes. Get out of here. What have you been doing?" All that in English, then she began shouting at them in another language—she later told Leila it was Kurdish. She explained that she was Aysun's daughter from a first marriage. When Aysun had told Yavuz about the American professor's dinner, he had made two phone calls, then ordered Estêr to meet the American student who'd been invited. Estêr had got herself invited too. She was to accompany Leila to the toilet, drop her bag, and Leila would be overpowered as she knelt down to help.

Estêr had told Leila that she would be transferred to a hiding place in Cyprus. The plan was to then feed me clues as to where she was, and I would fall into their trap. They could then ensure that neither of us revealed the existence of the artworks in Istanbul. Apparently Aysun was planning to go into hiding in eastern Turkey with Estêr, where they would both be safe.

*

Aysun had lied when she said the artworks came from galleries in Alsace. They had belonged to two wealthy Greek families who'd settled in northern France in the 1870s. For forty years they bought paintings and sculptures before the artists became famous. None of the works were publicly catalogued. But in 1915 the invading German army stole the collection and transported it to Constantinople. There it stayed. It was indeed the prize that Gottlieb had promised to Suzy, though it was doubtful that he could ever have delivered.

I had agreed to say nothing about the harem pictures on condition that the western canvasses and sculptures in the Green Gallery were returned to France, where I would try to ensure that they were returned to the descendants of the original Greek owners. After all, no-one else had a legitimate claim on them. The harem paintings were much less important and could be left where they were for the moment. I was surprised at how easily this arrangement was accepted.

A few weeks later we met Geoffrey in a cafe opposite the Louvre. He admitted that he had initiated the whole business by getting Aysun to attend my lecture and invite us to see the collection in Yavuz's museum. Apparently someone high up in MI6 was an art lover and wanted the existence of those paintings to be revealed.

He explained that two rival factions in Turkey were constantly warring with each other. Both had wanted to prevent news of the art from leaking out. The Islamists had for years been trying to destroy what they regarded as corrupt and offensive artworks, whilst the secular republican faction had always protected the collection. They had armed guards in the museum and simply wanted to keep all the paintings and statuettes in Turkey.

It was the republicans who had attacked us in the Roman pool, and the Islamists who'd set up the kidnapping of Leila with the intent of luring me into a trap. Geoffrey told us that Aysun and Estêr never reached their native Kurdish town. They were murdered and their bodies disposed of in the sea around Cyprus. Less than a month later Yavuz was found hanged in Aysun's office at the university.

Apparently Manfred Meyer had recently attached himself to a German delegation and was trying to ensure the collection would be sent back to Germany, not France. It was not clear whether he was trying to recover the art for Germany, or whether wanted to get his own hands on his grandfather's promised reward for Suzanne.

"What about Vincent?" I asked. "Is he interested in the Constantinople paintings? After all, they were promised as payment to his mother-in-law? And Delcia?"

Geoffrey said he didn't know. He had no reason to suspect that they were interested.

"Vincent has always been a lone wolf," he said. "He's clever and he's ruthless, and he could be a danger if he decides to harm you. He controls Delcia like he controlled her mother, but he can't do much about the paintings and sculptures. Unlike Meyer, who is getting the remnants of his Stasi men along with some younger recruits to do his dirty work for him, Vincent has no support, no means to intervene or get hold of the artworks."

I asked if the Turks were now a real threat to me, or to my family. He thought for a moment.

"The Islamists? I don't think so. They believe that if you manage to get the paintings and sculptures back to France, they will have more chance of destroying them here than if they remain in Turkey. They'll probably watch you but not harm you. But the Republicans, they certainly have the means to hurt you. Even more so than the Meyers. They are determined to keep their paintings, and to keep their secret, so you are obviously a threat to them. They have messed up once, and someone will have paid dearly for that. The next time, whoever is in charge will make sure they don't mess up again."

I reminded him that it was the Turkish army that had rescued Leila, not him or his 'team', of whom we had seen and heard no more.

"Yes," he said, "but that rescue mission was just a favour to a senior general's mistress. And it's you, the art historian, that they want to silence."

5. Champagne Moments

She was sitting alone at the table next to mine. She'd been explaining to the waiter that recently she had graduated from a 'Master of champagne' course in Reims. I turned to her and said that I had some curious little riddles concerning champagne. Maybe she could help?

She responded at once.

"Hullo. My name's Alessandra. Yes, my father sent me to Reims to learn everything about the production and marketing of champagne. He's convinced there are good openings for young women in the wine business. Since I came out top of my class and won an international wine-tasting competition, he's prepared to buy me the first small champagne house that comes onto the market. So what about your riddles?"

I must have looked at her with raised eyebrows. Champagne houses rarely came onto the market, and even the smallest would sell for not less than twenty or thirty million francs. She explained that her father was a diamond merchant in Rome. He'd always wanted the best for her and had sent her to Roedean, the select girls private school in Brighton, where she'd spent three years perfecting her English and acquiring a good all-round education. For the next two years she'd followed the master of wine course in Reims.

"What about your riddles?" she repeated.

I recited two short lines from the first one.

"Once we were five,
Now we are two..."

What could this mean, I asked, in the context of either Champagne with a capital 'C', the wine-producing region, or champagne with a small 'c', the sparkling wine itself?

"Mmmm," she concentrated for a few seconds. "Could be the different vineyard areas. Traditionally there are five, but today only two make really good champagne, the hills called the *Montagne de Reims* and the slopes of the *Côte des Blancs*."

"She's right," I thought, and asked her if there could be any other meanings.

"Let me think. My class notes, I always did a skeleton of them, and used numbers to remind myself how many topics there were in each section. So, *champagne, five and two...*"

She closed her eyes.

"Grape varieties perhaps. Nowadays only *pinot noir* and *chardonnay* are used for the best champagnes. There's a little *pinot meunier* in some, and they used to grow *pinot blanc* and *pinot gris* but these are hardly found these days."

"What else?" I insisted.

Eyes tight closed, her brow screwed up, she continued.

"Five? Five degrees of dry and sweet, *brut, extra-dry, sec, demi-sec, doux*. Only two are found today, *brut* and *doux*."

Amazing. This young woman was a walking encyclopedia of the vineyards and wines of Champagne.

"How about this?" I said.

"*Once we were five,*
Now we are two,
The upstart is vulgar
But my red's still true."

She didn't hesitate.

"It's Bouzy, *Bouzy rouge*. In the Middle Ages they made five wines. An ordinary red, an ordinary white, a classy white, a fine red, and a murky liquid with a fizz that they didn't like at all. Then they improved it and started promoting their 'upstart', the unique, now bright bubbly white champagne. At first it was considered a bit vulgar, all froth and frivolity. Today you can still find a little of the fine red known as 'Bouzy rouge', from the name of the village where it's made, but the other three have disappeared, long gone, and the upstart reigns supreme."

The first riddle had been solved in less than five minutes. Perhaps Suzy's 'treasure' hadn't been as well hidden as she'd thought.

*

I told Alessandra the clues were a game I was playing with my three grown-up children, a 'treasure hunt' that we played in the various wine regions. I asked if she would like to accompany me for a day out, with a meal in a good restaurant and the challenge of solving the riddles. She accepted at once. We agreed that I would collect her at half past eight the next Saturday. She gave me her address and phone number. By now I was no longer surprised at her readiness to give me her contact details and to join me on a day trip. She was so remarkably self-possessed.

My friendship with Leila had just hit a mini-crisis. I think we understand each other pretty well, but from time to time a heated argument will blaze up. There'll be a sudden disagreement, almost always about something that I consider to be trivial. She has a good line in withering sarcasm, distorting what I've said. She's particularly scathing when she's wrong. But five minutes later it's gone, and she'll be charming. We both know it's not worth coming back to the argument. The week before I ran into Alessandra, however, after what I thought was a minor spat, Leila flared up and left immediately. I didn't know what to make of her disappearance, but I saw no reason not to take advantage of the Italian girl's expertise.

I drew up in front of her flat at 8.30 sharp, in my old Toyota van. She was waiting on the pavement with a big folder of notes, a couple of books on champagne, and the *Quid*, a popular dictionary-cum-encyclopedia. This was in November 1997, before everyone had smart-phones with internet access.

"This should be fun," she said, sitting up in the front seat but still without a smile. She had a deep voice, rather masculine, and she spoke perfect English with long vowels and a rising intonation. The overall impression I can only describe as artificially natural, as if she'd been bred to appear at ease under all circumstances.

Suzy had written four clues for Champagne, some with more than one riddle. The first clue had five! Alessandra had already suggested Bouzy. The second riddle in the first clue was just one line.

Remember remember the fifth of November.

I explained about "gunpowder, treason and plot." Guy Fawkes. Alessandra said she knew that, of course, and pointed out that here we were, on our way to Reims, on Saturday November 8th.

She could find nothing in her memory, her notes or her books about champagne and the fifth of November. Then she took out her diary, looked at the calendar of saints, and saw that November 5th was the feast of Saint Lié. She suddenly turned to me and said:

"Saint-Lié, near the village on the hill, not far from Bouzy. There's a small stone chapel which has a beautiful statue of the

Virgin, and it's dedicated to Saint Lié."

First Bouzy. Then the nearby Saint-Lié chapel. What next? I showed Alessandra the third riddle, still part of the first clue.

The smiling angel's lost her head,
The beam just knocked it down,
But mine is safe, though it removes
Look under Sheba's crown.

She immediately recognized the 'smiling angel', a famous statue on the western front of Reims cathedral. She looked it up in her *Quid*, and explained that the cathedral had been bombarded in September 1914 by the Kaiser's artillery. The roof caught fire, and a falling beam knocked the head off the stone angel. It was restored in the 1920s. 'Sheba's crown', however, was a mystery.

As we approached Reims, I took the last turning off the motorway and drove along a narrow road then a winding country lane up to the Saint-Lié chapel. It was beautifully situated, the statue above

the door lit up by the low November sun. It was a young Virgin Mary, with long hair and a hint of a smile, more demure than the famous angel at the cathedral. We were looking up at her, when a group of chattering tourists emerged from the door below.

A tall, bald priest with a gaunt face was leading the group, but he stopped speaking when he saw us. Everyone else stopped, too, and stared at us. Did we want to see inside, he asked? The chapel was open only once a year, for two days, the weekend nearest to Saint Lié's day. They'd just erected this statue which was a replica. The original, recently restored, had been removed for safety to his church down the hill.

Two German tourists began chatting to Alessandra whilst I quizzed the priest. Was there any connection between the chapel and the Queen of Sheba? No, but there was a statue of Sheba on the western front of the cathedral. He believed that too was a replica. And of course the real original Virgin Mary, here at Saint-Lié, had been removed during the First World War. Fortunately, because the chapel had been destroyed by German guns in 1918. It had been rebuilt in the 1920s and 30s, and renovated again recently. But he thought the original statue had been lost.

"It's never been found?" I insisted.

No, he thought not, but we could go and look at his parish records if I was interested. He bade goodbye to his tourists, and led us back down the hill to the presbytery. I thought the eyes of the two Germans followed Alessandra a little too avidly.

The priest sat us in soft armchairs, poured three good-sized glasses of port, and held out a plate of dry biscuits. How could he help?

I noticed books and papers spread out on a table. I asked him about the chapel. He repeated what he'd just told me. The statue of the Virgin Mary was a replica, the restored original was now in his church, and an earlier statue had been removed in 1914 during the first weeks of the war, to prevent it being damaged.

"So," I insisted again, "the statue that was hidden in 1914 has never been recovered?"

He laughed, and said that the priest then in charge of the church and chapel had buried it for safety. Apparently he'd told no-one where he'd put it, and he was later killed by a German shell. The parish records for those years had been destroyed during the battles in 1918. Today there was no-one left in the village who could remember the Great War.

I thought that *Look under Sheba's crown* was the main clue to the whereabouts of the lost statue, so I asked him what that might mean, reminding him about the Sheba that he'd mentioned, on the western front of the cathedral. He said her crown had been badly eroded by the weather. Was there any connection, I asked, with Bouzy, the village on the south-eastern slope of the *Montagne de Reims*?

He laid his glass of port on the table, and started searching through the pile of documents. His fingers settled on a map, dated 1926, and he pointed to a spot on the hill west of Bouzy. *La grotte de Saba* was inscribed in italics. Sheba's Grotto. Then he found an old photograph of the cathedral statue of Sheba. Her crown was indeed eroded. It looked more like a flattish round cake.

We thanked the priest, and as we stepped out of the presbytery I noticed the two Germans leaning against a wall on the pavement opposite. Alessandra nodded to them and they acknowledged her gesture with a slight wave of the hand.

We were both feeling hungry so I suggested an early lunch at a restaurant I knew, hidden in the nearby woods. Our fillet steaks were accompanied by a bottle of *Bouzy rouge*, an ethereal, ghost of a red wine, very much at home alongside the best champagnes in vineyards overlooking Reims cathedral. Afterwards we left the van just outside Bouzy village and climbed up the gentle slope towards where Sheba's Grotto had been shown on the clergyman's map. We were soon lost. It was thickly wooded, with layers of prickly brown brambles from the previous summer. Suddenly I stumbled forward as the earth gave way beneath my feet, and I fell over a ledge. Winded, I sat down and looked around. I noticed that Alessandra was laughing. She asked cheerfully if I was okay.

"Look!" I said.

There was a hump of earth topped by... what was it? It seemed familiar, a big block of limestone. It looked... like a flat round cake. Sheba's crown!

Beneath the crown was a small cave. Brambles and branches had been pulled away and lay to each side of the opening. Rotting wood too had been pulled away and lay on the ground. It appeared to be the remains of a small door and its frame. Someone had been here recently. Very recently, for the flaking wood exhaled a fresh mushroomy smell.

The cave was barely big enough to stand up in. Not much of a 'grotto', but when I stooped and stepped inside, my shin hit a hard object. I blinked as my eyes adjusted to the darkness. There she was, the statue of the Virgin, much smaller than the replica on the chapel wall had seemed, but with the original crown, the hair and her demure smile. I lifted her outside without difficulty, but the head fell off as I put her gently on the ground.

Today's replica, with the crown, the hair, and the demure smile

Now what were the last two of the five riddles in Suzy's first clue, the riddles that I hadn't yet told Alessandra? I took the paper from my wallet...

Under the crown, the hair the hair
The hair the hair, when it's not there
My head is turned, it's your first share.

The last riddle heralded disappointment:

You see, all that glisters is not gold.

The statue had indeed had a large crown, attached to the back of the head by a thin rusted metal pin. It too had broken away, and the hair had split in two, each side, left and right, now lying on the ground. The hairless head was hollow. I put my hand inside and scratched around. Empty. No first share, no glister.

"Your children didn't make up those riddles, did they?" Alessandra snapped. "You haven't told me the truth. This is a hunt for real treasure, but someone else has got here first."

I was trying to work out who had got to Sheba's Grotto just before us. Surely not the priest, he must have known about it for years. But those documents spread out on his desk? And the two Germans, had they been questioning him before we arrived?

*

Suzy's second clue was another one-liner, this time in German:
im Keller bei dem Fräulein

A cellar belonging to a 'Fräulein'? Off we went to look round the vineyards north of Reims, the area that had been behind German lines from 1914 to 1918. We visited four properties, and I quizzed the occupants about their ancestors, the history of their vineyards, and those of their neighbours. Enquiries about a *Fräulein* were getting nowhere. Our fifth call turned out to be a big run-down house where a woman and two barking mongrels came out to meet us.

The dogs were a nuisance, jumping up and barking, so the woman tied them up. She apologized for her husband's absence, he wasn't well. I began quizzing her. How long had the vineyard been in the family? What did she know about its history? Had an unmarried woman, possibly German, ever held the property?

She looked at me, a probing stare. She appeared tired and harassed, but underneath was a brave, warm-hearted woman. She said I could call her Margot. But who was I? I said I was a university professor studying the history of Champagne, and that I'd come across a paper hinting at a store of wines hidden somewhere nearby. She started telling us about her great-grandmother Aline, who had owned the vineyard and kept it going even when they were surrounded by the German army during the First World War. The vineyard and winery had stayed in the family.

Margot had inherited it all ten years ago. It was hard, she said, with a husband who was always sick, especially now her daughters had left home. I bought two cases of her champagne. She said I would be welcome if I came back. "Any time," she stressed.

Again, however, Alessandra was not pleased. Why had I not enquired further? Why had I not tried to unravel the riddle? Why was I not being truthful with her? I said we had to hurry since it was nearing the end of the afternoon, and we just had time to work on the third of the four clues. This time no more rhymes, just three lines:

The Emperor's English mother's home (where did OUR Emperor die?).

It's in an outhouse...

Under the flames, where the salamander lies.

I explained that 'the Emperor's English mother' must refer to Saint Helen, whose son Constantine was the Emperor who converted Rome to Christianity. Of course our Emperor Napoleon died on the island of Saint Helena...

"It's the famous abbey at Hautvillers," Alessandra interrupted. "A priest stole part of Saint Helen's body from Rome, and brought it back to Hautvillers. We've got to find an outhouse, with a fireplace and a salamander sculpted in the stone mantelpiece."

The abbey was more than twenty minutes' drive away, near the top of a gently sloping hillside above the River Marne. When we arrived a young man at reception looked at his watch, smiled at Alessandra and said there was just time for a quick guided tour.

"I seem to remember," she lied, "when we came here with our class, there was a fireplace, with a salamander sculpted on the mantelpiece. It was in one of these outhouses..."

"That's odd," he said. "An old man was asking about that not long ago. He looked at a piece of paper and asked me about salamanders and fireplaces."

I asked what he looked like.

"Tall. Stiff. But... I don't know, he looked a bit unbalanced somehow, his arms moving about all the time."

So Vincent had got here before us. 'Not long ago.' That was strange. He must have had the clues for years.

Our guide went to the office, came back jangling a bunch of keys, and took us into a room at the end of what had once been a cloister. A bare room with a tiled floor, and a large fireplace with a salamander in the middle, right over the hearth. I would have to return alone. Only to discover that Vincent had already removed the treasure?

We were driving away from the abbey and it was getting dark when Alessandra remarked in an offhand tone, "There it is again.

I've seen it three times now."

"What?" I asked.

"A dark grey Mercedes, 4-by-4. A 'D' sticker by the rear plate. It goes everywhere we do. It's just behind us. I think it's those two guys who were at the chapel."

I looked in the rear mirror. The Mercedes was very close. On the narrow road running down from the abbey to Epernay, it suddenly shot out to overtake us, then cut in far too soon. If I hadn't braked it would have forced us off the road and into a ditch. I decided we should get on the road back to Paris. My Toyota van was far too slow and lightweight to compete with a Mercedes 4x4. I drove straight to the motorway.

I hadn't recited the fourth clue to Alessandra. She became quite angry.

"You're not telling me everything, are you? You think you have a valuable treasure, but you don't want me to know."

I was wondering if our meeting had really been pure chance. I recalled that she had arrived at the restaurant just after me, and had chosen to sit at the table next to mine. I also recalled her brief exchanges, of words and signs, with the two Germans.

*

Three days later I arrived at Margot's early in the afternoon. She came out of the house, hair unkempt and with the harassed look of a woman trying her best to cope against overwhelming odds. When she saw me she came running to the van. She tied up the dogs, smoothed back her hair, and took me into the kitchen.

"I know why you're here," she said. "We've been waiting for a long time. Have you got the paper with the riddles?"

I showed it to her. She told me the story of how Suzy had deposited a stock of wine with her great-grandmother Aline during the First World War. Suzy had said that it might have to be kept for some time, so Aline's family could drink the bottles that reached maturity, but could they please replace them with ones of roughly equivalent quality? She left quite a large sum of money to buy the replacements, and promised that she and her daughter would collect the wine later.

After the war Aline learnt of Suzy's tragic death. She vowed to keep the wines safely and wait for the daughter. But no-one ever came. In the end, the family drank and replaced almost all of the bottles. The secret was passed down to Margot, the fourth generation.

"We've had a lot of visitors since you were here," she added, "I've had to be very careful. Two old men came, one was English, like you. He said he knew you. The other was French. He had a paper like yours, but he was so unpleasant, I wasn't going to give him anything. And two Germans came an hour after you were here with that Italian girl. We would never give them anything either. They were aggressive, but they left us alone when I unleashed the dogs. Then some more Germans came too, a man and a young woman. They were very friendly, too friendly for strangers. I sent them away, saying we were closed for the week because my husband was ill. It's a long time since we've had so many visitors in one afternoon."

She took me out through the yard into a field. In one corner was an odd-looking hillock. In a ditch at the back was a door and after she had inserted and turned keys in three different locks, we walked down a staircase into the most immaculately kept underground wine cellar. There were several rooms, with hundreds of bottles, neatly laid on their sides and stacked row upon row in concrete bins, up to the vaulted ceilings. I turned and saw wooden cases piled against one wall.

"It was a Great-War German bunker," said Margot. "Aline converted it into a wine cellar. Most of the champagnes and burgundies had to be drunk long ago, and almost all the older Bordeaux vintages, Latour, Margaux and Haut-Brion, have gone. But all the old bottles have been replaced. The 45's and 49's are good, the 82's and 90's are still maturing."

The very best postwar vintages.

I drove into the field and stopped by the hillock. I put ten cases in the back of the van while she made up five more with a selection from the open bins. Dark grey and black clouds were looming and a cold wind was blowing.

"I'd better be off," I said, adding "for now. I don't want to get stuck if it snows."

"Well, I know you'll be back," she smiled, but there were tears in her eyes.

"Soon," I said, and drove off. She hadn't even asked me how I'd come by the clues.

Next morning, I made a list. It was a wine-lover's dream. Cases of the greatest vintages of the very finest French wines. Not Suzy's, but the best possible replacements. Then I saw that Margot's last case had twelve bottles of Suzy's originals. Lafite, Margaux, Latour, Yquem, from 1900 to 1915. I've tried only one so far, a Lafite 1914. Quite an emotional moment, opening and tasting a wine whose grapes had been harvested the very month Grandfather had first met Suzy, the young wine just beginning to mature during those years of their passionate encounters. Ruby red, spicy gingery nose, violets, smooth, the first mouthfuls were glorious... then slowly, second by second, the life drained away. The colour, aroma and taste evaporated. The wine was dead.

*

I called on Margot four more times, collecting the wines that I piled up in the cellar at home. I would soon have to store them elsewhere. By now Leila had come back. She just turned up one day, and neither of us mentioned any argument, rift or absence. She said nothing when I told her about Alessandra. The next day she looked at me very seriously, and said that her other friends were in passing, but we were for ever. I didn't know what to make of that.

There are times when I am mystified by her. I have occasionally wondered if she has attached herself to me with some particular aim. Several times I have tried to start a conversation that might help me see clearly what, if anything, is going on. But she always manages to turn the talk away, and she becomes very hostile if I insist, especially on any personal topic. I was later to learn that she had been in contact with her 'ex'. Geoffrey spoke to me about it.

"We know they have met. He is what I would describe as an Islamist, quite a militant and hostile to the West. We can't find anything to show that she shares his views, but she is a clever woman and she could be hiding her real beliefs. You need to be on your guard."

The next time I went to Champagne I decided she would come with me. After all she has proved her loyalty to me at more than one moment of danger. We started with a visit to the old priest at Ville-Dommange. I had two questions, and told him I'd been to Hautvillers and seen the fireplace and the salamander. Before I could say more he answered both my questions without me even having to ask.

"Oh!" he grunted, "There's a much finer fireplace with a sculpted salamander at Bouvillers. It's in the ruins of a big house on land that used to belong to the abbey." He stopped and scratched his head. "Of course, I'd forgotten." He looked very apologetic. "Few people know that there are also two salamanders sculpted on a stone in the crypt at Nestine. A beautiful little church. I was priest there in the 1960s."

In less than a minute he had produced what could be the answers to two clues. But then he added:

"I didn't tell the others about all this."

"What others? Who? About what?"

He started, then looked confused, and frightened. I tried to speak more gently.

"Have there been others asking the same questions?"

"Oh yes. There was Herr Meyer, a pleasant man, very friendly. He came with his daughter. Then there was the tall Frenchman who came a month ago. He talked about Bouzy and Sheba and salamanders, like you. And there was the old Englishman, what was his name? Gerald? George? He came after the two young Germans with shaved heads. When was it they came? I've been here so long, you know."

He paused.

"Perhaps it was last year," he murmured, "or was it last week?"

His memory for events, recent and distant, was evidently not to be trusted. Then his hands began to tremble, his face turned pale.

"All right," he whispered, "you can have it. It's yours by rights."

He pulled open a drawer in his desk, and took out a small linen bag.

"There you are," he said, pressing it into my hands, "I'd always known there was a mystery about Sheba and her grotto, and when you came and talked about it I had to go and look. I went as soon as you left. I found this. It fell out when I pulled the statue and her head fell off. But I've felt guilty, stealing it like that. And they all wanted to know why you'd called. I didn't tell them I'd found it. Please take it, I'll feel much better."

The bag jingled when I shook it. I took out a handful of little stones. Dozens of them. *Your first share. Shining and glinting. All that glisters is not gold.* Diamonds, the diamonds that Suzy had left here with the priest who shortly afterwards had been killed by a German shell. There were some coloured stones too, pink and red. Rubies? Some of the diamonds were quite large, not like the tiny ones that you see set in rings or brooches, though there were lots of smaller ones too. If these were genuine, what I held in my palm must be worth a fortune. And there were more palmfuls in the bag.

The priest took us to the gate and walked with us down the road. The dark grey Mercedes 4x4 with a German number plate was parked twenty yards beyond my van. The same two men with close-cropped hair that Alessandra and I had met at the chapel, and that had tried to drive us off the road. They were leaning on the Mercedes, smoking. They stared at Leila just as they had at Alessandra.

"Guten Tag," said the priest, waving to the men. They nodded, got into their Mercedes, and drove off.

Standing right behind where their vehicle had been parked stood a familiar figure. Tall, fists clenched, Vincent was staring angrily at me, as he had done in the Musée d'Orsay.

*

We set off for Bouvillers and Nestine, neighbouring villages three or four miles west of Hautvillers. The 'outhouse' was on the left hand side of the road, twenty yards past the BOUVILLIERS signboard at the entrance to the village. A big stone house behind a crumbling wall, the roof falling in, an overgrown garden.

I parked the van in the centre of the village. We walked back towards the house, hid behind a small copse, and waited for half an hour. The only vehicle to pass through was a tractor. We waited a couple more minutes, then climbed through a gap in the wall. Round by the side of the house I found some stone steps leading down to the basement. When we pushed the door at the bottom of the steps, it opened easily.

Upstairs there was a fireplace, with a big stone mantelpiece and a salamander right in the middle. *Under the flames, where the salamander lies.*

The hearth had been ripped up, tiles and bricks were strewn everywhere, and two feet below floor level was a narrow ledge in the side of a hollow.

"This is a mess, let's get out," said Leila. "We won't find anything here."

The priest's suggestion of the crypt at Nestine seemed promising. There were two riddles for Suzy's treasure here.

Salamander, salamander,
Over Benny's heart.
Crypt in the transept,
There you make a start.

'Benny' would be Saint Benedict, whose relics had been scattered around Europe. Reims cathedral might have seemed a more likely place, but the church in Nestine was within the jurisdiction of the Benedictine abbey at Hautvillers. The second riddle promised a specific treasure.

Gold, gold and silver,
Six bright bars,
Gold, gold and silver,
Three crosses full of stars.

Four gold and two silver bars could make three crosses. Maybe 'stars' were encrusted jewels?

We parked in the middle of the cobbled square in the shadow of the church tower. There was no-one in the presbytery, for the village had too few inhabitants nowadays to merit a permanent priest. A scrawled note on the gate said the keys to the church could be had from number 5 opposite. "Prière d'éviter les heures des repas," it added. At least something here was still sacred.

We rang at number 5, and a cheerful teenage girl handed us the keys. I said we wanted to visit the crypt. We'd been told we could see two salamanders and the relics of Saint Benedict. She stifled a laugh.

"There are no relics here," she said, "and you'll need candles."

"Okay," I said, "Please lock the church door, don't let anyone else in, and come back in twenty minutes."

She smiled, shrugged her shoulders, and handed us two candles. I wondered how a bright girl like her survived in this village. Down in the crypt under the transept, two salamanders were carved on a wooden beam, and 'Benny's heart' was there, cut in a stone slab that moved about half an inch when I tried to lift it. It took us nearly ten minutes to manoeuvre it to one side, revealing a deep hole. I tried to feel about with one hand, but I couldn't reach the bottom.

In the end I climbed right inside and felt around with both

hands. Hard bare earth. I scratched around, but the hole down in the crypt was empty.

The girl laughed when she saw the filth on our hair, shoulders and arms.

"Dirty business," she remarked, casually.

I gave her ten francs and she pouted.

"That's for the church box," I added, fishing for a fifty-franc note, "and this is for you."

As we drove away, I looked in the rear mirror and saw the girl standing hands on hips, laughing and chatting with the two Germans who'd been following us.

*

Leila was indignant. She had berated me for letting Geoffrey see the paper with the clues. We wouldn't see any more treasure now, she said. Without a word, I drove to Reims, and parked in front of a cafe opposite the cathedral. There he was, sitting at a table by the window, brown corduroy jacket, rimless glasses, bushy sand-coloured hair. A grandfatherly figure. Wasn't this our third 'chance' encounter, twice in Paris, and now Reims?

"Been doing your homework?" I asked. "It wasn't too difficult, was it, once you got started? Did you memorize the whole lot?"

"Yes, no trouble with that. Years of training. Instant memorization. Your riddles were so peculiar it was no problem."

I'd never thought of it that way. The riddles might indeed seem peculiar, but they were proving relatively easy to solve, for they had been intended to amuse Suzy's teenage daughter.

"I hear you've got one of our linen bags," Geoffrey continued, "and the wines. You know, we were well looked after during both wars. The British Secret Services have a strong tradition. We still have loads of gems from imperial days. They're currency for the most important jobs. India has been the main source of diamonds and other jewels for centuries. In the days of Empire, MI6 got regular deliveries. We still do, with occasional losses. An Air India Boeing crashed in the Alps in 1966. It was carrying two metal boxes full of little bags for us. Emeralds, sapphires, rubies, worth about half a million pounds today. No doubt the boxes will reappear one day at the foot of the Bossons glacier near Chamonix. We'd lost a load of gold bars in the very same place, Air India too, in 1950. Odd coincidence, don't you think, two Air India crashes in the same place?"

He didn't give us the chance to respond.

"Those stones the priest has just passed on to you were given as payment to Suzanne Burridge-Carnot in 1914. Now, you must beware of the young men who are with what used to be the Stasi. They have been recruited to work for Manfred Meyer. We know he has the paper."

"No," I said, "I have the Meyers' paper. Vincent has another copy." His head turned sharply.

"What? What d'you mean?"

Leila kicked my shin under the table. He noticed and looked askance at her, then at me.

"Well," he said, "if he has Suzy's riddles he can have found them only very recently. Remember, I told you that he, his granddaughter and his doctor friend are dangerous, but I didn't know that he'd found the clues to the treasure."

I asked him if he thought we should be armed to protect ourselves in any future meetings with them, or with ex-Stasi thugs.

"No," he answered firmly, "you'll be in more danger with a gun than without one. If they see you preparing to shoot, they'll shoot first. And they'll be faster than you. If you're not armed, you'll run less risk of being shot."

Then he suddenly winked at Leila, stood up and left. We tried to follow but there was no sign of him in the cathedral square.

*

The next week we went to pick up the last of the wine. Margot's dogs were tied up outside the house. They barked like mad when we drove up. I knocked on the door. Silence. I called out. Silence. Then I looked in through a window, and saw her lying face down by the cooker, blood all round her on the tiled floor.

"Don't touch anything. We'd better see if her husband's alive," Leila said. Her face was a ghastly grey colour.

We had a quick look round the ground floor. I opened a door into what turned out to be a large pantry. He wasn't there, and Leila said he wasn't in the living room. We crept up the stairs. There was a long dark corridor. Two doors on either side and one at the end. We pushed the doors open, one by one. No furniture, bare floorboards. I opened the last door.

There he was, lying on the bed. Head back, mouth wide open, a hideous grin on his face, a gash where his Adam's apple should have been. Dark red blood all over the dirty pillows and sheets.

I said we must go to Nestine. Twenty minutes later we pulled up in the church square.

"Something's wrong here, too," said Leila.

The doors were open, the church door and the door to number 5. Leila hesitated, then went into the house. I ran into the church. The nave and transept seemed undisturbed, but after I'd lit two candles and climbed down the stairs, what a sight I found down in the crypt. When I came back outside, Leila was already in the driver's seat. She had started the van and turned it round.

"Same story," I said, climbing into the front passenger seat. "The girl's in a pool of blood in the crypt." Just then the two Germans came running round the corner.

"Get going!" I yelled.

I didn't have to shout, she'd already got going. About half a mile down the road we could see no sign of them, so I told her to turn off into a narrow lane in the woods to the left. But the grey Mercedes appeared and quickly caught up with us.

The lane was narrow, the surface covered with damp leaves. My Toyota van skidded if you braked too hard once it had passed thirty miles an hour even on a dry road. We were doing fifty, and we couldn't go any faster on this road with its bends and the leaves. I thought the Mercedes was going to ram us, then Leila glanced in the rear-mirror and shouted, "He's got a gun, he's going to shoot." Our rear window shattered as she spoke.

Just ahead the lane widened enough to let two cars pass each other. Leila swung the van left, braked, then accelerated hard and swung back violently to the right. Our tyres screeched and there was a terrific crashing sound behind us. We were now driving the other way along the lane.

We stopped and I walked back to the Mercedes. It had left the road and was on its roof, the front smashed in against a thick tree trunk. I crouched down and looked at the two men, crumpled upside down in the front seats. I shrugged my shoulders, left both for dead, and climbed up into the van.

Leila drove to the main road, then to the motorway, towards Paris and home. At first we were too shocked to talk. We needed time to take everything in. Once we were on the motorway, she turned to me.

"Look inside my bag," she said. "This is what they were after."

The bag was still hung over her shoulder, dangling down between us. I felt inside, and took out another of Suzy's linen pouches! I shook it, and there was a clinking sound like tiny glass pebbles.

"It was on her dressing table," Leila whispered. "There was a piece of paper too. Look in my bag."

I took out the screwed-up paper, unfolded it and read out loud: "Mes petits cailloux trouvés sur les croix dans le crypte. M'apporteront chance, peut-être amour. Charlène." *My little stones found on the crosses in the crypt. Will bring me luck, perhaps love. Charlène.*

*

The newspapers, radio and television were full of the story for a few days. German criminals had committed four murders in villages near Reims, slitting the throats of a couple who made a modest champagne, of a teenage girl in Nestine and the priest at Saint-Lié. Yes, the priest too.

According to the media, the police believed that the victims had been punished for resisting thieves who were after silver plate in the churches and the wines from Margot's cellar, which appeared to have been emptied. There were traces of recent disturbances in a crypt and a presbytery. Two murderers had died in the front seats of a German 4x4 upturned in a narrow lane after an accident on a road surface made dangerously slippery by a covering of damp leaves. They both had blood-stained razor knives in their pockets and one had a revolver that he had fired recently. Skid marks found on a narrow lane had been made either by a rival gang or by accomplices who must have hurried back to Germany with the loot.

After a couple of weeks it was no longer headline news.

We knew that the four had been punished for letting us get hold of Suzy's treasures. It was a warning for us. A lot of blood had been spilt for those wines and gems we had. Were they worth it?

6. Gems in Rome

I had arranged to meet Alessandra again in Paris, hoping that if her father really was a diamond merchant, he might be able to trade the gems and make me a small fortune. At the very least he could check their authenticity and estimate their value. At first she was quite hostile, saying that I had tricked her into helping me solve the riddles.

"In any case," she explained, "Father only deals in substantial business. I'm sure your little stones would be of no interest to him."

I was disappointed. Then she suddenly said:

"I'm sorry, silly of me. Of course, it depends. One genuine diamond might be worthwhile. Fifty little pebbles wouldn't. I don't think you can have really valuable gems. Anyway, I'll ask him if he'll consider looking at your goods as a favour to me. By the way, I think you should trust me. I've been fair and open with you."

So Leila and I drove to Rome with a small sample to be examined by the diamond merchant. We settled into a hotel at the bottom of Via Cavour near the Colosseum. I gave Alessandra one large and two medium-sized diamonds, together with a ruby and a pink gem that I couldn't identify. I held back a few of what I thought were sapphires and emeralds that I'd also brought along, and six more diamonds, including another of the very big ones.

As she was leaving us in the hotel, Alessandra turned back and made a kind of confession.

"Look," she began, "I'll have to tell you this now." She stiffened, the first time I had seen her ill at ease. "I know you think I'm from a well-off background, Rome, diamond merchants, Roedean and all that."

I nodded, and listened.

"I know you think I'm serious and cold and perhaps rather snobbish. Well it's not quite what it seems. My father's background was very hard. A family history of betrayals and disappearances and unexplained deaths. Some people would say he's a criminal. A lot of his dealings have been very shady. But I'm an only child and he has looked after me. He always wanted to make sure I could enter decent, dignified, high society. That I'd be a sort of transitional generation, making the family respectable. I'm willing to try, though so far I'm not persuaded of the decency or the dignity of high society. But I want to do my best for him. Don't be surprised by anything you see or hear."

"Don't worry," I said. "We won't let you down."

Next morning we visited the Colosseum. As we left the arena, my head was full of gladiators, lions, and a baying crowd of fifty thousand Romans. We were walking along Via dei Fori Imperiali, aiming for a friendly *trattoria* I remembered, when my mobile rang.

"Can you come straight away?"

It was Alessandra and she sounded anxious, the veneer again breached for a moment. I wondered what was wrong.

"My father wants to see you. Now."

"Do we have time for lunch first?"

"No."

"Where do we go?"

"Where are you?"

I looked round and reported that we were opposite four big maps in grey stone on a brick wall, illustrating the growing Roman Empire.

"Don't move. A car will collect you in five minutes."

Four and a half minutes later, a large saloon with darkened windows drew smoothly to a halt by the pavement. A thickset giant in a black suit stepped out of the front passenger seat, looked around, stared at us, then opened the rear door and motioned us into the back seat. We found ourselves sitting next to a short fat man with curly hair and bushy eyebrows, smoking the tab end of a cigar. Leila said that she'd felt quite sick with the smoke, the lack of air, the tension.

The gorilla of a bodyguard settled into the front seat, his eyes clinically surveying the traffic at each crossroads. Who or what was threatening us? Should we expect a burst of gunfire to ricochet off the heavy glass windows of the limousine? The mahogany, leather and velvet interior felt unfamiliar and unsettling, with the two mini plasma tv screens, thick padded arm rests, and a drinks bar.

"My daughter says you are very kind."

So this was Alessandra's father. He spoke English with a faint

Italian accent.

"She said you needed my help. You must tell me more."

"Have you had time to examine my diamonds?" I asked, turning towards him and trying to sound calm. He nodded. I continued.

"Then I think you know why your help would be welcome. I have no contacts that I can trust. I've had some valued by Parisian jewellers, and they're apparently worth quite a lot."

"Yes, quite a lot." He nodded again and smiled.

The car sped over a bridge across the Tiber into Trastevere, a fashionable residential district, along a broad tree-lined avenue, then left into a narrow street and finally into a square where the driver stopped in front of two heavy gates that opened automatically. We moved silently into the courtyard of a splendid ochre renaissance *palazzo*. A footman led us up a marble staircase into a small private dining room, where the table was set for three.

We soon felt at ease with this man who had been presented to us as an underworld figure who did shady deals. We were to call him Gino, he would call me 'Rosso'—Red! As for Leila, whom he had barely considered thus far, he turned to her and said he would call her 'la Monna Leila', for he found her gaze mysterious like the girl in Leonardo's masterpiece.

He said my diamonds were very special and could make me a multi-millionaire. His information was that they had come to Europe from India during the British Raj. He was astonished to find two large coloured diamonds, one pink and one red. They were very rare and worth over ten million. I said I thought they were rubies. No, said Gino. Few such diamonds came onto the open market these days. White diamonds were almost commonplace, except for large, flawless, expertly cut ones like one of mine, also worth millions. If I was to obtain their full value he would have to have assurances as to their provenance. He could of course offload them, but only at about a third of the price.

I gave him the rest of the sample I'd brought to Rome. I'd kept them in my inside pockets, not trusting the hotel safe.

He said his commission would be fifteen percent at the most, maybe less, depending on circumstances. I had expected him to ask for a quarter or a third of the value. Over coffee he said he would transfer an initial deposit of one and a half million pounds. *An initial deposit!* He gave me a list of reliable Swiss banks, and recommended putting the sums I would receive into different accounts.

"Spread it around, Rosso, you must spread it around," he kept saying, and we were sure he spoke from experience.

"Enough business," he suddenly announced, standing up and showing us to an office upstairs, where he told a diminutive lady with outsize dark glasses to cancel his appointments for the rest of the day. She protested that two clients were already waiting.

"Filippo will see them," he ordered, "and any others you can't cancel."

The limousine drove us the short distance to the Gianicolo Hill, where it pulled into a large private villa with a big garden. We had more coffee on a terrace with a swimming pool, and splendid views

over the trees to the Victor-Emmanuel Monument and the hills beyond.

Gino explained that of his three shops in Rome and two in Milan, only two were genuine diamond merchants. The others were shopfronts covering shady deals, including smuggled gems. His money was 'spread around', in banks and property in New York, Paris, London, Milan and Rome. He had homes in each of these cities, as well as several holiday villas. He was a partner in various companies other than the diamond and jewellery businesses. He'd quickly discovered that he had to employ a couple of dozen strong men to protect himself, his family, and his businesses.

I told him about Geoffrey and the British intelligence services. I explained that the Meyers, Manfred and his daughter Barbara, were following us, and that they had the support of a team of ex-Stasi thugs who did not hesitate to kill. A man called Vincent was also pursuing the treasure. I mentioned the real threat that various Turkish groups represented because we had seen an art collection that they were hiding. Leila insisted:

"The army, and extremist Islamists. Both can be quite ruthless. They have already made two attempts to get rid of us."

He promised he would help with security. He told us how the diamond merchants in Rome had formed a syndicate to protect themselves from the mafia and other gangs. There was a sort of uneasy compromise which on the whole worked, with the occasional misunderstanding that might result in corpses being dumped in front of villas or shop windows being blown to smithereens. So he had his own bodyguards and security men, as well as the ones from the syndicate.

"You cannot go on ignoring the basic necessities," he said. "You need proper security, otherwise you will get robbed, and you, both of you, may be killed. There's already blood on this treasure. You must make sure there's none of yours."

We quizzed him about what we would need. He asked for a list of my properties, details of my children, where they lived and what they did. He wanted to know about Leila and her family. He thought we would need eight permanent guards and a couple more when we were away from home.

We would have to inform our head guard in advance of all our movements. I could pay for this on a month by month basis, fifteen to thirty thousand pounds. It was an expense that the sales of the treasure would easily cover for the foreseeable future.

He suddenly pressed a button on the arm of his chair and two seconds later a very masculine-looking woman appeared. Dressed all in grey, thick features, not pretty. Muscular. She barely smiled. Hair dyed blond. Scary.

"This is Severina," he said. "She will be in charge of your security. She's fluent in English and French, as well as other languages. She will brief you this afternoon and then you will only need to speak with her to tell her of your planned movements."

Severina nodded, bowed and left the room.

"One last thing," Gino said. "You need to be armed." He opened a drawer in his desk and pulled out two handguns. "One each."

"But," I protested, "won't that put us in more danger? If our enemies see we're armed, they'll shoot first."

"Nonsense," was the reply. "You must learn to protect yourselves. You must always be in a position of... what do you call it... top dog! These are Arsenal Firearms Strike One, known as a 'Strike One' or 'AF-1'. They are not yet in general supply. These are early prototypes that my Roman friends have procured. A joint Italian-Russian make. They are the fastest shooting semi-automatic pistols available. Be careful. Take lessons."

He invited us to stay the night in his villa. He said he had to go back to his office for a couple of hours, but Alessandra would soon join us. He would arrange for our things to be transferred from the hotel. In the meantime, perhaps we would like to take advantage of his swimming pool.

*

An hour later Severina reappeared as we relaxed beside the pool. She said she was to give us some important security advice.

"Never accept what any stranger proposes, offers or suggests, by way of entertainment or activity or gift," she said, with a slight Germanic accent that made her sound sinister, like the voices in post-war popular films. Or perhaps it was what she said. "Remember, 'Gift' means 'poison' in German. There will always be someone ready to poison you."

She continued, very direct, listing instructions with no emotion.

"Look three times both ways before you cross the street. Avoid routine. Never take the same route twice. When you book or reserve anything—plane tickets, theatre, restaurant, whatever—always change your seat at the last moment.

"Same with appointments. Make them at the last minute. Avoid them if possible. The more you make advance arrangements, the more likely you are to meet trouble. We will be there to protect you, but you must take simple precautions."

"Who is following us, and why?" Leila asked. We were astonished when she replied instantly.

"Here in Rome there are two sets following you. There are some Germans who think you can find what they want. They're using you to locate it. They can be ruthless. But they know that if they intervene too soon, they'll miss out on everything you haven't yet found. So for the moment they're just following you closely. There don't seem to be any ex-Stasi men here with them. The second group are British. They're more skilled, and they stay in the background. But the news will spread quickly. Then other gangs could be after you. I have no evidence that anyone from Turkey has been following you since you've been in Rome."

"I suppose we will be seeing quite a lot of each other," I added, looking at Severina. I was impressed. How did she know so much already?

"We will be seeing a lot of you. You will see as little as possible of us," she said gruffly.

"How do we communicate?" asked Leila.

"We will be there. All the time. We might have to warn you, instruct you to change plans. To avoid certain movements. You will know it's us. You must never appear to recognize us. We will use words that show we know you. Words or names that refer to past events in your life. Never the same ones twice. If you hear the same word twice, it means danger, that the others have picked up what they think is a regular code word."

"Give me an example," I said. Without blinking, Severina replied.

"Geoffrey. Nestine. Suzy. They all mean something to you."

How did she know that? How had she got this information in such a short time?

"And how do we contact you?" I then insisted.

"You won't need to. Our agents will be close by, and I get regular briefings and updates. We will give you one number in case of emergency. As soon as you have begun to call, our support will be activated. You don't need to say anything. Only use it in case of extreme circumstances."

She stood up, shook hands and disappeared, just as Alessandra joined us by the swimming pool.

"Severina is very cold, which is good," said Leila, "but I don't like this. They can't possibly protect us all the time against several gangs. How many are there with her? Eight, plus a couple of extras when we travel? That's not enough. They have to sleep, they won't all be on duty all the time. How do they look after both of us, and your children, and my family? It's simply not possible."

"Trust them," said Alessandra. "They've protected my father and our family ever since I was small. So far you've had some nasty encounters, but you've had no real protection until now."

"I will not tolerate anyone spying on me, watching without me knowing, interfering in my life," said Leila.

"Relax," barked Alessandra. I'd never heard her speak so harshly. It was as if her personality had suddenly changed. "They do not interfere, they do not in any way invade your intimacy. Besides," she continued, "you have very little choice now. You'll have to make a few concessions. Otherwise..." and she held two fingers to her temple.

"That's exactly what I don't like about it," Leila snapped in turn, "not having any choice."

"Incidentally," said Alessandra, the tone now cooler, ice cold in fact, "my mother and I also carry handguns wherever we go." She looked at Leila. "Keep it hidden in your pants. You need a special holster, I'll give you one. Only put hand to gun when you know you are, or are going to be, in danger."

We were to leave for Paris the next day. At dinner that evening, Gino said his chauffeur would take us to the airport in the limousine. Alessandra would come along to see us off. He had already calculated that the gems I had handed over could be worth millions of pounds.

"How many millions?" I asked him.

"At least fifteen, maybe more."

Apparently there was a very valuable blue diamond, as well as a pink one and a red one. All were worth far more than 'ordinary' white diamonds. He would send me the initial deposit as soon as he had confirmation.

I now believed that the gems from Champagne that I'd put in a bank vault in Paris could be worth tens of millions. Gino had a network of couriers whom we could use to get them to Rome. His agents would meet us in Paris, always in a different place, always somewhere teeming with tourists like the Louvre or the Eiffel Tower. The jewels would be delivered to Rome within twelve hours, and I would be paid as soon as he had found buyers and concluded the deals. I planned to open four new bank accounts in Paris, and three in Geneva. Gino was to declare that I was a consultant working for his company, tax on my earnings being deducted at source. His office would do the paper work.

I was surprised when Leila asked Gino if he dealt only in diamonds and other gems, or if he could dispose of gold ingots at anything like their face value. He seemed neither surprised nor very interested, but merely smiled a little as he spoke.

"Monna Leila, I can handle anything that makes it worthwhile to take the risks involved."

My life was about to be transformed. So easily, it seemed unreal. I had unexpectedly become very rich. I had Gino to sort out the logistics, Severina and her team to protect us, and Geoffrey to support them.

*

Next morning the chauffeur took our bags from the hall and out to where the limousine, engine running, was waiting for us. There was no sign of Alessandra, who hadn't turned up for breakfast. We assumed that Gino had already left for his office, for we had said our goodbyes after dinner the previous evening. So we were surprised to see him emerge from the house and join us in the back of the limousine. He ordered the chauffeur to switch off the engine. Was something wrong with Alessandra?

"There is a problem," he announced.

"In fact," he added, "there are three problems. First, there is no way I can identify these gems and their authenticity. I sometimes work with intermediaries for British intelligence. I buy from them, I sell and offload to them. My contacts tell me that your gems come from batches that they brought from India many years ago. But this cannot be proved without their confirmation. You see, nowadays diamonds have tiny laser identification markings, but that was not the case back in 1900. There is no way I can satisfy potential buyers of the provenance of these jewels without reputable documentation.

"Second, MI6 are refusing to provide proof of provenance. They might take back their gems, but only at something like one tenth of their real value. They drive a hard bargain, as you say. An inside source tells me that they do want their jewels back, and are willing to use force, blackmail, theft, whatever is necessary. So we are in danger. I am used to coping with this kind of situation, but it will be a big challenge for you.

"Third problem. Severina has discovered that a gang of criminals is trying to pressure your family. Not just you, but something to do with your daughter and the prosecution of a minister."

He got out of the car, ordered the chauffeur to drive us to the airport, and walked back into the house without another word. I felt that he had suddenly been transformed from an extraordinarily useful ally into an enemy. He still held my gems, and we could now no longer rely on his security team.

"There's a fourth problem," Leila said as the car moved off. "You have no right to those diamonds and any fortune that they might bring. They belong to Suzy's descendants. You know that Vincent is her son-in-law and that Delcia is her great-granddaughter. You can't keep the diamonds and the proceeds, or the wines. It all belongs to them."

"Vincent is a very old, very unpleasant man who has schemed his way to great wealth for decades," I replied. "He's always behaved threateningly towards me. Geoffrey says he's dangerous. You know what he's done to his wife and his daughter. I intend to make sure he can't harm us, and that he never gets his guilty hands on any of Suzy's gems. And quite frankly, I can't stand Delcia. I find her intensely irritating, her tears and her baby good looks."

"What you feel about them makes no difference to their rights," was the immediate retort.

"In any case," I said, "I doubt if we could get even ten percent of the value of the gems now. Only criminal gangs will look at them."

We didn't speak another word during the ride to the airport, nor in the lounge waiting for our flight. I still had those occasional doubts about her. There was a gap of a generation in our ages, and I had to wonder why she had so suddenly settled with me and stayed for so long. Now she seemed preoccupied. Once we were seated in the plane, she turned to me and said she had something else to say. I could see she was about to make a solemn announcement, of the kind I had been half expecting for some time. She looked at the floor, then at me again. She spoke slowly, saying she'd been thinking about our friendship. As she hesitated, I interrupted her. I'd already rehearsed the little speech to myself several times.

"Listen. I've always known that the day would come when you would leave. We cannot be 'for ever'. Since we met, I've lived for today, not tomorrow. But I know that I'm holding you back, preventing you from moving on. Our friendship cannot continue if you find someone with whom you could start a family, or if you decide to return to your husband. *I'll* survive, and *you* must move on."

We looked at each other. There was a long silence.

"We'll see," I thought, just as she said, "We'll see."

*

Back home that evening, we were about to turn in when the phone rang. I signalled to Leila to listen on the extension.

"*Buona sera*, this is Geoffrey."

"*Bonsoir*," I said, "where are you?"

"Oh, I've just got back from Rome," he replied, laughing, "making sure you were okay. Now you're a wealthy man, you're going to be much more vulnerable. You'll find there are several threats to your security, people who believe they have first claim on the gems, the wines and the art. Now you have some professional help, and fortunately we're here to keep an eye on things. That girl's team is good but there aren't enough of them. We will provide the necessary back-up. So you can relax. I will coordinate with her, otherwise the right hand will not know what the left hand is doing."

He was clearly unaware of what Gino had told us that morning, which struck me as odd since I'd imagined he was the person negotiating on behalf of MI6.

"Your little Leila was very good in Berlin and Nestine," he continued, "but now she will not be able to protect you all the time."

"*Little?*" Leila shouted out loud. "The cheek!"

"Why are you involved in this?" I asked. "It's a private affair. You're using the resources of the British government to watch over us."

"Governments come and governments go, but we have been looking out for our gems for over one hundred years."

"Well if they are to be sold on, you'll need an army to follow them," I said.

"No, no. We're good customers of Gino. We will recover those that you decide to part with. But he doesn't know who we are. In any case, I'm retired, so I don't owe the government anything. Now relax."

He hung up.

"I don't get it," said Leila. "He's retired, but he's still working for MI6? He's not aware that they aren't authenticating the diamonds?

He still thinks they're ready to buy back their own jewels? Why haven't they solved the riddles and collected the gems themselves? Why is he watching over us?"

I felt quite dispirited. My optimism had collapsed in just over twelve hours. I was tired, and soon fell asleep. For some reason, I was dreaming of ballet-dancers in Constantinople. Then I was suddenly awake and aware that Gino was standing in the bedroom, with Severina. She had two pistols and he had a knife. She took me hostage while he held Leila round the waist with the knife under her throat.

"I've really fooled you," he laughed, "now I have your jewels, and I've emptied your bank vault. If you are wise, you will not move. I'm going to take your girlfriend home with me, where she will be quite safe. With you her life is in danger. But I can protect her and will look after her."

He laughed again.

"I've left you the wines, you are welcome. They will console you for your losses."

He twisted Leila's arm behind her back and forced her downstairs while Severina pointed her pistols at me. They were ours, our new AF-1s. She'd taken them from the bedside tables.

"Let me see," she said, pulling aside the bedclothes.

I was lying there naked. I heard the limousine start up, and a horn hooted twice.

"I'm so sorry," said Severina, "I'll have to go."

She backed out of the room. I was sweating profusely, and ran to the window where I watched as Gino drove down to the gate, with Leila looking up at me. I turned round, and there was Manfred Meyer, standing staring at me. How stupid I was to have trusted Gino.

"Stupid," I shouted, "so stupid!" I wanted to cry out "Where's Geoffrey now?" but my throat felt blocked and I couldn't get the words out. I was struggling to shout.

"Easy," someone said, "take it easy, calm down." It was Leila, stroking my arm as she woke me. "Easy, it's okay, take it easy, don't shout. You're having a bad dream."

7. Frontiers in the Maghreb

"Well, look who's here!" she said. "What a surprise! He's here, he's there, he's everywhere."

We had decided to spend a few days relaxing in Marrakesh, and were having lunch at one of the open-air restaurants in the enormous, bustling Jamaa el Fna Square. We selected our dishes from the salads, roasting spittles and steaming vegetable bowls, and were immersed in the rhythms of the beating drums, the flutes of snake charmers and a constant buzz of human talk and shouts. Suddenly I noticed that Leila was staring over my shoulder.

I turned just as Geoffrey appeared and sat down beside me.

"What a coincidence!" he said. Leila and I looked askance. "No, really. I'm here for a few days' holiday, looking up old friends."

"And contacts?" Leila suggested.

"Oh no, they're mostly long gone, though there are still a few. Actually," he continued, leaning forward and looking very serious, "you're right. Of course it's not a coincidence that I've come across you just now. I want you to go to Leila's home near Sétif, and see what you can do about what's left of the gold bullion that Mohamed and Idir re-buried. I have my contacts, but I can never get as close to the ground as you can in Algeria."

He was looking at Leila, who shook her head. She hated anyone prying into her family life. He continued, unperturbed.

"Your great-uncle Idir left quite a lot once he thought he had enough for everyone. We believe there are still gold ingots buried somewhere up in the hills. The Stasi has never got anywhere near it. Nor has anyone else. *We* can't. We've tried sending in local spies we've hired, but our Kabyle agents side with Idir and his network every time. I think you should have a go."

"We can't get direct from Morocco to Algeria," I said. "I've tried many times, but I always have to go back to Paris or shuttle around via Malta or Marseille or Istanbul. The frontier with Morocco has been closed for a decade now, since the troubles began in Algeria."

"Oh it's very permeable," he replied, "I can soon have that sorted. Give me a couple of hours and we'll find you a car, guards and a driver. I'll get you tickets and a visa so that you can fly direct from Sétif to Paris. By the way," he added, "do leave your hand-guns at home. Rely on your guards. Let them get shot, that's their job, to be in the front line. They're there to make sure *you* aren't killed, and you're taking unnecessary risks. I told you that before."

He took our passports, and returned them two hours later with Algerian visas, stamped as if we had flown in to Sétif that very day. He gave us plane tickets from Sétif to Paris, dated one week later. We were to leave early the following morning, driving from Marrakesh in western Morocco to eastern Algeria, a distance of over eight hundred miles, he said, adding that his arrangements were quite safe.

"*Quite* as in *completely*, or *fairly*?" Leila muttered.

Geoffrey told us we could do the journey in two days. Leila was very doubtful, and we were aware that although we would have a modern air-conditioned vehicle, comforts would be minimal.

"What's the real reason he wants us to go to Algeria?" she asked once he had left us. "Why does he insist we do it this way, and how does he know about the gold bullion? It's none of his business."

"MI6?" I replied.

"None of their business either," she said. "It belongs to my family now, and some of it is mine by rights."

*

Next morning an Audi 4x4 was waiting for us outside our hotel, along with an old jeep for our two bodyguards. The security arrangements were more visible than before, and seemed more unnerving than reassuring. We set off with a driver and a guide sitting in the front of the 4x4, and us in the back. They communicated on a walkie-talkie with the guards in the jeep. They spoke only Arabic, and could have talked with Leila, but they just looked at us very coldly, quite aggressively in fact. I was beginning to let my irritation at their attitude show. She told me to calm down, since we would be no match for the four of them.

Before we left Marrakesh, Leila looked at a map of the route we were to follow. It was much further than Geoffrey had said. She became quite angry as she discovered that his claim that it was an eight-hundred-mile drive was in fact based on the distance by air.

By road it was eleven hundred.

"Either he hasn't done his homework—which I do not believe—or he's misleading us. We can't possibly do it in two days, not on these roads. What is he up to? I've never trusted him."

A few minutes later she burst out laughing.

"I've just phoned a travel agent about routes from Marrakesh to Stif. They said it's over three thousand kilometres, with an itinerary going via Tangiers, driving up the eastern coast of Spain and taking the boat from Marseille. Total three thousand three hundred and sixty two kilometres. They obviously know the border is closed."

Then she became quite convulsed with laughter.

"From Oujda in Morocco over the border to Tlemcen in Algeria is seventy kilometres on the map, less than fifty miles. They say it takes three days and they gave me the same route, Spain and Marseille, two thousand nine hundred and seventy five kilometres! This is crazy."

In fact the roads were well maintained, straight strips of tarmac cutting through parched, semi-desert scrub with cultivated fields near the villages and views of the Atlas mountains. By mid-afternoon we were already approaching Fes. I was disappointed to discover that we wouldn't see the imperial city, for we turned off eastwards on a route which took us rapidly through the hills, at first covered in trees but then very dry and bare, the road skimming over the heights. We'd soon covered the three hundred kilometres from Fes to Oujda.

On the outskirts of the town, the last before the border with Algeria, our driver turned right and took a southward-bound road with an uneven surface, much worse than any we'd seen so far. It didn't seem to be leading anywhere. Leila asked him where we were going, and he told her we were to go fifty kilometres or so south before crossing the border on a desert track. We were surrounded by a flat stony landscape. Thick clouds of dust rose behind, making us visible for miles around. Our driver had to keep swerving hard to avoid potholes. Finally he turned onto the track which the guide said would take us across the border without any frontier police or army.

The sun set behind us, and soon it was pitch dark. The driver turned off his headlights and slowed down to about ten miles an hour. He strained forward, his face pressed against the windscreen.

The guide in the front seat turned to us and grunted, in English "No road!" He told Leila in Arabic that we would have to stop for the night and wait until shortly before sunrise. If we showed any lights it would attract attention, and it was too dangerous to drive on because the track wasn't visible. If we missed it, we might find ourselves marooned in the sand.

So we were stuck in the dark with four armed men whose loyalty to us was doubtful, and whose hostility towards me in particular was obvious. I suggested to Leila that we take it in turns to sleep for two-hour stretches. The moon, a thin crescent, shone faintly through a film of cloud. We were both awake and on edge every time we heard the guards talking, but the night passed and before sunrise they made tea. We were soon ready to move on.

When the sun's rim appeared on the horizon, it shone directly into our eyes. The blinding light made it impossible to see the track ahead. It was worse than trying to drive by night. We slowed down to a snail's pace. After almost half an hour the track veered left and our driver was able to speed up slightly as the sun rose higher.

We must have been doing around thirty miles an hour when we heard a distant droning sound which quickly grew louder. A helicopter swooped into view and we watched it circling overhead. Then it dipped and flew away. Within two minutes it was back. We stopped and our guards shouted over their intercom then pulled down the canvas top and sides of their jeep, revealing a revolving turret with an antiquated anti-aircraft gun. We were ordered out of the Audi and pushed underneath, just as two men leaned out of the helicopter and began firing with automatic rifles.

The guards were heroic, maintaining fire although they were fully exposed to the bullets raining down onto the sand and stones. Then the helicopter swerved and roared away. The battle had lasted less than half a minute. We rolled out from under the Audi. Leila asked the driver who had attacked us, and he shook his head. No-one he knew, not police or army, who could have had a helicopter but wouldn't have fired on us. Not local *caïds*, nor the usual kind of bandits, they would never come in a helicopter.

We wondered about radical Islamists, but Leila said not here, though we might encounter them in the hills of Kabylia. No-one had been injured, and we decided that whoever it was, they had deliberately fired wide, wanting only to give some kind of warning.

The track turned north and we were driving at a steady fifty miles an hour when we reached a tarmac road. In less than half an hour we were nearing Tlemcen.

The guide told Leila that we would be turning off before the town, to drive eastwards to Algiers. But now she took over, instructing him to drive straight on to Tlemcen and take us to what turned out to be a large house on the southern outskirts. After a loud argument over the intercom, the jeep followed.

Tlemcen was a sizeable town surrounded by green hills. It was a remarkably human, restful and congenial place. Ochre and white buildings, a mixture of ancient and modern, more varied than Marrakesh and without the hordes of tourists.

We were welcomed into the house by Kamel, who was introduced as a childhood friend from Leila's summer holidays spent *au bled*, in her parents' town. He hadn't appeared at all surprised to see us. I wondered what kind of friendship this was, since she had never mentioned him, but that was not unusual since she rarely spoke about her past. We showered and had a late breakfast. Leila then had an animated talk with the drivers and guards. She explained to me that they were very reluctant to take orders from a woman.

Kamel intervened, and Leila's plan was adopted. The guards, the Audi and the jeep would continue as planned, following a route to Sétif via Algiers on well maintained roads. But we were to take Kamel's BMW and drive a rougher route directly eastwards to Leila's home town. We paid driver, guide and guards an advance on what we were to give them when they arrived in Sétif, and we left Tlemcen shortly after eleven.

The guards had apparently disapproved very strongly of Leila and me travelling together. They had watched us carefully and not been able to find fault, except that we seemed to think it so natural to sit next to each other and chat and laugh. Kamel said that he thought in fact it was just that—the way we lived our friendship as if it were normal—that they couldn't understand. He said that if I'd touched her they would probably have shot me. Or her, more likely.

We felt safer in the BMW, believing our enemies, and perhaps our 'friends', would still be keeping an eye on the Audi and the jeep. Kamel, who was apparently some kind of regional government representative, gave us a stamped pass which he said we were to show if the army stopped us.

"Likely to happen regularly, you have a long way to go," he said.

This was the 1990s, a troubled decade in Algeria with tension at its height and hundreds of thousands of casualties in the war between the State authorities and the fundamentalists. But the pass worked like a magic wand in front of young, low-ranking soldiers. We drove fast on decent roads with little traffic, and we arrived at Leila's town, Bordj Bou Arreridj, just as the light was beginning to fade.

Her grandmother Kahina lived in Bordj. Some of her aunts, uncles and cousins also lived there, others lived in villages and hamlets in the surrounding hills. She was to stay with her grandmother and her mother's sister, Malika. I would be lodging with Great-Uncle Idir next door.

He was, said Leila, the only person who would accept our friendship. She'd already told him about me. The other male members of the family, especially the younger ones, would certainly not understand, and if they suspected that we were close friends they'd be extremely hostile. Leila would take care of the women, with whom I would never be alone.

We parked in front of Kahina's house, and Leila took me straight to Idir's. He was waiting on the doorstep, an erect figure with tightly curled grey and white hair, dressed in a short-sleeved open-necked shirt, khaki trousers, and sandals. He bowed, extended a hand, and welcomed me in perfect French. One of those old men who inspire respect. He was the patriarchal figure for the extended family. After independence, he'd been president of the municipal people's assembly and mayor of the *baladīyāt*, the town district, for twenty years. His elder son had succeeded him and had now held the office for almost ten years.

Idir said that he guessed one reason why we had come was to make enquiries about what he called *le butin*, the booty. He said he had already recovered far more than he needed. No-one else, apart from Leila and his two sons, knew about it. He would show us the hiding-place. His sons were already quarrelling over it. He was disappointed in them. After all, they'd already profited quite enough. He added that he would ensure Leila had her share, for she was a direct descendant of the Spahi Mohammed who had buried it.

He said this with no trace of emotion, and announced that we were now to meet the family at Kahina's. Leila led us into a large room with wide doorways on either side leading into two smaller rooms. One was for the women only, the other for the men, with the central room mixed. A tidy arrangement.

As we entered the main room everyone stopped talking and turned to look at us. Idir guided me into the men's room and introduced me to them one by one. Little groups started talking again, but there were frequent long, heavy silences. I had been to many Arab, Berber and Kabyle homes in Morocco and Algeria, but I'd never met an atmosphere like this. I felt everyone inspecting me and I guessed that even if they tried to appear polite, they were hostile because we'd arrived together, just the two of us.

I stuck near to Idir and his two sons, who had been told to be my escorts for the evening. Eventually Leila approached and said she would introduce me to Grandmother Kahina, Great-Aunt Nora, and Aunt Malika.

Kahina and Nora, the two little girls who had sat opposite my father on a train to Algiers in 1942. Fatima's daughters. Idir and I moved towards the women's room and met them right in the doorway. Kahina spoke in Kabyle which Leila translated, then hesitant French which I had difficulty in following. All conversations had stopped. Everyone was looking at us. Nora stood there, too, but she just bowed and didn't say anything. Then she suddenly smiled and said in French, "I've seen you before, the English man on the train, the man at the station when Mother ran off." Her sister led her away. Idir explained that her mind had been wandering for years.

There was still that hush throughout the three rooms as everyone observed the scene. I was relieved when Idir took me by the arm and escorted me back to his home.

We talked as he served mint tea and cakes. The last thing he mentioned took me completely by surprise. He spoke of Leila's father. I realized that she had never talked about him, and it had never occurred to me to ask her. I don't know why.

"Yes," said Idir, "he died when she was ten. She was an only child, unusual in our family, but there were complications and they couldn't have any more children. He'd always taken special care of her. She loved going to his allotment with him, planting and picking vegetables and fruit. We never understood what happened. She found him in his shed with a bullet through his temple. She's never recovered from that. We're not supposed to mention it, and she never does. I did my best to look after her, but you can't replace a father. Soon her mother took her away to France, and I only saw her for a month every summer. She grew up so quickly."

*

Next morning we were to go with Idir to have a look at some huts up in the hills. I suggested we take Kamel's BMW, but he said the roads were rough and it would be better to take his battered old Mercedes. He'd already put shovels and a pick-axe in the boot.

After a couple of miles we left the main road and took a winding track through scrubland. We arrived at a small plateau above the clouds, with rocks and stones and a thin covering of grass. I could see no huts.

Idir stopped the car and we looked around. There was a breeze and it was quite cool. He took the pickaxe and shovels and went straight to one of the rocks. He struck hard into the grass and began removing the earth. Soon he stopped and growled angrily. He moved to another rock. Then another. Then he looked at Leila and shouted to her.

"He says someone's been here," she announced. "The earth is loose and the boxes have gone."

She took his hand. We got in the Mercedes and she drove us back to town. When we got to his house we went inside while he went to look for his sons.

"So," Leila said, "this particular treasure hunt ends here. Disappointment, and anger."

We were wondering who could have removed the last of the gold. Idir's sons? Local gangs? After some reflection, Leila said she wondered about her 'ex' husband Mourad, who could also have been behind the helicopter scare. He obviously had, she said, a triple motivation. Revenge on her, spite against me, and some valuable loot. In Algeria he had all the logistics he needed to attack us.

But she had also been busy on another front. The previous night she was up very late, talking with her Aunt Malika and her cousins. She'd done some detective work on Fatima.

I was pressing her to tell me what she'd learnt, but before she could reply, there was a loud detonation, the sound of breaking glass, and dust everywhere. Choking, we felt our way along the walls of a corridor to the front door and out into the street where Kamel's BMW had exploded and yellow flames were licking all round what remained of it. There was an acrid, sulfurous smell. All the other cars had broken windows and two more were on fire. There was a body curled up motionless in the road. Men were running and shouting. A boy was crying.

'this particular treasure hunt ends here'

Idir suddenly appeared. He took Leila to one side and whispered that his sons had betrayed him. He said he would recover what, if anything, was left of the bullion they had taken. He would ensure that all the proceeds he could get back from them would now go to her. That could make her very wealthy, just as my own prospects of making a fortune from Suzy's gems were fading.

Idir said he was sorry but we would have to leave immediately. There was a crisis. Then the sons arrived. They began to shout at Leila. Idir ushered us away, and fifteen minutes later we were in a car on the way to Sétif airport.

*

On the plane back to Paris, Leila said she'd found two old women who remembered Fatima and Mohamed's wedding. She'd also found a young woman whose mother and aunts had passed on their stories about what had happened fifty years ago.

They all agreed that there had been two Fatimas. That explained the message Delloula left when she was dying, "Tell Leila that Fatima wasn't Fatima." Mohamed married the first Fatima in 1935. Kahina was born in 1936, Nora in 1937. He went off to join the Spahis in France the next year. Their mother was killed soon after he came home in 1942. She was knocked down by a German army lorry. Mohamed was acting as their guide. *We* know that they were carrying the gold bullion. They drove dangerously fast and with little care for the locals. Fatima was run over when she was going to fetch her daughters from a neighbour's house.

The two oldest women, however, were sure that she'd been murdered by her husband. He'd found her in bed with the German officer. Hans Meyer. Mohamed told the story of his wife being killed by the lorry, but the women said he'd strangled her and then got a German army driver to run over the body. She was buried the same day.

Only the closest female relatives saw her corpse. Whatever the truth, Kahina and Nora had lost their mother. A servant girl who had lived with the family took over the household. The two little girls began to call her Fatima. Soon they forgot their mother, and Mohamed accepted the name thinking it would shelter his daughters from their mother's death.

There was a veil of mystery surrounding the second Fatima. Apparently Mohamed was very rough with her. He forced her to marry him. She ran away when they were on that visit to Algiers. She soon came back to him, but then she left him and his daughters again. She kept disappearing, Mohamed knew not where, but some women in the family must have known. Probably the only person who knew the full truth was Delloula.

The women said they all knew the second Fatima had been a prostitute in Algiers. They believed Delloula had persuaded her to come back and work in the big city. There was so much business, with all those soldiers and sailors passing through. They claimed that she'd been working for Delloula in Algiers for some time before she came to Bordj.

So the Fatima with whom my father had had his Algerian adventure was not Leila's great-grandmother. She was not the Fatima that Hans Meyer had known. She was a prostitute, or former prostitute, who sent messages for MI6.

*

Geoffrey's information, and at times his protection, have perhaps been vital. But in both Turkey and Algeria we felt he had put us needlessly in danger. Is he friend or foe? Is the support that he has at his disposal being used for or against us? I determined to discover whether he really did work, or had worked, for the Secret Intelligence Service.

I myself sometimes do minor jobs for French agencies. Nothing very spectacular, mostly taking part in consultations, using my specialist experience of the Muslim Mediterranean, gathering news from my university networks. During the trip to Turkey I collected information about the potential takeover of government by emerging Islamist movements. In Marrakesh I met a contact who updated me on the penetration of universities in Morocco and Algeria. In admitting this I am not giving away any great secrets or putting myself in danger. But my contacts have enabled me to ask, for want of a better expression, my 'handler' here in France to enquire at the British SIS. She has reported back that MI6 have never heard of Geoffrey. Of course they would say that, wouldn't they? They never admit to knowing or having employed any of their agents. But apparently he was not listed anywhere in their archives of past and present personnel. An ultra-confidential list, only known to two or three people with the necessary authority. My source contacted one of the top two or three, and I'm inclined to believe her.

If he is not connected to MI5 or MI6, he must have the backing of some organization. He has substantial funds and he is well informed. He has agents and contacts out in the field. He knows all about us and our movements. So who *is* he working for? Why is he interested in us?

I intend to find out.

8. Vineyards and Monasteries

Three months after Gino had said that he wouldn't be able to get anything like the market value for the gems, he called me to announce that MI6 were ready to buy them back at seventy-five percent of the going rate. He advised me to accept. Someone had looked in their archives, traced the payments in kind that the original 'Section 6' had made to their agent Suzanne Burridge-Carnot during the Great War, and authenticated the jewels.

I immediately started working on the Burgundy riddles. Soon I found myself thinking about them at all times of the day and night. In the kitchen, in the shower, lying in bed. They looked more sophisticated than the Champagne clues. I remembered that Suzy had written them for a grown-up Delphine, not for the teenage girl. There were three sets of what I had by now worked out were interlocking puzzles. I repeated them so often that I soon knew them by heart.

Visit ye brothers, who live with five sisters.
On finding the chapter and verse,
Give to each in his language, his colour that glisters,
And he will then give you the purse.

Look up, look down, look round,
The castle, the cellar, the church,
The gate to the plot, and the grandest house,
Then match them to finish your search.

Near these Five Heads:
  - Welcome to the white one of ill birth.
  - On this one, his church he built.
  - Not far from the good ponds.
  - Look by the street, the High Street.
  - Wealthy, not Edwin, nor Johannes.

'Chapter and verse' sounded biblical, so 'ye brothers' would be monastic, their language Latin. 'The purse' was surely another of

Suzy's little bags of gems.

Somewhere there must be references to wines. Burgundy is a mosaic of tiny but precisely delineated vineyard plots, painstakingly defined by the Cistercian monks. It is said that they tasted the soil as well as the grapes when they drew the boundaries. A few yards either side of a pathway can make all the difference between a simple village label and a famous top-growth wine with its own name, worth fifty times more. It was the first line of the 'Five Heads' riddles that set me on the right track.

Welcome to the white one of ill birth was surely a reference to the famous vineyard with the curious name of Bienvenues-Bâtard-Montrachet. The Mont Rachet is a rather bare hill with too much hard limestone for the great red wines produced in the nearby slopes above Beaune. But around the hamlets of Puligny and Chassagne to the south-west, the stony ground combines with the chardonnay grape to yield some of the world's greatest white wines.

After decoding that first line—we were to look 'near' the Bienvenues-Bâtard-Montrachet vineyard—I deduced that 'Five Heads' must refer to five top-growth vineyards. Until the 1930s, when the *grand cru* label was introduced, the finest wines of the region were each known as a *tête de cuvée*, 'head of the vat', the best juice to trickle from the press. So Suzy had called them 'Heads'.

We had to look 'up, down, round' for a castle, a cellar, a church, a gate and a big house, near five *grand cru* vineyards. Four of the locations were easy for anyone who knew the Burgundy vineyards.

Welcome to the white one of ill birth. Bienvenues-Bâtard-Montrachet, of course.

Not far from the good ponds would be Bonnes-Mares.

Look by the street, the High Street must be La Grande Rue.

Wealthy, not Edwin, nor Johannes pointed to Richebourg (not Edinburgh or Johannesburg).

But I couldn't understand *On this one, his church he built.* It seemed an obvious reference to Saint Peter. I spent hours looking at maps with the names of all the vineyard plots. Their names rarely if ever changed over the years. I studied maps dating from the 1900s as well as the present-day plot names. There was no Saint-Pierre.

*

We drove down to Beaune the last Saturday in March 1999, arriving just before midday. The perfect excuse to start by taking the road to nearby Volnay for lunch at one of my favourite restaurants, *Chez Nathalie*. As we worked our way through five courses and I sampled three different wines, Leila suggested we ask Nathalie if 'five sisters' meant anything to her. She seemed to be thinking hard as she supervised her cooks and waitresses and customers. By the end of the meal she hadn't found the answer. We had coffee, and she asked for my mobile number saying she would call me if she "had any ideas". Leila looked curiously at her. As I paid the bill, standing up at the bar, I remarked to Nathalie:

"I'm sure we met somewhere before I started coming here, but I can't place you."

"Yes, me too. Must have been in one of our previous lives."

"Well," said Leila, "Perhaps you'll meet again in one of your future lives."

She smiled at Nathalie and guided me towards the door.

It was a short drive from Volnay to Puligny and Chassagne, the two villages that have attached to themselves the famous name of the limestone hill. We stopped at the roadside and looked at the Bienvenues-Bâtard-Montrachet vineyard, a small plot where each square metre of ground was worth more than in the most select districts of Paris. We looked around for the five landmarks suggested in the clues. The church spire at Puligny was just visible. We drove into the village, and I parked the van in front of the church. We found the door unlocked. Recently renovated roof beams, bright stained-glass windows, a series of embossed brass shields depicting the Way of the Cross. Obviously a wealthy community. On a step leading up to the altar, there was a carved Latin inscription:

Et vidi et ecce ventus turbinis veniebat ab aquilone et nubes magna et ignis involvens et splendor in circuitu eius et de medio eius quasi species electri id est de medio ignis. Ezekiel 1:4

Was this what we were looking for? I realized that my Latin was rusty, not up to the challenge. Leila walked to the back of the nave and took a book off a table by the door. She opened it, turned the pages, and read out loud, in vibrant tones that echoed round the small church:

"And I looked, and, behold, a whirlwind came out of the north, a great cloud, and a fire infolding itself, and a brightness was about it, and out of the midst thereof as the colour of am-

ber, out of the midst of the fire."

She had found an English Bible, and we had found in a *church*, by the *Bienvenues-Bâtard-Montrachet* vineyard, the chapter and verse to be *given* in Latin, with the *colour that glisters*, the amber hue of the famous white wine, source of the wealth of this village.

I felt a vibration in my pocket. It was a text-message from Nathalie about the five sisters. "5 Cistercian offshoots," it read, "small monasteries east of Beaune, in woods that had once been marshlands."

*

We searched the Michelin map for the five monasteries. We'd soon located four, but the fifth was marked as a site in ruins. The map led us to a small wood with a stream running through the middle. We followed the stream on foot and found the ruined abbey fenced off, with a sign reading "DANGER DE MORT". We walked round the outside wall and soon came to what had once been an imposing entrance with a gatehouse. In the stonework was the name of the monastery, inset in dark yellow stones. Dark yellow, for the 'amber' quotation we'd identified?

We drove to the nearest village and sought out the local priest. He turned out to be a pleasant young man who said the monastery had been unoccupied since the 1960s.

"Where might we find any brothers who were there when it closed?" I enquired.

"Oh, there must be a few survivors... Yes, of course, there's old Frère Jérôme who lives in the next village, in the presbytery that hadn't been occupied for years. He should have gone to one of the other monasteries, but for some reason he chose to move there when the abbey closed."

Ten minutes later we were sitting with Frère Jérôme, a sprightly eighty-year-old who was clearly taken with Leila's shining eyes. He wasn't paying any attention to me, so I firmly read out, in my best latin, the amber verse from Ezekiel that I'd written down in the church. He swung round and faced me, his steel grey eyes glinting behind his spectacles. The little ruddy patches in his cheeks faded, and he took short, hurried breaths.

"You are the second," he said. "It is too late. The first came only two days ago. A tall, disagreeable old man."

"Did you give him the purse?"

"Yes. I had no choice," he replied. "How strange that you should both come in the same week, after all these years. Ever since my monastery closed down, I have kept the purse. It had been handed down from abbot to abbot. There was always one other brother in the know. I was the one, and then the abbot died and we had to close down—you see there were only five of us left. They said I couldn't take it with me if I went to any of the four surviving houses. They said only one purse per monastery. So I chose to live here in the presbytery and keep it safely with me. One brother was told where to find it, should anything happen to me.

"When the man came the other day, I had to obey the instruction. He recited the verse, so I had to give him the bag. I never knew what was inside. We had been richly endowed when it was entrusted to us. No-one could have kept the secret better."

"Let's see," said Leila, "there's..." and she reeled off the names of the other four monasteries we'd found on the map. Frère Jérôme smiled.

"Now," she continued, "what colours are the others?"

"Colours?" he said, "What do you mean?"

"You know," she continued, "here you're amber. The amber is in the lettering of the name over the gate."

She spoke as if Frère Jérôme were still in his monastery.

"They're not colours," he retorted angrily, "they're gems, precious stones. The stones in the crown of our brotherhood. A symbol of what we have relinquished on earth and will find in Heaven."

Not discouraged, Leila didn't hesitate.

"Now remind me," she said, "what gems are the other four monasteries?"

He told us each one: ruby, sapphire, emerald and amethyst.

So now we knew where we had to go and what we had to do, all the while fearing that Vincent, the 'tall, disagreeable old man', had probably got there before us. And we first had to locate four more Latin verses.

*

We drove through Nuits-Saint-Georges, then walked between the newly pruned vines in plots above Chambolle-Musigny and Morey-Saint-Denis. I noticed a very big house on the slopes at the edge of one of the villages. It had a *gîte* sign on the gatepost. We rang the bell, and were welcomed inside by a couple who looked anything but Burgundian villagers.

The man was about fifty, tall, bald, and very self-assured. He told us he'd been executive director of an international oil company, that he'd cashed in his stock options and bonuses, bought the grandest house he could find on the vineyard slopes, invested in some new winery equipment and bought the most prized plots that were available. Around here plots rarely become available, but there'd been a family with an inheritance problem that needed sorting quickly.

He said he'd made quite a few changes to the house. Most of the woodwork had been rotten and he'd rebuilt some parts in the old style but with new materials. His wife showed us round. In one room that hadn't been refurbished, over the fireplace was a long strip where the wallpaper was lighter.

"What was hung up there?" I asked.

"A long wooden plank with a carved biblical inscription in Latin," she said. "He's anticlerical. He wasn't having that. He took it down and threw it out. Put it down in the cellar, I think."

I asked him if we could go down to his cellar to taste a selection of his wines. They were all clean, modern versions of good first-growth reds from the Côte de Nuits. I bought two cases. Just as we were climbing back up the stone stairs into the courtyard, I turned round and saw what I was looking for.

Fortunately he was carrying my wine, so I was able to pretend to lose my balance. I fell off the side of the steps, and grabbed a long plank leaning against a wall. I held on to it, and before he'd hurried back down the steps to help me, I had read the first three words carved in Latin: *aleph mulierum fortem...*

"Are you hurt? I'm sorry, those uneven stairs, and no bannister."

"I'm okay," I said, "I missed my footing."

We spent a pleasant evening with our hosts. I asked if I could consult the internet on his computer. In his office I searched for an *aleph* verse in the Bible, and eventually discovered, Proverbs 31:10. In Latin, "*aleph mulierem fortem quis inveniet procul et de ultimis finibus pretium eius.*" The English translation was "Who can find a virtuous woman? for her price is far above rubies." In fact the Latin text does not specifically mention 'rubies', which feature only in the King James Bible. Other English versions mention 'pearls' or 'precious stones'.

Curious. The big house we were now in was by the vineyard called Bonnes-Mares, the 'good ponds' formed where springs emerged from the hillside. Suzy must have known that an alternative name was Bonnes Mères, the 'Good Mothers' of a nearby convent who had looked after the sick. Virtuous women, worth much more than rubies, pearls or precious stones?

Next morning, we headed straight for the 'ruby' monastery.

The gateway was a replica of the amber one, but with red stones forming the lettering of the name. We rang the bell, and after five minutes a young monk came out of the gatehouse. He looked at me, and averted his gaze from Leila.

"I have an urgent message for the abbot," I announced.

"Again?" he said, and my heart fell. We were taken into a cool room with red-tiled flooring. An austere old monk in black and white robes, standing before a lectern, continued reading silently, his lips moving. The novice motioned us to wait, then left the room. A quarter of an hour passed. Maybe twenty minutes.

Finally the abbot looked up, took off his glasses, and scrutinized me without speaking. I coughed, and recited Proverbs, Chapter 31 verse 10, in my hesitant Latin:

"*aleph mulierem fortem quis inveniet procul et de ultimis finibus pretium eius.*"

He stared hard at Leila, then looked puzzled. Had we got it wrong? At length he responded.

"You are the second."

"I feared so," I said, "a tall old man, a few days ago?"

"No, not tall."

He closed his eyes and his lips moved again.

"Yesterday. An old man. An Englishman, like yourself."

My accent still gave me away, after thirty-four years in France.

"An Englishman?" said Leila, looking at me reproachfully, then to the abbot, "Did you give him the purse?"

"Of course. I had to." He spoke slowly, articulating each syllable. "We were sworn to this bond for more than eighty years. The first person to enter and, without further comment, pronounce the Latin verse, would get the purse. My predecessor insisted on this latter condition. I have no idea what was in the bag, but we have waited loyally for that moment."

He looked as if he could have waited for eternity.

We drove back to Beaune and retreated into a café in the main square, armed with the clues and my map. I shouldn't have been surprised to see Geoffrey sitting there perfectly relaxed as he scanned the morning paper. He smiled when we sat down at his table.

"I'm sorry, I couldn't resist it," he said. "Yes, I got the ruby gems yesterday. The old Father Superior, or whatever they call them, wasn't pleasant. But he had no choice."

"Abbot," I said. He nodded.

"Well of course, I recognized the linen bag as one of ours from decades ago. I'd solved the clue and the instructions. You see, I followed you to the amber monastery and then to Brother Jérôme's. I went to see him after your visit. He explained what you had done, and he told me about the tall stranger who had collected Suzy's 'purse'. I must admit he helped me a little with the quotations, without realizing what he was doing.

"Now listen carefully. I have a lot to explain. You are in some danger, but my people are keeping an eye on things, and so is that woman, what's her name, Sarajeva, Savarona...?"

"Severina," I said, "and what is the danger?"

"First you must beware of the Meyers," he replied. "I've seen Manfred and Barbara this morning in Beaune. Savarina is watching them, so they aren't an immediate threat. But they have a back-up of two ex-Stasi men, and we know that *they* can be really dangerous.

"You see, Manfred discovered the rivalries between your grandfathers and fathers only when old Frau Meyer, Gottlieb's wife, died in 1983 aged a hundred and three. Their son Hans had committed suicide in 1977. He left a note explaining everything, saying he felt ashamed at his own weakness, unbearable for a former member of the Hitler Youth and the Waffen-SS. But his mother found the note and hid it, along with a photocopy of his wartime notebook. Manfred found Hans's documents in the old lady's flat after her death. He was incensed by what he read. He swore vengeance, and went to Sheffield to look for William Wright.

"He found the school where your father had taught, discovered that he was retired, got his address and visited him at his home. He pretended he was a German school inspector on an exchange visit, so they talked schools and then your father told Meyer all about his time in the war. He showed him the diary he'd written, 'From Normandy to Berlin.' "

"How come you know all this? It sounds impossible!" I said. He ignored my question.

"Meyer decided to leave this old man, now feeble like his own father had been. He realized that he would derive much more satisfaction if he took his revenge on you, his own generation. Your father was perhaps confused, because he gave him your old address in Montmartre. Meyer hired a man with ex-Nazi contacts to murder you in Paris. Over ten years later he discovered you were still alive. He then ordered his former Stasi agents to trace you and bump you off during your Magny-Cours weekend."

"How did they know I would be there?" I said.

"Search me," he replied. "But Manfred's daughter Barbara has recently decided you are worth far more to them alive, leading them to the different hoards of treasure. You see, they've never had the clues. Manfred Meyer believes all these treasures belong to him."

"How do you know all this?" I repeated.

"We have a mole inside the Stasi," he said. "But wait, one thing at a time. Of course I'll give you the bag. I don't need the gems. They're worth a fortune, but I have everything I need. I've put them aside for you. And to compensate for the scare I've caused, I'll show you the other clues, the quotations I mean, and we can see if the rest of the gems are still there."

"One of *your* linen bags?" I said. "But who are you? What organization are you really working for?"

"By the way," he replied, "the driver, guide and guards I hired to look after you in Algeria. Of course you never saw them again. They were shot on the road from Algiers to Sétif. They were ordered to stop by the army, but they accelerated on and were gunned down at the next checkpoint. I'm afraid they were not as professional as I'd been told."

At that moment Severina suddenly appeared. In her East European accent, she quickly informed us that we were being followed by the Germans, "the man and his daughter, and two of his agents." Vincent too was following us. They had all been on our trail since we had arrived in Burgundy, and Vincent had already got one of the purses.

"Wait," said Geoffrey, "I think Sav... well, whatever her name is, I think her teams and my men should be enough to keep you safe. I've got some of our people from Lyon to come up here. I'll show you the castle, the cellar and the gate. I can probably save you a lot of time. I had it all worked out before nightfall. Habit, you know. And I do know my vineyards."

"Where is Saint Peter?" I asked. I told him I'd looked at maps of every wine parish in Burgundy.

"*On this one, his church he built* isn't Saint Peter," he said. He reminded us of Matthew chapter 16 verse 18. " 'And I say also unto thee, That thou art Peter, and upon this rock I will build my church.' Of course," he added "in the French Bible, there's a play on words that doesn't work in English: 'Et moi, je te déclare: Tu es Pierre, et sur cette pierre j'édifierai mon Eglise.' It's not stone, *pierre*, but 'rock' in English. The Clos-de-la-Roche in Morey-Saint-Denis."

I'd wasted a lot of time looking for Saint Peter in Burgundy.

The fun had now gone out of the puzzle-solving, and all that mattered was seeing if the 'purses' were still there. We hadn't eaten, and it was nearing lunchtime. I was about to ask for the menu.

"Let's go," said Leila, getting up and walking out of the cafe. Geoffrey followed her with his eyes, and nodded.

"We're going," he said brightly.

*

He instructed me to drive from Beaune to Nuits-Saint-Georges, only a few miles. After Nuits he directed us up the slope to the village of Vosne-Romanée where we stopped by the Grande Rue vineyard. We looked around and saw a walled enclosure, with a stone inscription carved over the entrance. "Exode 39:12".

We drove back down the slope, past the world-famous Romanée-Conti, the first leaves barely emerging from the vines on this sunny Spring day. Next stop the nearby Richebourg. Not far along the road our old spy-cum-guide showed us some stairs leading down to a cellar.

"See what's carved on either side of the staircase?"

On a headstone to the left were carved the initials "E.Z.", on the twin stone to the right the date "10 janvier 1772."

"E.Z. is Ezekiel, the tenth of January is '10.1'. Chapter 10 verse 1 of Ezekiel is the sapphire verse."

He finally showed us, visible from the Clos-de-la-Roche in the village of Morey-Saint-Denis, the courtyard of a small *château*, where we saw over the doorway an inscription from Revelation 4:3, "Et le trône était environné d'un arc-en-ciel semblable à de l'émeraude."

... from La Grande Rue back down the slope, past the world-famous Romanée-Conti, the first leaves barely emerging from the vines on this sunny Spring day, on to Richebourg ...

Following his instructions as he sat in the back of the van, we set off towards the sapphire monastery. On my insistence we stopped for a quick lunch in Nuits-Saint-Georges. Geoffrey recited Ezekiel 10:1 to us in English. "Then I looked, and behold, in the firmament that was above the head of the cherubims there appeared over them as it were a sapphire stone, as the appearance of the likeness of a throne." He tore a sheet from a pocket-book, and wrote down the Latin version that I was to recite to the abbot.

I asked Leila to drive, and she soon exclaimed that we were being followed. She slowed down and an Audi drew up close behind us. She muttered that she recognized the driver.

"It's Barbara Meyer."

I turned round and saw a man whom I didn't recognize sitting in the passenger seat.

"Must be her father," I said.

"Just drive normally, not too fast, not too slow, and keep going to the monastery," said Geoffrey. "Don't worry, they won't be able to follow us all the way."

I was reading the map and giving instructions on the route. I protested that we were leading them to the treasure, but he insisted we continue. He was holding a mobile phone to his ear. The Audi stayed thirty yards behind us. After the last turning we drove up towards the monastery, parked and waited. The Audi didn't appear. We waited a few minutes. There was still no sign of the Meyers.

"I told you. Now go ahead and see what you can get," said Geoffrey. "Don't worry about the Meyers, my people will look after them."

We pulled the bell chain, and were shown into the abbot's room. I recited the Latin text Geoffrey had written out for me:

"*Et vidi et ecce in firmamento quod erat super caput cherubin quasi lapis sapphyrus quasi species similitudinis solii apparuit super ea.*"

The abbot bowed, turned, went through a heavy wooden door, and returned a minute later with one of Suzy's bags. He handed it to Leila, waved dismissively as I thanked him, and told his companion to see us out. That was all, after eighty years that the linen bag had been in their care. Leila felt inside, and pulled out a handful of diamonds, with a few sapphires. She handed it over and I put it in a pouch that I had brought for the purpose, attached to a sling that I wore under my shirt.

Outside there was still no sign of the Audi.

"You see," said Geoffrey, "I told you my man from Lyon would take care of them."

As we drove off and turned the corner, we found Barbara Meyer standing behind her car, holding a gun aimed at our windscreen. I saw the man who must have been Manfred standing beside her. He too had a gun, pointed at our front passenger window. We had no choice but to stop. Manfred ordered us all out of the car.

"At last," he said. "Now will you kindly hand over that little bag. I think it's time we had one of those."

Geoffrey had let us down again. But before we could move, a Volvo screeched round the corner and rammed the Audi. Two young men leapt out of the car brandishing revolvers in the direction of the Meyers. An older man stepped out and ordered Barbara and her father to drop their guns. They hesitated, then he dropped his. She grimaced, bent down, and put her revolver on the tarmac in the middle of the road. The older man told us to get back into our vehicle.

Geoffrey ordered Leila to drive away. He lowered his window and shouted "Everything OK?" One of the men nodded.

"Our man from Lyon," said Geoffrey, "I still have influence."

"We can see that," Leila said, "but where are the Stasi agents? And you still haven't told us who you're working for."

"All will be revealed tomorrow," he replied, smiling brightly.

"Look," I said. "We know you don't work for MI6, and probably never have. I've carried out extensive enquiries."

He smiled again.

"You'll see," was his response. Then he looked me straight in the eyes. "If you work for them, they're not helping you very much. You are fortunate that I have been around to look after you."

Perhaps he was right.

The emerald monastery was only a quarter of an hour away. As we stood before the gate, the little green stones that formed the lettering of the name glinting in the sunlight, a gruff voice behind us shouted, "Haut les mains! Mettez-vous contre le mur." Hands up! Stand against the wall.

The Meyers must have escaped the agent from Lyon.

"Don't argue," Geoffrey hissed.

We did as we were told. For a few seconds nothing happened. Then a shot rang out, then another, from somewhere to our left. I turned to look behind us, and caught a glimpse of a tall man holding a revolver and looking at where the shots had come from. Behind him, a slim figure ran up and held his arms and waist in a tight grip. Two men came running from the other side, snatched his gun and knocked him to the ground. The slim figure was Severina.

"Quite close," she said, "but Vincent is too slow. Please go ahead to the monastery."

The threat of our 'dangerous' rival had been easily countered.

Geoffrey rang the bell. A monk came to the gate and enquired of our business. A few minutes later, we were standing before a rather overweight abbot.

"*Et qui sedebat similis erat aspectui lapidis iaspidis et sardini et iris erat in circuitu sedis similis visioni zmaragdinae.*"

Once more reading Geoffrey's crisp handwriting, I had some difficulty in finishing the sentence. My breathing was by now quite uneven, for I was much disturbed by the scene we had witnessed a few moments earlier.

"I thought you would never come," said the abbot, mopping his brow with his sleeve, "after all these years." He was smiling. And perspiring. He looked at Leila and translated the verse into English. "And he that sat was to look upon like a jasper and a sardine stone: and there was a rainbow round about the throne, in sight like unto an emerald."

"Revelation chapter 4, verse 3," he added, then asked, "But why has it taken so long?"

Leila looked at me, alarmed. He was talkative, we wanted the purse and to get away to the amethyst monastery. I looked stern, and repeated:

"*Et qui sedebat similis erat aspectui lapidis iaspidis et sardini et iris erat in circuitu sedis similis visioni zmaragdinae*."

"Ah," he murmured, and withdrew. After two minutes he came back, purse in hand. He gave it to me, wiped his brow and asked again, "Why has it taken so long?"

Leila stepped forward, bowed, and put a finger to her lips. He looked at me, then sighed.

"Of course," he said. He rang a bell, and the first monk showed us out. This time Leila found a few emeralds among the diamonds. Small emeralds, large diamonds.

Geoffrey gave me instructions on the amethyst quotation, Exodus chapter 39 verse 12, which he translated: "And the third row, a ligure, an agate, and an amethyst."

Leila and I were shown in. Geoffrey had said he would stay outside to watch for Stasi agents.

"*In tertio ligyrius achates et amethistus*," I said, slightly stressing the last word.

The abbot stiffened. He coughed. He looked from me to Leila and back again.

"Er, I'm afraid," he mumbled, "I'm afraid you are not the first one. We had kept the bag as requested, but earlier this morning an old man appeared and spoke the verse, exactly as you have done. That is it. Our compact is over. We've kept it safe, and now it is his."

He looked us up and down.

"I'm sorry," he said, and began telling a story. "We had a very loquacious old abbot, who told us what happened years ago. He'd been in charge for more than half a century. He was there when the bag was left in our care. 'A delightful lady', he used to say, 'a delightful lady'. For years afterwards the rest of us used to laugh, and repeat in prayers *domina iucunda*, 'a delightful lady'. It always made him blush.

"The lady had said she was sure that in the keeping of the monastery it would be safe. The old abbot used to pray every day to protect the treasure... and the lady."

As we walked back to the van, we could hear monks chanting Cistercian plainsong. I stopped to listen.

"I'm not remotely religious," I said, "but plainsong, the monks chanting, that always takes me out of myself. I become aware of the timelessness of it all, the same chants today as were sung over five hundred years ago. In the same place. Today, yesterday, five hundred years. It makes no difference."

Leila looked at me.

"You don't understand," she said. "If you're a believer, you don't need plainsong to know about eternity."

"But daily prayers don't seem to protect our friends," Geoffrey retorted. "They may protect the treasure, but they didn't save Suzanne. And they haven't kept her treasure safe for you. I stayed outside because I'd received a message saying that the ex-Stasi replacements were waiting for us. But there was no sign of them. Maybe they'd been following Vincent?"

Maybe they had. But whilst he seemed to be less of a physical threat to us than we had been led to believe, Vincent had proved that he was clever enough to have got hold of two of Suzy's little Burgundy bags.

We dropped Geoffrey off and he said to meet us at our usual café half an hour later. He would bring us the gems from the ruby monastery. We waited an hour, two hours, three hours. I activated his number. No response. We decided to drive back to Paris with the gems we'd collected, for two Stasi agents were still lurking in Burgundy. Why had Geoffrey not turned up?

9. Miss Fortune, Murder in the Louvre

This was surely the most splendid urban home I had ever seen. I'd received a fancily printed invitation for two, to a house-warming party at an address in a street above the Luxembourg Gardens in central Paris. It was for 3 p.m. on Monday 21st June. Midsummer's Day.

Adam and I walked down from the Port Royal underground station, and found tall iron gates closing off a private, tree-lined road. We showed our invitation to security staff who let us through the gates then into the garden.

High walls surrounded lawns, bushes, fountains and a tennis court. A protective double row of tall fir trees was planted down both sides of the garden. The four-storey house had a stone facade with sculpted decorations, leaded-glass windows, wrought-iron balconies and turrets on round towers at each corner. I was soon to see that the upper floors overlooked the Luxembourg Gardens as if the latter were part of the property, with the Senate building forming an elegant horizon four hundred yards away down a gentle slope.

Guests were standing or sitting in groups on the lawns, drinking champagne and nibbling *canapés* and *petits fours*. We had been told we might meet an actress who had played the lead in several popular films. "Dark curly hair, bright eyes, unlikely adventures in jungles and tombs and distant eastern lands," Adam informed me, adding, "and, at least on the screen, 'un corps de rêve', as we say in French."

As I looked around the lawns, I saw her. Rebecca Fortune, the film star, surrounded by a group of young men. Adam couldn't take his eyes off her as we circulated amongst the guests, some of whom recognized me from my tv programmes. We noticed that Rebecca hardly smiled. In fact she looked bored, and she seemed to wince more than once as the young men around her joked and flattered. A footman approached us and announced that Joshua and Hettie Strauss wished to be introduced to me. He guided me to a table in the middle of the lawn. The Strausses were the lucky new owners of this magnificent property. And they were the parents of the beautiful and famous Rebecca Fortune. They were with a lady who smiled graciously and shook my hand. I congratulated them on their new house. The smiling lady was called Ruth. She was a doctor and, she soon informed me, had been a widow since her husband's sudden death from a heart attack five years earlier. The small talk and the introductions didn't last long, as Joshua Strauss took my elbow and pulled me aside.

"We have very much enjoyed your latest series on the history of western art. Our daughter has just been appointed patron of an association that has for years been working to have Jewish property that the Nazis plundered returned to the children and grandchildren of those who were despoiled and murdered. We would be most grateful if you could help with the identification and authentication of a number of paintings."

"I'm sure we can arrange something," I began, when he interrupted me.

"Forgive me I cannot talk now. There will be urgent business to discuss. Please stay until my guests have left. You must excuse me for the moment."

I nodded, turned to Ruth, and caught a glimpse of Rebecca across the lawn, still surrounded by a group of admirers. I noticed that Adam was now one of them. But Ruth was very chatty and demanded all my attention. She kept touching me as if we'd known each other for years. She asked all about my work, children, marriage, likes and dislikes. I learnt that she was born in Prague, had lived in Montreal then Paris, and now had a big house in Auvers-sur-Oise, the village where Van Gogh had lived his last few days.

I listened to this entertainingly merry widow, but my mind was trying to focus on the appointment with Joshua Strauss. I could see Rebecca Fortune talking to Adam, her hand on his arm. Yes, she was very pretty.

When the last few guests had gone and an army of servants were clearing up, Joshua and Hettie took me up to the second floor, to a library with an authentic Louis XVI desk and chairs and the view down the Luxembourg Gardens to the Senate. Ruth came along too.

"So," Joshua said, with quite a pronounced Germanic accent that I hadn't noticed earlier, "so, you are the foremost Parisian expert on nineteenth and twentieth century European art." He was terse, and came straight to the point. "There are paintings that were taken by the Germans when my parents were deported."

"Why have I been selected to help?" I asked.

"It was Rebecca's idea. She is the delight of our lives. She was born at a time when we thought we were too old to have children. She's become a very successful actress. She worked hard, trained at RADA, changed her name and has done well. She's settled in Paris, and bought this home for us with the money from her last two films."

He beamed with pride. At that moment Rebecca came into the library, with Adam.

"It's all right my dear, we've finished," said Joshua. He beamed again. Was that all? It *was* to be all for now. Rebecca looked at me, a wave of the hand acknowledging my presence.

"God they're tiresome," she announced. Not a trace of Germanic accent, but a slight mid-Atlantic drawl. "Not one of them is sincere. Money and sex, sex and money. And the house now. Their mouths watering, their paws pawing. I'm sorry," she looked at me, "we haven't met. I'm rather tired."

"Fame has its drawbacks," I said, without thinking.

"Bores, all of them. Bores and boors. They think they're so funny, so original, so irresistible. But they're all the same. Always the same lines in chat."

"Well, I see you've met my son. I hope he hasn't been a boor and a bore?"

"No, actually," she hesitated, then grinned at Adam, "he's okay."

Adam blushed. Joshua reminded his daughter why I had been invited.

"Where do you live?" she asked.

When I said that I lived in the suburbs she suddenly said she would take us to the train. I shook hands with Joshua and Hettie, and got a suffocating hug from Ruth. We followed Rebecca downstairs to a garage at the rear of the house.

We got into a red and yellow mini and she set off. Adam sat in the back and I was in the front passenger seat. She was wearing a short white summer dress with an orange flower pattern. She had dark glistening eyes and smooth tanned shoulders, arms and legs. She drove fast, slaloming through the Paris traffic. In the end she took us all the way home.

We chatted, I can't really remember what about. Adam spoke sparingly, Rebecca a lot. She looked at the road in front mostly, but occasionally turned her head and looked at me, then glanced in her rear mirror at Adam. She dropped us off at home, and as I thanked her, she gave him a kiss, then put her hand on my shoulder and said, "See you again."

Adam said he would stay the night with me. Later that evening he came up to the loft.

"Listen Dad, I'd rather you didn't mention Rebecca to Jordan or Jessica. She was very friendly, and we're going to see each other again. I tried to be, you know, normal, but I was very much in awe. She soon had me talking as if we were good friends. But they'll tease me and I don't want to look foolish if she doesn't want to know me any more. Let's wait a while."

"Okay," I said. He looked a bit sheepish. I hoped he wouldn't get badly burnt, but I was pleased that my reasonable son, the serious one, had attracted a famous actress. A 'midsummer enchantment'. Would it soon be undone?

*

The next month Ruth called and said I must come to her house at Auvers to see Joshua and Hettie. And Rebecca, she added. Perhaps I could bring Adam. We were to arrive for dinner and stay overnight, since there'd be a lot of 'serious business' to talk over.

At Ruth's dinner, Joshua talked non-stop about the Old Testament, the history of the Jewish people and the politics of the Middle East. There was no room for frivolity. Nor interruptions, nor second opinions. It had been planned that we would talk business after the meal, but he became very drowsy and fell asleep without finishing his dessert. Adam and I carried him upstairs. Hettie and Ruth put him to bed.

Rebecca took Adam by the hand 'to show him round the house.' Ruth served coffee, and soon suggested we all go to bed since Joshua was no longer available. We would have our business talk next morning.

I slept soundly, and didn't wake until nearly nine. I was about to get dressed when there was a knock on my bedroom door. It was Adam. He came in and sat on the bed.

"Look, I have to talk. I'm bursting. Last night I took some time to doze off, but it was still dark outside when I awoke. Something was different. My mind was in a cloud. Gradually, very gradually, I realized that I wasn't alone. She was curled up in bed with me, entwined around me, her head snuggled under my chin. Her perfume was exquisite, and she was completely naked. So was I.

"I put my fingers through her hair, hugged her, and slowly stretched each part of my body as we moved together, clasped tight. I don't think I woke up fully. I wanted this to go on for ever. I held her in my arms, kissed her forehead, put my hands through her curls again, and stayed in this blissful state for... I don't know, an hour, two hours? She kept half waking and gave me little hugs and pokes and light caresses then went back to sleep.

"As a faint daylight showed around the shutters, we woke up. She kissed me. We made love and then slept. When I woke again, I put my arm round her. She turned, looked at me, wrinkled her nose, and made a short speech about how she liked me and said we could meet again. Then she announced, 'I'll have to go. I'm late. For God's sake don't say anything. To anybody.' And she was gone. Please, don't tell the others what's happened. At the moment, I really don't know where I stand."

We went down for breakfast. Adam started when he saw Rebecca sitting there, a cup of coffee in her hand, waiting for us. Didn't she have an appointment? She said "good morning" in a matter-of-fact tone. Ruth said there was a delay in delivery of the paintings and there was nothing much they could do now, except wait for news. That seemed to be all the business? Was that why we had been invited out for an overnight stay?

Rebecca stood up and announced that she had to leave. She kissed her parents and Ruth, and shook hands with Adam and me. Not a flicker of recognition. Adam hung his head, and his shoulders drooped. I began to wonder if he *was* going to get hurt. After agreeing that I would wait for instructions, we made our excuses and left.

A couple of weeks later I was on my way home when there occurred one of those coincidences that occasionally happen in a metropolis. There are several million inhabitants so it's always a surprise when you see someone you know in a cafe or in the street. At the Châtelet underground station Adam and Rebecca got on my train, but they didn't see me. They stood facing each other, close, holding hands. Then she put her arms round him, grasped his shoulders, and gave him an affectionate kiss.

*

Only a few days later Leila and I went to the Strausses house by the Luxembourg Gardens. Ruth, Rebecca and her parents were waiting for us. I was surprised to find Adam there too. Rebecca immediately announced, "We'll leave you to check everything." She took Leila and Adam by the hand, and led them out of the room. A team of domestics brought in about twenty paintings. I recognized none of them. But there was no mistaking the artists, although some canvases were badly damaged. Chagall, Salvador Dali, Picasso, Kandinsky... I wrote out a list for Joshua and Hettie.

Ruth suddenly took me aside and I thought she was about to make a suggestion as to what to do next. Instead, she started quizzing me about Leila. Who was this girl? What was she to me? Didn't I realize how ridiculous it looked, going around with a woman half my age? What did my children think? Couldn't I see how embarrassed Adam was? And Rebecca obviously noticed the awkwardness. Ruth finished with a tirade.

"You claim you're just friends, but you don't fool anybody. You must know that."

I gave her short shrift. Indeed, I was quite rude.

"I don't give a toss what you think. You can mind your own business. And your own business doesn't seem very proper. But that, I can assure you, is no business of mine."

She burst into tears. Perhaps I had been a bit unfair. Maybe she was only articulating what others thought but never said out loud.

*

The next day Geoffrey phoned.

"I must warn you," he announced, "that you are wrong to ignore us and to count on Savarona and the actress's bodyguards. We are far more effective. You really need us. I don't have much time right now, but you need to know that a gang of criminals is tailing your family. You, your sons and your daughter. They have located your home and are following all your movements. Apparently your daughter's case is about to proceed. My source tells me that 'not only the witnesses are in danger'."

He rang off abruptly. Rebecca had bodyguards? All of us being followed? I would have to speak with Jessica and the boys.

As usual Geoffrey seemed to know what was going on every-where. Leila claimed that he was playing his own game, using us as pawns, or as bait. True, he didn't keep his promises, and he'd rung off before I had time to mention the ruby monastery gems.

A few minutes later Adam called.

"Hi Dad, just to bring you up to date. After her filming in Egypt, Rebecca invited me to join her for a few days break at Deauville. We were walking along the sea front when a young woman bumped into us. I was sure she'd done it deliberately. She was aggressive, and seemed to want to pick a quarrel. Suddenly what looked like two thugs, real muscly types with crew cuts and leather jackets, appeared and confronted us. Then an older man came up and spoke to the woman in German. Rebecca understands German. She said he was obviously the woman's father."

"Don't tell me," I remarked, "Herr Manfred Meyer, his daughter Barbara, and two ex-Stasi toughs again! The meeting of the fourth generations?"

"You can hardly say we met," Adam replied. "The toughs led Re-becca and me away. I hadn't realized until then that she was always followed by two bodyguards. Her very own security team. They saved us from what had looked like a nasty situation. At any rate, I feel secure now, at least when I'm with her."

*

We were to meet Adam and Rebecca in the Louvre. As Leila and I took the winding staircase down to the big hall below the glass pyramid, I was surprised to see Jordan standing there too.

"Hello. Adam told me you were meeting here, so I've decided to take the day off. Hope you don't mind."

What was he up to?

Our appointment was for 10 o'clock with a curator called Aurélie Touret. I'd looked for her on the Louvre website and hadn't found her name, but she appeared at two minutes past ten. She took Jordan by the arm and guided us through Greek, Etruscan and Ro-man Antiquities, past Coptic Egypt, through a heavy door marked 'INTERDIT AU PUBLIC', and down a flight of stairs. We were in the cellars of the Louvre, on the level of the twelfth-century ramparts that used to protect the city.

We found ourselves surrounded by stone walls with arrowslit

windows that now looked out into darkness. We were inside part of the old fortress. The floor was a wooden platform, three feet or more above the hard earth. It took several seconds to adapt to the dim lighting. I could just make out rows of paintings stacked against the walls, with more on easels or piled on trestle tables.

"This was part of the wall of the original moat," said Aurélie, as she led us through a door into a cramped room that felt, I said, like a cell for condemned prisoners. She told us that was exactly what it had been, not all that long ago.

'We were in the cellars of the Louvre, on the level of the twelfth-century ramparts'

"My office," she continued. "A lot more of the medieval castle survived below ground than has ever been officially revealed. The fortress, moats and dungeons were excavated long before a small part of what's known was opened to the general public. There's a network of passages and rooms. They connect with the catacombs via miles of underground galleries and old quarries. There have been some macabre events down here, and not just in the Middle Ages."

Our project was to research and catalogue the paintings and little sculptures from Istanbul that had at last arrived in Paris, as well as several hundred important works of art that had, mysteriously, been hidden in the Louvre basement for over fifty years. Rebecca had joined us since she was the patron and public face of a new charity for the restoration of art plundered by the Nazis. Aurélie gave us a mini-lecture on the works of art that had been stored here since the 1940s and whose owners had never been traced.

"At the beginning of the war," she said, "the Louvre was almost empty. All the most valuable paintings had been tucked away in provincial *châteaux*, safe from the bombs. But after Paris was occupied by the Germans, stuff taken by the Nazis began to come in. Loyal French museum employees put what they could in this underground maze, to prevent it going off to Germany. Most of what they hid was never found by the Germans. At the Liberation, it was all taken to the Jeu de Paume. But when the Impressionists were installed there, over two thousand paintings that hadn't been reclaimed came back here. They've stayed underground ever since. Efforts have been made only recently to contact possible owners."

I saw some of what Hitler had labelled 'degenerate' art, works by Klee, Kandinsky, and Chagall. Then about fifty paintings and over a dozen of the smaller statues from Yavuz's Green Gallery. We spent two and a half hours sorting the paintings into related groups. We started with the Impressionists from Istanbul, hoping to trace early sales records in order to identify provenance and previous owners. We found no references and I was beginning to conclude that they had never been exhibited in western Europe. I was also concerned about some of the paintings now that we could examine them closely. There were odd details of brushstroke and technique that were unusual. Then Aurélie suddenly reappeared.

"I'm going to have to kick you out now," she said. "We close for lunch, and this afternoon I have to meet a Chinese delegation. I suggest you come in two or three times a week until you've finished."

Jordan said he wanted to stop at the bookstall on the way out. I was looking at a new catalogue of Delacroix's Moroccan sketches when I heard Leila talking. I looked round and saw she was with Delcia.

"What are you doing here?" she said when I went to greet her, as if we had no right to be there.

"Consultancy, down in the basement," I said. "And what are *you* doing?"

"I've been tracing images of Aphrodite. I have a contract for a book. Pictures of me alongside famous paintings and statues of women in seductive poses. It's called *Images of Aphrodite*."

I introduced her to Adam, Rebecca and Jordan.

"Why don't we all have lunch together?" said Delcia, and so we sat at a table for six on the terrace of the Cafe Marly, overlooking the cobbled courtyard, the pyramid, and the crowds queuing to get into the Louvre. Delcia suddenly looked at me.

"Don't you have a daughter too? A barrister. Where is she?"

That reminded me of what I'd been putting off for some time. I knew I must contact Jessica. Here were her brothers participating in my affairs, with Leila and Rebecca too, but I still hadn't told her what was going on. Why not? We hadn't seen much of each other for the previous year or more. I was away a lot, and she had been busy with that high-profile case. But I knew that the real reason was my fear that she wouldn't accept my friendship with Leila. The boys had found out, and they didn't seem to give it a second thought. So why hadn't I told Jessica? Why was I scared that she would take it badly?

As I was ordering coffee, I realized that Jordan and Delcia were talking together. An earnest conversation, it seemed. When we stood up to leave, they touched hands and kissed each other. It was a little more than the customary peck on the cheek.

*

Should I have been surprised? I was unaware that Jordan and Delcia had already met, exchanged mobile numbers, sent messages, and called each other, so he knew he would find her at the Louvre that day. I've never found out how they first made contact, but soon they were meeting every day.

"Yes," he said, "we've been seeing a lot of each other. Of course, we were very much aware of the involvements of you and her mother Laurence, not to mention my great-grandfather John Henry and her great-grandmother Suzanne. You'd never said anything about that, but she told me. We were both fearful of getting too close, because we knew how those relationships had ended. Both women were murdered, weren't they? We tried to take our time, but... why hold back? Last week I moved into the Boulevard Saint-

Germain flat."

They hadn't held back for long. So one of my sons was going out with a film star, the other was dating a model whose face appeared on billboards and magazine covers.

Jordan told me about himself and Delcia. He said that one day they'd been stopped in the Louvre by a man with a camera, a famous American photographer. He'd offered them twenty thousand dollars if they would pose for him in different parts of the city. Apparently his work sold well and twenty thousand dollars was chicken-feed to him. They'd accepted. They were a beautiful couple, I must admit, ideal for a portrayal of young lovers exploring Paris.

He showed me photographs of them holding hands and looking into each other's eyes by the Arc de Triomphe, the Eiffel Tower, in front of Notre Dame, on the banks of the Seine. They'd been promised further contracts, modelling for fashion magazines.

The next week they were away on a photo-shoot, full of excitement. They borrowed the Ferrari. A month later Leila showed me a perfume advert in *Cosmopolitan*. There were Jordan and Delcia, sitting in front of the Doge's Palace in Venice, in *my* Ferrari.

*

We worked in the Louvre basement three or four times a week, listing the artworks, cross-checking them with an inventory of paintings plundered during the war and with catalogues of works missing from museums and private collections all over the world. Aurélie had internet access to most national databases, to Interpol's art theft listings, and to auction records going back to the 1920s. Adam and Rebecca were helping us almost every day. She wasn't filming that month, and he had taken two weeks holiday to be with her. One morning he took Leila and me to one side.

"I'm not sure but I think I've just seen that Meyer man and his daughter leaving Aurélie's office. She shook hands with them and showed them out."

I decided to confront her immediately.

"Oh no," she said, "he's a colleague from the Pergamon in Berlin. He had an assistant with him. He was asking about what we have down here. Of course we vetted them first. His visit was arranged at a very high level, the German Ambassador prepared everything through the Quai d'Orsay and our Ministry of Culture. I've no reason to doubt his credentials."

We had always suspected that she was hiding something. She never looked us in the eye, though Jordan claimed she had a slight squint. Her behaviour was curiously irregular. I started watching her more closely. She often went upstairs, absenting herself for half an hour or more, leaving us down in the basement. Delcia was in the Louvre every day for her Aphrodite project, so I asked her and Jordan to take a bit of time to follow Aurélie. At first they kept losing track of her, but they soon became more skilled at shadowing and discovered that she regularly visited an office on the top floor. Delcia said it belonged to a curator who was in charge of cultural exchanges with museums throughout Europe.

Then one morning—it was a Tuesday, the day when the Louvre is closed to the public and so our security was lighter—Jordan came running to the room where we were working.

"We've just seen Manfred and Barbara going into the cultural exchanges office with Aurélie," he announced breathlessly, "then Barbara emerged with her, and they came down here to the galleries in the cellars. I've left Delcia keeping watch. You *must* alert Severina."

At that moment Aurélie appeared and called us all into her office.

"I can see you don't trust me," she said gaily, "so I'll tell you a few things about myself, and my work here."

"You'd better be quick, and convincing," Leila said impatiently. "We know you're in contact with Manfred and Barbara Meyer."

"In contact?" Aurélie queried. "Not exactly. We know who they are, and after encouraging their rather amateurish attempts to get hold of some of the artworks you are checking, wherever they go in the Louvre, and outside, we have them followed."

"Who's *we*?" I asked.

"I'm not really a curator at all," said Aurélie, "and my name is Anastasia, not Aurélie. I've been posted here for the last five years to supervise this collection. We've been watching over it since 1945. And we've had reinforcements to our team since your stuff came in from Istanbul."

"*Who*," Leila repeated, "*who* is *we*?"

"Like you, I work for the French Secret Services," Anastasia replied, very cool and self-assured. "But for me it's in the family. I'll tell you a story. My grandfather was a doctor, a Jewish doctor. During the war he survived because he treated a German officer for syphilis. Injections once a week. He hid his Jewish identity. Of course, he was circumsized, so he said he was Muslim. It worked. He studied his Koran and had to feign the Islamic rites from time to time, but he survived the war. His German officer survived too. Until the last few days. I'm afraid Grandfather's last injection killed him."

She smiled.

"So who was your grandfather working for?" asked Rebecca.

"No-one. He'd come from Lithuania in 1931 to study medicine at Rouen. In the war he was alone in Paris, and was concerned about saving his own skin. He married after the war, and had a son, my father, who became an intelligence agent. He spent a lot of time in Eastern Europe. One day they found him hanging from a bridge in Leningrad. I made up my mind to avenge his death. One day I will."

She shrugged her shoulders, looked at Leila, then at me, and began speaking very slowly.

"I'll give it you in a nutshell. Since I've been here, watching over these plundered works, there've been contacts with the security organizations of several foreign governments. At first we thought MI6 were very interested, but it turns out it's only an old man who apparently has his own agenda. There've been former KGB and Stasi agents, including Herr and Fräulein Meyer. Recently, we've had Greeks and Turks who are both trying to persuade us to hand over what has come from Istanbul. We think, by the way, that the old man has been working with the Germans. I overheard him speaking German with them. We can't work out what he's doing, but he's certainly very eccentric.

"Thanks to you, we now have recovered part of the collection that was taken to Constantinople in 1914. The Germans regard these with particular interest, and your Meyer friends have been very active. They're certainly motivated. It would appear that their funds are starting to run low. That is why their interest in you has recently been more manifest. They need to find more resources to fund their activities. But we are not so concerned about them. It's the art we're interested in.

"Our aim is to secure the artworks here in France, and for the French government to be seen to be foremost in the restitution of a some of them. That is my role, to protect and return these artworks.

On the other hand, one of my superiors seems to regard it as his mission to frame and discredit the German agents. The Meyers will shortly be arrested, and a dossier of entirely false information about them distributed to the press. They will be treated as common criminals, and there will be a trial. In return, the role of official German agencies in hiding Nazi loot over the years will be played down. As will our own rather discreditable record in that regard.

"And I have news for you. The bad news is that we suspect some of the paintings that have come from Turkey are forgeries. Some but not all, and as you know attempts are being made to get the genuine ones back to Turkey, or taken to Greece, or Germany. Until all such attempts have been eliminated, you are in need of special protection since they hold you responsible for revealing the existence of the collection.

"The good news is that we have been protecting you ever since the Meyers arrived here in Paris. They seem to have a vendetta with you. The daughter Barbara is particularly dangerous. She believes she has a mission, 'woman to woman', someone heard her say."

Forgeries? I should have thought of it, that the Turks wouldn't let the originals go. And I was about to ask why Manfred and Barbara Meyer had not simply been arrested and locked away, when we heard a shriek and a lithe leather-jacketed woman came running in.

"She's dead, I'm sure she's dead," the woman shouted.

"Who?" demanded Leila, "who's dead? Where?"

"After the second gallery, the one that leads to the catacombs," the woman screamed, "a body, a woman, the young woman who's with you."

I looked at Leila, and realized that 'the young woman who's with you' could be Rebecca...

"This way," said Anastasia.

We followed her down to the catacombs. It was pitch dark. She flashed a torch along the walls, and there we found a body. Delcia, slumped in front of an alcove full of thigh bones and skulls. Adam moved forward and touched her.

"Her neck's broken," he muttered. A pause, then turning to us he whispered, "Where's Jordan?"

There was no mobile signal underground, so I told everyone to go upstairs, where we first called Louvre security, then the police. The blood had drained from Leila's face.

"They've got away," said Anastasia, one ear on her mobile phone. "It seems the Meyer girl broke the woman's neck with one movement, while her father held off one of our agents. They've both got out through the catacombs. We'll catch them, don't worry."

So far they haven't been caught.

Why Delcia? We don't know. Maybe she just got in the way. Or perhaps they'd mistaken her for Jessica, or Leila, or Rebecca?

Four deaths. Four murders. There was a curse on the Burridge-Carnot women. Two killed by the Meyers, two by Vincent. That evening, I found myself thumbing through Grandfather's diary, and I noticed that Delcia had died eighty-five years to the day—perhaps to the minute—that John Henry Wright had first set eyes on Suzanne, in a train on the way to Southampton. Mid-morning, August 19th 1914.

THE FOURTH GENERATION

10. Vincent's Vendettas

"I need some more coffee," Jessica announced. "I've been up since half past five."

They went downstairs to the kitchen. While Jessica was making the coffee Leila disappeared into the cellar. When she reappeared half a minute later she was with an overweight rottweiler that followed her eagerly into the kitchen. Jessica looked at the dog.

"Where did he come from?"

"*She*. She's mine. Bonza. She guards the house fine."

"It's easy enough to poison or shoot a dog. Any common burglar can do that."

"We don't just rely on her," Leila replied. "The garden walls are covered in security equipment, every room in the house has cameras, every door and window has sensors."

"All that hasn't prevented Father from disappearing off the face of the earth after he'd left the house. And it didn't stop me coming in this morning, did it?"

"I was expecting you, I was in the cellar, and I saw you arrive. There's a full set of screens down there as well as in the hall and in his bedroom. The alarms were switched off."

"How come I didn't meet Bonza?"

"I leave her out all night in the garden. She would bark if she heard anything unusual. But I took her down to the cellar before you arrived and kept her quiet..."

Leila was cut short as Bonza suddenly jumped up and began barking. They heard the security gate clang shut. Leila stiffened and Jessica noticed how alert she had immediately become.

"It'll be my brothers," said Jessica, opening the kitchen door, "I called them this morning and told them to come."

Leila didn't bat an eyelid. Bonza barked again, and Jessica noticed she was wagging her stump of a tail. She ran off round the house to the front drive. A few seconds later Adam appeared. Bonza was making a fuss of him, putting her paws on his thighs and licking his hand.

"She's no good as a guard dog," thought Jessica. She turned to her brother.

"Dad's friend," she said, her outstretched palm indicating Leila.

There was a moment's hesitation. Jessica was sure she saw a gleam in Adam's and Leila's eyes as they shook hands.

"You two have met before," she exclaimed, glancing from one to the other, "and Bonza knows Adam."

"Yes, Leila and I do know each other," Adam admitted. "We've met a few times. We've done things together with Dad and with Jordan. And Rebecca. We know about the threats to Dad's life."

Jessica hesitated for a second.

"Who is Rebecca?"

Adam ignored her question.

"Why have I been summoned for 'an emergency'?" he asked.

Just then the doorbell rang. It was Jordan. He too got a friendly welcome from Bonza.

"Why have you two kept me in the dark over all this?" Jessica said angrily, looking from Adam to Jordan. "Father is in danger, and he's now been gone three days. You should have told me."

"We must go to La Châtaigneraie," said Jordan. "Grandfather Vincent is a dangerous old man with more than one reason to kidnap Father. Delcia often talked about him and his *château*. I don't know where it is, it could be in the middle of nowhere, the ideal place to hide a prisoner. But if it's in Picardy we can be there in less than two hours. We must find it and leave now."

"Wait," said Jessica sharply. "What is La Châtaigneraie? Who is 'Grandfather Vincent'? Who is Rebecca and who is Delcia? Why have you never said anything to me?"

Adam took her aside and explained, while Leila and Jordan started searching for La Châtaigneraie. They had soon found more than a dozen hamlets and manor-houses of that name. Oak copses were common all over northern France. They found four in Picardy.

"The envelope!" Leila suddenly shouted. "He must have kept her letter, there'll be a postmark."

She recalled how Redmond had told her that the day after he'd heard the news of Laurence's death, a letter from her dropped into his mail box. She'd started writing it before setting off for La Châtaigneraie. She'd posted it from the village as soon as she arrived with her father. A letter full of love and hope for the future.

Leila said he kept his personal mail in a desk in the living room. She came back two minutes later with the envelope. She read out the postcode, 80295. It was just over an hour's drive away, on the main road south of Amiens.

Adam and Jordan were surprised to see their sister apparently so much on edge. They could feel the tension whenever Leila spoke. Jessica suddenly whispered to Jordan.

"She annoys me. She's had Dad completely in her pocket. She's taken over his life."

"Don't you believe it!" he replied. "He knows what he's doing. He goes along with her, but he has everything under control."

Jessica looked hard at her brother. What made him think that?

*

La Châtaigneraie turned out to be one of those hamlets typical of northern France, stretching along either side of a main road, apparently bereft of any life. Two lines of low brick houses, doors and shutters closed as the traffic thundered by. Not a person to be seen. A café and a general store. No sign of, nor signs to, a *château*. Adam stopped the car and Jessica and Jordan were bending over a map spread between them on the back seat when they were startled by a sharp tap on the rear window. They all turned and looked back. No-one. Another tap, this time on the window by the driver's seat.

Someone opened the door and Adam found himself face to face with a dwarf-like figure huddled in a wheel-chair. He was clutching the door handle.

"What do you want?" he croaked, a deathly-white face staring at them. A skull of a head, deep eye sockets and hollow cheeks. A ghost, not a man.

They asked for directions. He said two kilometres down the road and turn left. Another kilometre and they would come to the gate.

"Thank you," said Adam, "thank you Monsieur..."

"Moreau," he squawked, and in a rising tone, "Monsieur le Docteur Jacques Moreau." He saluted, an ironic, mocking gesture, then spun his wheel-chair round and sped away.

*

The gates to the *château* were open. They drove down a broad tree-lined avenue, over a bridge above a moat, and into a courtyard of gravel and cobblestones. A tall, erect man emerged from an archway fifty yards or more away, to the left of the main building. As they got out of the car, Leila muttered "that's him" just as her mobile rang.

It was Geoffrey.

"Watch out for Vincent, Laurence's father. He's ruthless and he's vindictive. You're walking right into a trap. He's mad, but beware, he's clever. The doctor is very ill, not far from death, but he can still cause you problems. We'll be with you soon."

The courtyard and main buildings, La Châtaigneraie

Before Leila could ask any questions, her mobile cut off. Vincent strode towards them, his face scowling and his fists clenched. He towered above them. Adam noticed that Leila was no longer there. He looked round, but couldn't see her anywhere.

"Wright," said Vincent as he stood before them, "Redmond Wright. You three look just like him, you must be his children. Jessica, Adam and Jordan, isn't it? What are you doing here? What do you want?"

If Moreau had appeared sinister, Vincent did indeed look as if he were mad, quite unpredictable. Perhaps it was the way he swung his arms about as he spoke, and his rapid eyes movements in all directions. He looked like a strong and well-preserved man in his sixties, certainly not an old man born at the end of the First World War.

"This way," he snapped without waiting for them to answer, "I'll show you."

He led them round to the right of the main building into a smaller courtyard, where he guided them inside a little chapel. Jessica shivered. It was cold and dark. There was an altar with two candles flickering in the draught. He ordered them to sit in the first of three rows of wooden pews. He took a heavy silver candlestick, inserted and lit a candle, then stood holding it above Jessica's head.

"It's time you knew," he announced, and began a long monologue. He explained that the day after Laurence's death, he'd hurried down to Paris to the Musée d'Orsay. He'd stood by *Le Déjeuner sur l'herbe*. His anger was overflowing. But he decided to wait. For the moment it was more satisfying to see Redmond suffering, believing Laurence had jilted him. He had enjoyed that. After half an hour, he'd returned to La Châtaigneraie, and supervised the funeral.

"Yes," he said, "Laurence was Suzanne's granddaughter. Suzanne would have been my mother-in-law if she'd lived."

He explained that he was a nephew of the mayor of Senlis who'd had Suzy's body brought back from her first wartime burial near Reims in 1922. When he was a schoolboy in his teens his uncle gave him a holiday job sorting out the municipal archives. He'd found an envelope which had been lying under a pile of documents since the end of the Great War. It contained a one-page police report suggesting that there was substance to the rumours about Suzanne Burridge-Carnot leaving a vast hoard of treasure, and that the key lay in Oxford.

He'd asked his uncle to pay for him to study at the College where Professor Burridge had been Master. He arrived in 1935, aged eighteen. The Professor had died soon after the First War, but Vincent's uncle had managed to get him enrolled in the College where he was taught by a group of dons who'd been Burridge's protégés. He was soon convinced that they too were looking for Suzy's treasure, and he was hot on the trail when they suddenly accused him of cheating in an end-of-term exam. They got him sent down.

He believed they'd conspired to get rid of him because he'd married a French widow he'd met at a fund-raising event for the

College. She died soon after, bequeathing him her two properties in France and a trust fund that brought in an annual income of fifteen thousand pounds, a considerable sum in those days.

"I knew that Suzy had had a daughter, Delphine. I now believed that she held the key to the whereabouts of the treasure. I went back to Senlis, found her, and within three months we were married, but she soon declared there was no treasure. She said she'd barely known her mother, who'd been away for most of the war."

Vincent admitted that he and Delphine were never very close, but after eight years of marriage, a daughter was born in 1945, Laurence.

At the mention of her name, Adam stood up. He knew Vincent could hit Jessica with the heavy candlestick he was holding, so he grasped it and pressed it against Vincent's shoulder. The old man resisted. His body was like a rock, an enormous frame for one of his age. As he was pushed away Adam felt a sharp pain in his lower back.

"Don't move," said a voice behind them. It was Moreau, who had silently wheeled himself into the chapel and, Adam surmised, was now holding a gun to the base of his spine. A shot rang out, a loud crack and a sharp echo in the small chapel.

For an instant Adam couldn't understand. He had felt nothing but a slight movement behind him. Then a familiar voice.

"You, don't move," said Leila. She had aimed a shot in front of Moreau's feet. "Just to scare them both," she said later. Moreau hadn't been holding a gun, but was prodding a walking stick into Adam's back.

"Now, go on with your story," Leila hissed at Vincent, "and you," to Moreau, "you stay where you are."

Coldly, calmly, Vincent explained that in the mid-1960s, he had come across Josette in Senlis, the same Josette who'd worked at the *Grand Cerf*. Now a very old lady, she told him about Suzy, Gottlieb, and John Henry. He traced the Wright family and found out that Redmond was now living in Paris.

He said that he'd found a young Redmond in a cafe next door to the Bibliothèque Nationale, that they got chatting, and so he knew Redmond was going to the Jeu de Paume the next day. Vincent said he'd arranged for Laurence to bump into him. She was given strict instructions to hook him. Vincent was furious that she let him get away from the Jeu de Paume and the Orangerie. But he'd had him followed and managed to get her to run into him again in the Rue de l'École de Médecine.

"But if you didn't want them to see each other, why did you arrange for them to meet?" Jessica asked.

He said that since Redmond was the grandson of the man who had been the lover of Laurence's grandmother, he thought he would know about Suzy's treasure. And that was also why he ended their 'affair', because he soon discovered Redmond knew nothing about it and could be of no use to him after all. He added that if in 1968 Redmond *had* known about it and had had the clues to its whereabouts, he would have been willing to let Laurence marry him.

"What about the treasure?" Leila asked, "I know you got two of her little purses in Burgundy and one in Bouvillers. Where did you find Suzy's clues and riddles? How did you know where to look?"

Vincent hesitated, sighed, and suddenly began explaining again.

"I found the clues when I went through Laurence's room here at La Châtaigneraie after her death. It had been under my nose all the time. It was a copy that Suzy had dictated to Delphine in her hotel room during the war. Delphine was about eight or nine years old, and she'd obviously forgotten whatever her mother had told her about it at the time. For her it had probably just been yet another dictation to help her learn to write English."

He said he'd been searching for the treasure for the past three years, often in the wrong places. Although he'd found the priest at Saint-Lié, he was looking in the abbey at Hautvillers and in Reims cathedral. Yes, he'd got a little bag from beneath the hearth in the 'outhouse' at Bouvilliers, thanks to the priest, who'd told him about Nestine too. But he found nothing in the crypt there, and Margot had refused to hand over any of the wine.

"You got two of the five bags of gems in Burgundy," said Leila.

"Yes, but one of the abbots took a dislike to me, and ordered the others not to hand them over."

"He tried sending *me*," Moreau rasped, "with the Latin quotations." He paused for breath. "But they wouldn't budge, they said the contract was broken."

"And you must have got them," Vincent added, "the wine, the other bags full of diamonds and rare gems. You got them, when it should belong to me."

Leila suddenly raised her gun and pointed it at Vincent.

"Where have you put him? Where is he?"

Vincent frowned and looked at each of them in turn.

"What do you mean?" he said.

"No time," said Leila, turning to Jessica, Adam and Jordan. "I'll hold the two of them here. You three go and search the buildings and the grounds."

*

The sun was low in the sky over the avenue of trees leading to the main gate as they went back to the *château* and began as thorough a search as they could. They shouted for Redmond and listened. They split up and looked on the three floors, in the different wings and down in the cellars.

In the kitchen Jessica found two men and two women sitting at a large wooden table. They looked terrified. They turned out to be the cook, the housekeeper, the butler and a handyman-gardener.

"Where is the prisoner?" Jessica demanded.

No-one answered. They sat stiffly, looking down at the table.

"What are you scared of?" she asked. "We've got him cornered and he can't harm you."

Still no answer.

"Well," she said, "if you're not going to say anything at least you can help us look round. We will soon need torches. You must have some in here."

The housekeeper stood up and went to a wall-cupboard. She took out three torches and a bunch of keys.

"You'll need these," she said.

"Where is he?" Jessica insisted again.

"We don't know anything. We haven't seen anyone. If there was someone hidden, I would know for sure," the housekeeper said.

The butler glared at her. Jessica shouted for her brothers, met them in the hall and gave them each a torch.

They searched the outhouses, the stables and some wooden huts in a yard behind the vegetable garden. Again and again they shouted, listened and looked, but could find no sign of their father.

"Either he's not here," said Jordan, but he didn't finish his sentence.

They went back to the chapel, where Leila was still holding Vincent and Moreau at gunpoint.

"Look at that," she said, pointing to a plaque on the wall behind the altar.

It was dark, and they couldn't see what she meant.

"There, above the roses in the vase," she said.

Jessica approached and slowly read out, "A la mémoire de mon oncle Vincent, 1917-1947." In memory of my Uncle Vincent...

"He's not Vincent, he's his nephew," said Moreau. "He's an imposter. Most of what he told you about Vincent is true. We knew all about that because Vincent talked endlessly about Oxford. But Delphine was weak, always sick, perhaps mad. I treated her often enough."

Moreau began to cough and seemed to be searching for breath. After a couple of minutes he continued.

"She liked it here. She said it was peaceful away from all the noise and bustle of the towns. So she lived at La Châtaigneraie with Vincent, but she kept her own name, Burridge-Carnot. She was proud of it. Then Laurence was born. But Vincent died of liver failure in 1947. He'd always been a heavy drinker."

He paused again, and they all looked at the giant of a man that Adam and Jordan held by his arms.

"The man you are looking at who has called himself Vincent since he moved in with Delphine is Maurice, Vincent's nephew," said the doctor. "He was only eighteen at the time, but very astute and determined. With my help we declared that it was he, Maurice, who had died. No-one round here questions my statements. I wrote the death certificate and no-one looked in the coffin. The *gendarmes* are very cooperative. He put up the plaque with Vincent's name only last year. No-one but he and I ever come here. The servants aren't allowed in.

"Delphine didn't tell little Laurence that her father was dead. She said he was away on business. A few years later, when Maurice was a young man, he came to live with them. He was accepted as the returning father. He wanted to marry Delphine to get hold of the treasure his uncle had always talked about, but she refused to acknowledge that there was any treasure. I've told you, she was ill most of the time, half mad, and she never really understood what had gone on in her life. In the end they didn't marry, and he killed her after Laurence had left home."

"Why are you now betraying your friend Vincent... I mean Maurice?" Jessica asked.

"Because he raped my wife. She told me only a few weeks ago. And she told me yesterday that he is the father of our son, of *my* son!"

"That's enough," snapped Leila. "We must get out. It's getting late."

"First of all I'm going to get the police to come here, hold these two, and make a proper search for Father," Jessica declared. "I'll call my senior partner and get him to make sure it's the police who come, not the local *gendarmerie*."

She went outside to make the call. An hour later the police arrived with sniffer dogs, floodlights, a team to search the buildings and grounds with pick-axes and spades, and a scientific unit ready to examine any evidence that might be uncovered.

As Jessica drove them over the moat, down the avenue of trees and back to the main road to Paris, Adam was trying to make sense of what they had heard.

"So Maurice is the 'old Frenchman', not Vincent. But for over forty years he has been Vincent. It's like in the end he can't tell the difference between himself and his dead uncle. He's taken his properties, here and in Paris. He's taken over his wife and their daughter, and eventually some of his uncle's deceased mother-in-law's treasures. But Maurice isn't Suzy's son-in-law, since he never married Delphine. Does anyone have a claim on that treasure?"

Jordan suddenly intervened.

"No. Since Delcia was murdered, none of Suzy's descendants are left. There was a line of daughters who are now all dead, with no brothers or sisters, no surviving legal spouses, no descendants."

"That," Adam said slowly, his eyes narrowing as he looked at Jessica, "that makes a considerable difference to Father."

Jordan seemed to smile, just very slightly.

"Actually," he said, "if I had married Delcia, which we were contemplating, I would now be a widower with a claim to the inheritance."

Jessica was wondering if her father could be the victim of a *terrorist* kidnapping? Had his books on orientalist paintings excited the hostility of some extremist Islamists? Hadn't Leila talked of threats concerning supposedly 'corrupt' western art? She'd also mentioned some gold that was at the heart of claims and counter-claims, some sort of family dispute. And there was 'Mourad', one of the names on her father's list of dangers.

"What about your husband, or ex-husband or whatever he is?" she suddenly asked. "You've hinted that he could be a threat to Father, and to you."

"Well," said Leila brightly, "I've told you that I am, or rather was, married. I had been completely, blindly, slavishly in love. We went out for three months, and then got married. A brute, but handsome and very clever. He laid on treats and surprises. He was what we call a 'bad boy'. I was in bondage. And you might call him an 'Islamist'.

"But he cheated on me. He had a series of one-afternoon stands after we were married. When I found out I nearly killed him, and I left that same day. However..." she paused, "I got over it very soon. I'd found him out the week before I went to Magny-Cours. That was why I went, with my boss. I had to get away, if only for a weekend. And there I met Redmond."

Leila saw that they were all looking at her.

"We haven't divorced. I've never sorted out the remnants of the marriage. It's a black hole that I don't want to look into. I ran away from a failure that was my fault, I shouldn't have married him. I've never sorted out the mess because I've been otherwise engaged."

What Leila was keeping hidden, however, was more important than what she was telling them. She thought of Mourad as a *caïd*, with gangs in Algeria, and no doubt in France too. Despite his own infidelities—or more likely because of them—he had been a very jealous husband. He was now motivated by personal vengeance. She had recently had a text message from him.

"Come back to me now, or I'll make you both pay. He will pay with his life."

She knew he was hard. Not only hard, but clever, manipulative, not the kind of man who would let anything or anyone stand in his way. He would never accept defeat, and would take revenge on anyone he imagined had crossed him. He had a network of subordinates that was spread very wide, gangsters who would carry out his orders. She now believed that he was behind the attacks in Algeria. The helicopter had been a warning, but the car explosion was meant to injure or kill them.

She hated him now, because of the way he'd treated her, a hatred that was equal to the blindly passionate love she had felt until the moment she had learnt that he had betrayed her. Perhaps something remained of that love, denied and deeply hidden. But above all, she was afraid, now that Redmond had been gone for three days.

"And Geoffrey," she said, turning their attention elsewhere. "You see, I'm right, we can't trust him. He knew we were here. He knew about 'Vincent'. He said he would soon be with us, but we must have been at La Châtaigneraie for three or four hours, and he didn't turn up."

11. A Terrorist Attack

A siren wailing in the distance. Getting louder, nearer. Then silence. It had sounded very close to the house. Jessica grunted, turned over and looked at her mobile.

"Two minutes to six," she sighed.

The sound of voices nearby. She dragged herself out of bed and looked through the window. Bonza was jumping up at the security gate and barking.

She decided to investigate. Down the stairs to the front door, where she found Leila studying the video screen. Two police vans with revolving blue lights. A woman and four men, uniformed, one with an automatic rifle, all looking up towards the house. Bonza still jumping up and barking.

Jessica pressed the intercom button and asked what they wanted.

"Good morning. There's been a death. We need to question four people who are in this house."

Leila opened the door and called Bonza. Once the dog was safely in the cellar, Jessica opened the gate and the police vans drove up to the garage.

"What's happened? Who's dead?" Jessica asked.

"Identities," snapped a policewoman.

Adam and Jordan appeared, and all four identity cards were checked with a rather surly scowl.

"Yesterday you were, all four of you, at La Châtaigneraie in Picardy. We were called to look for a missing person, a Redmond Wright. We've found a body in the chapel."

"We were in the chapel yesterday," said Adam. "There was no body there in the afternoon when we called you."

"We found a man with his throat and his wrists cut. It looks like suicide."

"That can't be Redmond Wright," said Jordan. "Father would never kill himself."

"We've heard that so many times before," said the policewoman with an exaggeratedly polite smile. "People are always surprised when it turns out to be true. But the man has been identified by a local doctor, Moreau by name. He says the body is that of a man called... well, there seems to be some confusion... Vincent, or Maurice. And the doctor has certified that it is indeed suicide."

"You'd better check," said Leila. "That doctor has already been in gaol for a number of false statements. And," she added, "for complicity in murder."

"*We* will decide what needs checking," said one of the policemen. "What were you doing out there yesterday?"

Jessica explained that she was a barrister and her brothers worked at the Finance Ministry and at a top bank. She recounted the reason for their visit to Picardy. She noted that the officers began to speak more courteously. One of them even saluted when he turned to speak to Leila. It transpired that the police had found the body as soon as they had arrived at La Châtaigneraie yesterday. Once Moreau had identified him they'd begun to search for Redmond. They spent the rest of the day and half the night combing the property, which they said was 'extensive', but they had found no trace of him. In any case, Moreau had said that he wasn't there.

Just then there was a crackling sound, and a message came on the radio in one of the vans. The policewoman went to check, and came back two minutes later. She frowned.

"Our police doctor has examined the body. He says it's murder, not suicide. They're carrying out a more detailed examination. But apparently the old man called Moreau has confessed. He says he'll be dead himself in less than two months time so he doesn't care about the consequences. He has killed Vincent... or Maurice or whoever it was. Something to do with the doctor's wife and a series of assaults many years ago."

Adam's telephone vibrated in his pocket. It was Rebecca. An emergency. He turned up the loudspeaker and they all listened.

"I'm at Charles-de-Gaulle airport. There's been an explosion in the underground car park. My bodyguards saw it happen. They say it's Redmond's old Toyota van. Blown to pieces."

"Again!" said Leila, recollecting Kamel's BMW.

The two police vans, sirens blaring, ferried them all to the airport. They went straight to the underground car park at terminal 2F and found an area cordoned off. The police made a way through for them. They found Rebecca with her bodyguards in discussion with two airport security officers.

In her mid-Atlantic drawl, she explained what had happened.

"I just got back from Cairo this morning. My security met me and said there was a problem in the 2F parking lot. They'd come to collect me and stopped next to what one of them recognized as Redmond's Toyota Lite-Ace.

"There were wires poking out of the rear door, so they immediately moved my limo well out of the way. Before they got back to the van there was an almighty explosion. They called airport security and police and went back to find the smoking remains. The question is, was he inside? My man said he hadn't noticed anyone sitting in the van, but someone could have been hidden on the floor or in the space behind the back seats. The police are waiting for the scientific team to arrive and analyze the wreckage."

"Airport security cameras will show if there was anyone in the van," said Leila. "And we must check the air company records to see which flight he was on."

Jessica went with Jordan to start enquiries at the Air France desk, whilst the others accompanied two policemen to try to find out what the car park cameras had recorded. The response was mixed.

According to Air France, Redmond had been on a flight to London the previous Saturday morning. He had booked to return yesterday, Tuesday, on an open day-ticket with no particular time or flight. He had twenty-four hours available for last-minute booking. But he hadn't taken any of their flights yesterday.

"What about overnight and this morning?" Jessica asked.

The woman behind the desk looked baffled.

"That's odd," she said, "the screen goes blank immediately after midnight. It's jammed. There must be a computer glitch. I can't find any passenger records for flights from London. I'll check. Come back in ten minutes."

When they returned they were met with a refusal to give any information.

"We're not allowed to say anything," said the girl who ten minutes earlier had been very helpful.

The others had met with no greater success. The policemen who had accompanied them had been able to insist that they should see what the security cameras had recorded. They saw Redmond arriving at the airport on the Saturday and parking his van in the 2F carpark, then going up to the departure area and disappearing into the lounge half an hour before his flight was due to leave. But no footage was available for the last twenty-four hours.

CDG airport 2F, where Redmond's van had been parked

With Jessica the barrister, a top civil servant in Adam, and Rebecca the world-famous actress, they were shown into a VIP lounge and told to wait. After half an hour an airport official arrived to announce that no camera footage was available for that day.

"Why not?" demanded Jessica. "All the cameras can't have failed. You must have some evidence."

They were made to understand that there was no way anyone at the airport could show them the footage. Airport security themselves were not allowed to see anything. It had all been put under embargo and sealed.

Adam said he would go and find out what was happening.

"Who are you going to contact?" Leila asked.

"The Prime Minister's aides. If possible, the Prime Minister himself. Failing that, the Minister of the Interior. I'll get someone who can explain."

He said he was going to use a scrambled phone network, and suddenly he had disappeared.

Ten minutes later he was back in the VIP lounge. Slowly, he sat down on a plush sofa and looked at the expectant faces scrutinizing him.

"Well," he said, "I've got an answer. Of sorts."

He paused again. No-one spoke.

"*Secret défense*," he declared. "Top secret military intelligence."

Leila raised her hand and spoke slowly and deliberately, not in her usual quick-fire tone.

"Can they tell us *nothing* about him?" she asked. "They *must* know if he was in that van."

"No," said Adam. "I can't get anything more out of them. I'm going to go to Paris to find out what's happening."

*

They all piled into the limousine that had come to collect Rebecca and set off for Adam's desk at the Foreign Ministry. He said he would be able to use an encrypted phone line and perhaps find some direct contacts who might have information about Redmond.

The journey to central Paris took only half an hour, yet in that short time there was a flurry of speculation, new information, and confessions.

They started by going over the list of possible kidnappers. Geoffrey and his organization, whatever it might be? Leila's 'ex'? The Meyers? Criminal gangs, some kind of mafia? The Turks? At least 'Vincent' was no longer a suspect. But Jessica announced that she was now worried about the repercussions of her corruption case. She knew that at least one gang notorious for kidnap and murder and linked to the minister she was prosecuting had been threatening the two principal witnesses she was calling to the court. Were they trying to threaten her by targeting her father? She herself was protected by special forces, but her father and brothers were no doubt more vulnerable.

A call to Leila's phone interrupted the speculation.

"It's Redmond!" she shouted.

It turned out to be from his phone, but it was Geoffrey. He appeared to want to reassure them, but his message had the opposite effect.

"Geoffrey speaking. I'm using Redmond's phone and I just want to say that you needn't worry about him. We know where he is and he's not in any great danger. I'm calling because..."

"Where are you?" Leila shouted, but his voice continued then he suddenly rang off.

"It's a recorded message," she announced.

She said Geoffrey had claimed that Redmond would be home within two days. But his voice had sounded hesitant and she thought the recording could have been made under duress. Were they both being held in captivity? And why had Redmond himself not spoken to her?

Then she suddenly admitted that Redmond and she herself had both been helping a branch of the French secret services. Every so often they would be given a specific mission.

"What kind of 'mission'," Jordan asked.

"Making contacts. Collecting or passing on information."

"Can't you be more specific?" Rebecca insisted.

"In Morocco, one of his university colleagues had information about a new network that was being set up to monitor French government computers and to engage in cyberattacks. In Algeria, Idir gave us details of the local conflict in the war between Islamist groups and the army. The country has been in a state of civil war for almost a decade now."

Leila's phone rang again. She turned pale as she listened intently. They could hear a man's voice. It sounded gruff and terse. After what seemed a long three minutes, he rang off.

"Mourad," she declared. "My ex. He says that Redmond's van was blown up this morning by militant Islamists living in Paris. They've left a message declaring that they know there's gold bullion still hidden in Algeria and that Idir must hand it over to them. But they've got that wrong. In fact Mourad, who has an efficient network used to passing frontiers undetected, has arrived in Paris with a present from Idir. A few gold ingots that he recovered, plus a bag full of money that the sons had made from selling most of what was left of the gold. In the end Idir had confidence in Mourad, after he swore allegiance to me and the family. He was going to leave everything in the van at the underground carpark. Fortunately he decided to wait. Now he wants to meet me to hand over my 'inheritance'. He says he's willing to take me back on condition I leave Redmond."

*

"You'll have to wait here in the entrance lounge," Adam said as soon as they arrived at the Foreign Ministry on the Quai d'Orsay. "It will take me at least half an hour, depending on what I can find."

An hour later he returned.

"Frustrating," he announced. "I've got a bit of information, but there's not a lot. It's all very hazy."

He had discovered, from a 'low-level' secret service source, that a terrorist attack at Charles-de-Gaulle airport had been suspected for some hours before the van was blown up. The information confirmed what Mourad had told Leila, but didn't add much detail. A cell of radical Islamists in northern Paris had been under surveillance for several months, but the level of activity had been estimated as 'near-dormant' until the previous day. A level-3 alert had suddenly been issued, as a number of individuals had simultaneously seemed to go underground. It emerged that they had converged on the airport, but the information about their movements had been collated too late. It was not clear why Redmond should have been the target of the attack. Although he had worked for the French services, he was not on any current mission for them. When Adam told them that his father had disappeared, they could find no trace of recent movements.

"That", he was told, "is the problem with the freelancers. Regular contact is not maintained, and they sometimes go off the radar."

Jordan suggested they go to the Louvre and try questioning Anastasia. She had seemed to hold an important position working for the French government and she might have contacts that could explain what had happened to Redmond. They walked from the Quai d'Orsay to the Louvre, and found Anastasia apparently free and pleased to see them.

"I've missed you," she said, "and with your father you did a very good job in cataloguing all those paintings. What can I do for you?"

It turned out that she was able to do quite a lot. She sent them to the cafeteria while she made enquiries, and they were amazed at what she was able to discover in less than half an hour. She was evidently an agent of some importance.

"Your father was on a mission to see a contact in London, but he didn't turn up for the meeting. As far as we know he hasn't returned from England, and we can't locate him. Apparently he called at MI6 headquarters last Saturday. He made enquiries about the man you call Geoffrey, then he disappeared when they could tell him nothing. Like I told you last time we met, 'Geoffrey' doesn't work for MI6, and he never has. He doesn't work for us, either. He seems to be some kind of half-crazy head of a sort of elite club. My chief thinks he's not of much interest. We have more disturbing things to worry about.

"The German woman, for example. Barbara. We still believe she killed your friend." Anastasia was looking at Jordan. "But she has disappeared. We can't find any trace of her in France, and our German colleagues can't find her. We've been holding her father, Manfred. He's been a thorn in our side for some time, interfering with the recovery of the artworks from Istanbul. He is cold and ruthless, though perhaps less so than his daughter. He hates your father, and now he just wants revenge for what he considers to be a feud between your families. It goes right back to the First World War. But you needn't bother yourselves about him. He won't escape from where we're holding him. It's his daughter who is the main concern."

"Never mind Barbara," said Leila. "We'd better get back to the airport, and find out more about that explosion. We still can't be sure that Redmond wasn't in his van."

*

"There were no human remains in what was left of the Toyota," said a police officer who seemed to be in charge of the scene. "We're holding two suspects. They were arrested as soon as they tried to leave the airport. We'd followed them on the security images we later confiscated. By the way, there's a foreign blond woman who wants to talk with you. She's waiting for you by exit number 12 in terminal 2F."

They found Severina standing by the exit, drinking coffee from a plastic cup.

"Bad news," she said. "Your father is in danger. There've been problems in Rome."

They listened as she explained what she had just learnt. She took out her phone, pressed the loudspeaker, and played a message from Gino.

"I'm in hospital. They shot at us. Alessandra is seriously wounded, hit in the chest and shoulder. Her mother has died. They missed me apart from one that clipped my arm. Our security has let us down. It's connected to Professore Rosso. You must warn his people. A gang is after him and his gems, his money and the valuable works of art."

"We should go to London," Leila announced. "At least two of us. We could get the next available flight."

"Go where, in London?" Jessica asked. "We haven't a clue where he is."

Leila was determined to get to London, to try to locate Redmond. Jordan agreed to go with her, but when they approached the Air France desk they were intercepted by two armed policemen.

"No travel," they were told. "You are to go to Redmond Wright's house and you must not leave the Paris region until we give you permission."

12. Face to Face

Jessica was surprised when the doorbell rang. They'd all got up at seven so as to get an early start this Thursday morning. Adam and Jordan had gone to Paris to enquire if Redmond had removed any money or valuables from his banks in the previous week. Leila was out buying cigarettes. She should be back any minute, but she had the keys to the security gate so she wouldn't have rung the bell.

Jessica went into the hall and glanced at the small screen by the door. A woman was standing at the gate, looking at her watch. There was no-one else in the street. Jessica pressed the intercom button.

"Hello?"

"Good morning. I have some important information about Redmond Wright." Blond hair, a slight accent. East European? Leila had said that the security teams kept a close eye on the house.

"Severina?" thought Jessica. She pressed the button to open the gate. News of her father at last? She opened the front door, and watched as the woman walked up the path, looking left at the garden, not up at the house as most people did when they approached. Jessica stood at the top of the steps and held out her hand. She suddenly felt uneasy, and wished Leila and the others hadn't gone out. Where was Bonza?

"Good morning," said Jessica. The woman's hand was cold. She had close-cropped hair and a hard face. It was her faint smile that made Jessica anxious.

"Aren't you Severina?" she asked.

"No, I'm Barbara... Barbara Meyer."

*

Redmond walked down Broad Street past Blackwell's bookshop. He hadn't been to Oxford for three years. He glanced in the window, and saw his latest book *An Orientalist in Algeria* displayed prominently. He didn't even smile, but strode on, turned left into Cornmarket Street, and followed a tortuous route through the narrow lanes to the College gate.

He'd left France five days ago. An urgent message from Geoffrey to come to London, to MI6 headquarters. He was to wait on the pavement by the main entrance on the Albert Embankment. Drop everything and come, he was told. We will inform your security teams.

He'd flown to Heathrow, and taken a taxi to Vauxhall Bridge. He was early, and decided to go inside and make enquiries. But they wouldn't let him past the first control barrier. Of course they'd never heard of Geoffrey. There was no record of any appointment. That confirmed his misgivings. He'd been ushered outside, then a car had pulled up by the pavement where he was standing. Two young men got out, said they were security and that they would take him to Geoffrey.

He'd spent the following five nights and four days a prisoner in a house somewhere in the Oxfordshire countryside. They'd emptied his pockets, taken his laptop and his phone, leaving him only his clothes in his suitcase. He'd been cut off from the outside world. He'd had plenty of time to think, but had been quite unable to act.

Twice he'd tried to get away—once by running towards the gate when he was allowed out for exercise, then by climbing down the fire-escape from his bedroom window in the middle of a moonlit night. Each time he'd been set upon by three burly youths who looked more like rugby-playing students than hard-faced guards. He almost got away the second time, but they had called on reinforcements and had managed to hold him down. He had tried to make a third attempt to escape when they'd bundled him into a car this morning.

They'd driven him the short distance to Oxford, dropped him at the corner of Parks Road, and given him a note with instructions on the route to a College where he was to show his card at the porter's lodge. The two men who had sat either side of him in the car were following a few steps behind.

He showed his card to the porter, a burly, friendly man, who said "Roight you arre, sirr," and showed him down a cloister to a quadrangle and into what looked like a Senior Common Room. There were comfortable armchairs and low tables with the day's newspapers laid out. The smell of pipe tobacco, like Grandfather's.

"Ah, here you are."

Geoffrey rose to greet him, and guided him to a group of three aged professors, sitting in deep armchairs by the window. All men. "Not retired yet?" thought Redmond. He took one look at them, and christened them Sleepy, Dopey and Grumpy.

"You can help us," said Geoffrey, "we were discussing sweet white wines from the Loire Valley. We were arguing the merits of the Coteaux-du-Layon. Two of us favour Bonnezeaux, and two are firmly for Quarts-de-Chaume. I think you have the casting vote."

Redmond glared at Geoffrey. He'd been kidnapped for more than half a week, and he was here under duress. All Geoffrey could find to talk about was sweet white Loire Valley wines. He decided to temporize briefly, to see what the man really wanted. He took the only possible line.

"I can't accept the premisses of your argument."

The three professors looked mildly interested.

"You don't have to choose between two good things," said Redmond. "You can have both. I refuse to say that I prefer Burgundy or Bordeaux, blonde or brunette, London or New York. If you *do* have to choose, it's a question of the occasion. And your mood. Not of 'better' or 'the best'."

Three pairs of eyes and three furrowed brows closed in on him. He guessed he was about to be demoted to a lower second class degree. They began to fire questions at him about sweet Loire wines, but Redmond was only half listening, as he focussed on the questions *he* wanted to ask. Then Geoffrey rang a bell and the butler appeared. Black jacket, winged collar, white gloves and a silver tray. Geoffrey ordered morning coffee for five.

Redmond could wait no longer. He took Geoffrey aside and spoke firmly.

"What the hell are you playing at? I want explanations. Now. And a phone to call Leila and my children. Why have I been kidnapped?"

Geoffrey looked unruffled.

"To protect you. Because Manfred Meyer was about to kill you. He was waiting near your house. I'd talked with him in the Louvre and I knew he was about to pounce on you. I decided it was too dangerous for you to stay at home."

"I don't believe you. You didn't have to entice me to England and kidnap me to protect me. There's Severina, and your lot. And what about Leila? She's in danger. What about my children?"

"Do calm down. He won't kill them. It's you he's after."

"What about his daughter? She's ruthless."

"She's in Berlin. She can't do them any harm."

The butler appeared, carrying a silver tray with five cups and saucers, a coffee pot, sugar and milk.

*

Jessica stiffened. The fourth generations were face to face. She'd made a mistake. She should have checked before opening the gate. Bonza stuck her head round the door, and growled. Jessica put her hand on the dog's neck and felt the raised hairs as it sat beside her, studying the intruder with an air of canine distrust.

"You'd better come in," she said. She showed Barbara into the patio. "What do you want?" she asked, knowing that she sounded hostile.

"I come in peace," was the answer. Jessica sniffed, and waited. Bonza growled again, and the hairs on her neck stiffened once more.

"Why doesn't Leila come back?" thought Jessica. Barbara Meyer was dangerous. What did she want? How had she found them? That would have been easy, so the real question was *why?*

"I know you don't trust me, but I tell you I come in peace," Barbara began. "I know all about the family rivalry, between the Wrights and us. I want to explain a few things, one at a time. For example, when your father and his girlfriend came to Berlin they saw the Stasi archives. I guess you all believe that your grandfather and mine crossed paths in the Ardennes in December 1944. Well, I have news for you. Your grandfather didn't shoot mine. In fact they were nowhere near each other in 1944."

"But the Stasi found his regimental records," said Jessica.

"No," came the reply. "My father Manfred visited your grandfather William, in Sheffield, in 1985. Your grandfather told him all about what he'd done in the war, and showed him his diary. So my father knew where your grandfather had been in the Ardennes at Christmas 1944. Some years later, he went to the Stasi headquarters and altered the archives. He made up the story about Hans Meyer being in the Ardennes and getting shot. In fact he was in Berlin, where he'd been ever since he'd returned in 1942. He *was* wounded, but he'd been shot by his boss Gustav Keller, who took off with a load of loot to South America as the war was ending. My grandfather Hans was never the same after that. Physically weak, always tired, mentally crippled. He couldn't be bothered with revenge against the Wright family any more."

"But your family has never forgotten that John Henry Wright shot Gottlieb Meyer in 1918," said Jessica.

"Of course not," said Barbara, "but it was many years before my father took up the cudgels on the family's behalf, when his grandmother, Gottlieb's widow, died and he found his father's wartime notebook and suicide message. By then he'd moved up the ranks in the Stasi and he had a lot of influence. That's how he was able to change the archives, without anyone knowing. Now, I'm not saying this to scare you, but my father has been released, he's on the loose and he's dangerous."

"I think *you* are dangerous," Jessica replied, "probably more dangerous than your father. You killed Delcia."

Barbara shook her head. That set Bonza growling again.

*

Dopey and Grumpy drank their coffee quickly and withdrew. Sleepy fell into a deep, snoring slumber. Geoffrey looked at him, put his finger to his lips, and stood up.

"Please go and stand to the left of the fireplace," he whispered. "Put both hands on that medallion with the three lions, and push."

Redmond hesitated. What was this new game?

"Go on," said Geoffrey, a little louder, so Redmond did as ordered. He went to the left side of the fireplace, and pushed.

"Harder," Geoffrey said, as he himself pushed at the medallion on the right-hand side.

Redmond heard a click from the door.

"Automatic lock," said Geoffrey, "so that no-one can come in."

Redmond began to feel anxious again.

"Don't worry, I'm not going to kill you," Geoffrey laughed, "all is about to be revealed."

Redmond heard a slight grating sound. He turned, and saw the bookshelves opposite moving. He stared in disbelief. They revolved and stopped at thirty degrees to the wall, revealing a room beyond. The sleeping professor hadn't moved. Redmond followed Geoffrey through the gap.

"Same again, please," said Geoffrey, indicating medallions on either side of another fireplace. They pushed, and the bookshelves slid back into place.

"You have to be two for these manoeuvres," said Geoffrey, "so that none of us can do it alone." A wall-lamp shone a soft light on a dark painting. Redmond gasped. A Rembrandt self-portrait. They were in an oak-panelled room, but it had no windows. There was a staircase leading down below, and winding metal stairs going up to a floor above.

"Our wine cellar," said Geoffrey, indicating the downward staircase, "I'll show you later."

Redmond followed him up the metal stairs, into a large room with skylights. There were paintings, bookshelves and filing cabinets covering every inch of the walls. Ten dining chairs were spaced around a heavy central mahogany table. Redmond glanced quickly at the paintings. Botticelli, Velasquez, Goya... were they originals? And a Cézanne landscape, a *Montagne Sainte-Victoire* that Redmond was sure he'd seen in Istanbul.

*

"Why did your father alter your grandfather's war record?" Jessica asked.

"Shame," replied Barbara, without hesitation. "Wounded filial pride. He'd been ashamed of his father ever since he was a little boy. Hans was weak, an invalid, with a mind that couldn't concentrate for more than a few seconds. Other boys mocked him, and teased Manfred endlessly. As he grew up, Manfred realized that his father had not been much of a war hero. Keller had fooled him, turned him into a physical and mental wreck, and taken the loot. And when the Russians arrived in Berlin, Hans had hidden himself away and left his mother to fend for herself. The last straw was when he committed suicide, six years after I was born.

"When my father decided to spare your grandfather and to look for Redmond, it took him some years to catch up. But now he's ready to finish his mission. That's why I'm here. To warn you. I think we should put an end to all this killing."

Jessica thought that Barbara was making a good job of sounding sincere. But hadn't *she* killed Delcia in the Louvre? Jessica's mobile vibrated. A text message. From Leila? No, it was Adam. *Father not been to first 2 banks. 2 to go. Back after lunch.* She quickly tapped in a reply. *URGENT. Barb Meyer here, Leila not home. Come back NOW.* As she finished, she was aware of a movement. Barbara Meyer had stood up, and seemed about to throw herself forward. But Bonza had barked and jumped at her, knocking her over and pinning her to the floor.

There was another movement, which Jessica saw from the corner of her eye. It was Severina, who came running into the patio, gripping in both hands a gun that was trained on Barbara.

*

"Sit down," said Geoffrey, "and I'll tell you the whole story. It won't take very long, because you're already aware of most of the details. But you don't have the keys. I'm afraid I haven't been entirely frank with you."

"We've been aware of that for some time," said Redmond testily. "Now will you please get on with it, and stop treating me as if I were a child or an imbecile."

"First, these rooms have been the operations centre for the Cabal for more than eighty years."

"What," said Redmond, "is 'the Cabal'?"

"Be patient," Geoffrey replied. "I said it won't take long. I—we, that is—have no official connection with MI6. From time to time, one or two of our men may work for them, and some have had a full career in the Secret Services, MI5 or MI6. So we are able to use their networks and logistics for our own purposes without anyone realizing, officials or the government. But we're just a small team, and we have to sub-contract some of the security."

"Who and what are 'we'?" Redmond asked.

"It all began with Professor Burridge. He was a rare species back in 1900, a modern languages professor. He knew every modern European language. I believe he was one of the last persons alive to understand Dalmatian, though no-one spoke it by the end of the nineteenth century. He gathered around him a team of brilliant young Fellows. But they weren't taken seriously here as academics. Only the ancient languages counted then. Greek, Latin, Persian, Arabic, Sanskrit.

"Burridge had married a Mademoiselle Carnot, a beautiful *Paris-*

ienne whom he met on a trip to France in 1887. He brought her back here. The next year they had a daughter, Suzanne. Burridge's French wife died suddenly, in 1900, of a rare liver infection, leaving him with a twelve-year-old daughter. She too grew into a very beautiful and intelligent young woman. Burridge devoted himself entirely to looking after her and bringing her up to be independent.

"In those days College duties were very light. He arranged special coaching for her from his colleagues. Rumour had it that she was very precocious, and was playing off the dons one against the other by the time she was fifteen.

"Burridge was worried about what would happen to Suzanne if he fell ill or died. He wasn't in good health. So he founded a club, with nine of his colleagues. There were always to be ten of them, sworn to absolute secrecy. They were to look after Suzanne. When any one of the ten died, or was declared incapacitated, a replacement would be selected among the Fellows at the College. There was a head—Burridge at first—and a deputy-head ready to take over. New members and the deputy were selected by the head.

"Burridge fixed up this hideout, with the help of a porter by the name of Templar, who never knew what its purpose was. One porter has always been let into the secret of the hidden rooms ever since, but none has ever known what they were for."

Redmond was still very angry, but he wanted to know more and so he let Geoffrey continue without interruption.

"Suzanne had long been difficult to follow, to control. With her language gifts, her looks and her brains, she'd been recruited to British Military Intelligence before the war. She had a daughter, born in 1909 after an affair with the elder son of a champagne merchant, Chancel from Épernay, though some said the father was Chancel himself. She had to leave the child with an English family in Senlis, while she travelled all over Europe on her intelligence work, spying on the French and the Germans.

"When war broke out, she was twenty five, nearly twenty-six. Burridge made five of the College Fellows volunteer for intelligence work, just so that they could keep watch on Suzanne and protect her. They were recruited into what was called the Secret Service Bureau, Foreign Section, where his daughter and several of his former students already worked. Burridge had no problem in getting them recruited into espionage, because of his contacts and, of course, their language skills and their intelligence. But their first loyalty was always to the College, to Burridge himself and to the task of following and protecting Suzanne. One was killed in May 1915, at the second battle of Ypres. Another at Thiepval Ridge, the final flurry on the Somme in 1916. Burridge sent out replacements. He pulled strings at a very high level."

Redmond was shocked. He recalled how his grandfather's diary had recorded Suzy saying that these men were 'amateurs'. She was right, but they were out in France to protect her, and two of them had died trying to do that. She had thought they were after her treasure.

Geoffrey explained about his College and the Cabal.

"We had influence. We still have. Former students of ours are in government, the armed forces, the top civil service, international banking and business. And as I've said, MI5 and MI6. Our reach stretches a long way, and very deeply. We've had several cabinet ministers, and one prime minister. So there's a powerful network that the Cabal can manipulate, counting on loyalty to the College. Apart from our own select ten, none of them know that we exist and that they're working for us. It's just doing favours to old College boys. And," he added hurriedly, "girls in more recent years. Most of them are sharper than the men. All the information comes back here, where the head follows and records everything.

"Old Burridge had been distraught at his daughter's affair with Chancel's son, and he was very reluctant to take any interest in her daughter, Delphine, who had been born when Suzanne was only twenty. And he was furious about her affairs with your grandfather during the war. He wasn't so bothered about the German Gottlieb. That he considered to be in her line of duty to her country.

"No doubt he would eventually have come to take an interest in his granddaughter, but when Suzanne was killed at the end of the war it finished the old man. Templar found him one morning, dead in his armchair. Heart attack? Maybe.

"Thereafter the deputy took over, and the nine, soon to be ten again, began calling themselves 'the Cabal'. They had been recruited to follow and protect Suzanne, but now they took an interest in only one thing, recovering all of her treasure, the wines and the jewels in Champagne and Burgundy, the paintings and sculptures in Constantinople."

*

Jessica and Severina bound Barbara's hands behind her back and tied her to a chair. They found a knife in her bag and a gun in a holster on her body. Severina said that she herself had been tied up and dumped in the garden. Her head felt very sore. She hadn't been able to get help from her two colleagues, who'd been stationed in the street. Maybe they too had been immobilized.

A lot for one woman, thought Jessica. Barbara was surely not alone. They must have got Leila when she'd gone out.

"Where's your father?" she asked.

"He's not far from here. He's gone to a place called La-Roche-Guyon in Normandy. There's a castle there that was Rommel's headquarters towards the end of the war. He's been looking through the archives again, and is persuaded that Rommel himself had a hoard of treasure."

"Do you know where my father's friend Leila is?" Jessica asked.

"No, I don't know where she is. But if my father finds her, he'll kill her. You'd better contact her."

They heard the sound of the front door opening. Leila at last, thought Jessica. But it was Adam and Jordan, who had raced back to the house. There were now four of them, and Bonza, to keep an eye on Barbara. Jessica quickly updated her brothers about what she had just learnt.

"You do realize," Adam announced, "that in fact there was no rivalry between Hans Meyer and William Wright. It skipped the second generation. Two different Fatimas, and no Hans in the Ardennes."

"A red herring, so disappointing," Jordan remarked. He grinned, and added, "Maybe Grandpa William *did* kill a German soldier after all."

Jessica took out her mobile again and called Leila's number. She had called several times and tried to leave messages, but got a recorded voice each time. All her text messages were marked "undelivered".

*

Redmond said nothing. He guessed that he was to learn more from Geoffrey in half-an-hour than he had in the previous two and a half years.

"The Cabal had no idea where Suzanne had hidden her rewards.

Nor that she'd written the clues for her daughter. She must have known they were watching her, and she got her gems and wines hidden away without them knowing. She was always a step ahead. Ever since she was a teenager, she'd been used to escaping their clutches, if and when she wanted. During the war, they couldn't keep close to her all the time. And they knew she'd been rewarded by the Germans too, with modern paintings and sculptures and statues. One of them discovered these were now in Constantinople, and he went off to inquire. He never came back.

"For some time after the war, the Cabal kept an eye on your grandfather and his family. Waiting. They knew the treasure was of inestimable value, and they were persuaded that someone had the secret. After five or six years, they decided that John Henry Wright didn't know where the treasure was hidden, so they stopped spying on him.

"By the mid-1930s, the Cabal was more or less moribund. They thought they would never find any treasure, and they were riven with political and personal disputes, like most Colleges during that decade. Some were fascists, others communists, the odd one Conservative, Liberal or Labour. They were always fighting each other. But they'd kept the rewards they had accumulated in World War One from the Secret Service Bureau Section 6. Diamonds and gems from India, mainly. Sales of the stones gave them plenty to finance all their activities.

"For fifty years the organization was more of a clandestine drinking club, consuming the first-class wines they'd been steadily accumulating. Selling the odd diamond now and again to maintain their funds. Then in the late 1980s my predecessor as head began looking more closely at the archives, and decided it was time to re-activate the Cabal in search of the lost treasures. That was shortly before I became deputy head, but my role then was minimal. When I became head, four years ago, I went very thoroughly into everything. You see, the head is the only one who has access to all the records and incoming information. We were two short, so I immediately appointed two smart recruits. I got them into MI6 posts where they had access to full resources. We've used them efficiently for three years now. They've been following you very closely."

Geoffrey paused, looked at his watch, and declared it was time to return for lunch. By a different route, for his three colleagues would now be eagerly waiting on the other side of the wall. He took a bunch of heavy keys from his pocket, and showed Redmond through a double door at the far end of the wine cellar. They walked along a dark damp passage, through a heavily reinforced gate which Geoffrey opened with his keys, carefully locking it again behind them. They emerged into an enclosed courtyard. From here they were able to rejoin the cloister Redmond had taken that morning, and walk through to the Common Room.

*

They took Barbara up to the loft and strapped her to a chair, with hands and feet bound. They let Bonza sniff around her, growling, and set about interrogating her.

"Where is my father? And where is Leila?" asked Jessica. "You must know!"

"I've no idea. I thought they were here. I last saw them in the Louvre..."

Jordan interrupted her.

"... where you murdered Delcia. Why did you do that?"

He was scowling, and looked as if he was about to hit Barbara. She hesitated.

"No... No, that wasn't me, it wasn't us... We escaped into the catacombs, they were following us..."

"Who was following you?" Adam demanded. Barbara quickly recovered her composure.

"I don't know. A woman who was working with Anastasia, the one who was supposed to be a museum curator. She came after us. I didn't know your friend had been killed."

She hesitated, then continued.

"If your father and Leila hadn't come to Berlin, where they called at my flat, I'm sure neither my father nor the Stasi would have even known that your father was still alive. It was that visit that alerted them. They thought he'd been killed ten years earlier."

"I don't believe a word of what you're saying," Jessica interrupted, "and I want to know why you're here. You're not alone. Someone knocked out Severina. Someone knocked her on the back of her head. And that was in the garden not out in the street. You've got Stasi support here. You *must* know where my father and Leila are."

Barbara shook her head. Jessica stood up and walked around the loft. She tried calling Leila again, but there was no response apart from a recorded voice. "Please leave your name and I'll call you back as soon as possible." She tried Redmond's number, and got the same response.

They all stared as Severina, usually silent, suddenly spoke.

"Geoffrey. He manipulates everything."

There was a long silence. Jessica looked at the little clock above the Eiffel Tower on Redmond's mirror. Thursday 30 September 1999. One o'clock.

"Let's go and get something to eat," she announced. They went downstairs, leaving Bonza to guard a dishevelled and tiring Barbara.

"Now we know she's lying," said Jessica.

"How do we know?" asked Adam.

"Because the Stasi tried to kill Father twice during the Magny-Cours weekend, presumably on the orders of Manfred Meyer. So they knew he was still alive a month before he and Leila went to Berlin."

*

A clock in the quadrangle outside struck twelve. Geoffrey stood up, announced it was time for lunch, and led the way into a small staff dining room.

The lunch and the wines were excellent, the conversation very dull, thought Redmond. He glowered at Geoffrey throughout the meal. After a fifty-five-year-old Armagnac—sweet, plummy, rounded, great depth—which did nothing to improve his mood, and cigars, which he declined, the three professors dozed off, so he began questioning Geoffrey again.

"How old are you," he enquired, "you don't look your age. You must be in your nineties."

"Oh no, nothing like. I'm not much older than you."

"But," Redmond interrupted, "you said you worked at Bletchley Park during the war, deciphering Enigma."

Geoffrey laughed.

"I only said that to make you think I might be able to help you with Suzanne's clues. I was born in 1929, and could hardly have been decoding Enigma at the age of thirteen. I was elected a Fellow here in 1961, joined the Cabal in 1970, became deputy head in 1989, and took over as head when my predecessor died in 1995."

Geoffrey looked at the three snoring old men, stood up, and signalled to Redmond that he was to go over to the fireplace and repeat the manoeuvres of that morning. They went through the sliding door and closed it behind them.

"We have a very detailed record here of everything we've done since 1910. That was the year Burridge started his diary, the year after Suzanne had left Oxford to have her baby. His diary was the start of our archives."

He pointed to a row of leather-bound books, took three of them off the shelves, and put them on the table. They had dates on the binding. "1914-1916", "1939-45", "1986-1996". Redmond opened the last one. In neat, tiny handwriting, seventy pages of short paragraphs with dates and underlined headings. On the last three pages, a hand-written index. This was an amazing record. He looked at the other two volumes. Similar tiny neat manuscript. These were exercise books that had been bound when each 'volume' was completed.

*

Over lunch, while they left Barbara Meyer upstairs, guarded by Bonza, they quizzed Severina about Geoffrey, who had been supposed to cooperate with her and her team. She said he was difficult. He interfered, didn't give her enough information, and had made some serious misjudgements. She had been surprised because he'd seemed so efficient when they'd met in Rome.

By the time they got to Beaune, she felt he was deliberately misleading them. She now believed he was dangerous, a threat to both Redmond and Leila, though she didn't know what his motives were. She believed that he was in cahoots with the Meyers.

She was puzzled about what had happened that morning. She'd had two of her team with her. They had been outside in the street, while she had been in the garden. She had a vague memory of a blow on her neck, and of waking up, lying by the wall behind a laurel hedge. Her colleagues were not answering her messages so she knew they must have been put out of action. This had never happened before. She contacted Gino for reinforcements, but got no answer. She had tried to reach Geoffrey, but he hadn't been responding for the last few days. Redmond's security had gone haywire since his disappearance.

After another fruitless attempt to call Leila and Redmond, they went back upstairs. They had decided not to question Barbara, but to leave her alone and talk amongst themselves, trying to disconcert her and provoke a reaction. "She's hard," thought Jessica, as they discussed who could be responsible for their father and Leila's fate.

"You know, I think Leila is younger than she says," Jessica suddenly announced. "She claims to be in her mid-thirties, but everything about her is more like someone in their twenties. I guess she's had to pretend that she's older than she is. I've been wondering since yesterday. I know she lies about their relationship."

*

"Yes," said Geoffrey, "we got it all wrong. Until I had the idea of introducing you to Leila."

"All these lies, half-truths and secrets," said Redmond. He seemed to have missed Geoffrey's last remark, as he continued. "There's a saying in French, *Il n'y a que la vérité qui fâche*. Only the truth hurts. I don't believe that. Lies can hurt more than the truth. In fact, both can hurt."

"Indeed," said Geoffrey, "I remember a colleague whose wife had been unfaithful to him. They divorced, and she drew up the most frightful list of lies about him. He had simply told the lawyer what she'd done, with no malice on his part. Eventually, he said to her, 'Look. I'll do a deal with you. If you stop telling lies about me, I'll stop telling the truth about you.' "

"I could have used that line," thought Redmond.

"And you do realize," said Geoffrey, "that... but of course, you *don't* realize, you weren't listening a moment ago, that if it weren't for us, for me, you would never have met Leila."

Redmond stared at him.

"No. We met one weekend, quite by chance, and became friends very quickly."

"*By chance?* You surely don't believe in chance after all that's happened? No, we arranged that you should meet her."

"I don't believe you. How could you have arranged that?"

"Simple," said Geoffrey. "We'd been watching you for a long time, and knew you were going to Magny-Cours. We'd located Leila, who lived not far from you and had exactly the profile we wanted. It was easy enough to get her invited for the weekend by her boss and his brother."

Redmond thought for a moment.

"She had a profile?"

"Yes. Despite the revival of our Cabal interest in Algeria when I took over in 1995, we never managed to penetrate the Kabyle network that had kept the loot that stayed in the hills near Sétif. Then we traced Mohamed and Idir's family to the Paris suburbs, and found Leila. Ideal. The family connection, on both sides. Her and Fatima, you and your father. You worked on orientalism, and liked women with an exotic touch. She was tough, and could look after herself. We were fortunate to find someone living not far from you who had a connection with your father's Algerian tryst. If it hadn't been for us, you would never have met her."

"Does she know you'd arranged this? Is she working with you?" Redmond sounded very alarmed.

*

"You refuse to see the obvious reason for Redmond's disappearance, and Leila's failure to return," said Barbara.

"I think we've overlooked the question of motives," said Adam. "Remember the North African adventure? The guards who they never saw again after Tlemcen? The helicopter attack and the car bomb? Someone was after Father and Leila, and now we believe that it was her husband. Maybe he's kidnapped both of them."

When they'd got back from Picardy two evenings ago, Leila had told them about her own fears and suspicions, and that her husband had made promises to her, but threatened her if she didn't respect his wishes. He'd also admitted to organizing the attacks in Algeria.

"You're wrong," said Barbara. "The real threat is your man Geoffrey. He's been after the treasure for himself, for a long time. He is your father's enemy. He's been using him. He told us that. He talked to us at the Louvre, let us know his plans. He's used your father and Leila to locate the different treasures. Now he's going to take over all of your father's wealth. Which should be yours, too. He's ready to pounce. I think he's going to bump off Redmond and Leila and take everything. He controls people in high places. You must release me and let my father sort out Geoffrey. I'm sure we can come to an amicable agreement that will put an end to a century of rivalry between our families."

"He knows all about you," said Jessica. "He's been following you, and he must have been collaborating with your father."

"I don't know," Barbara said, "and I doubt if you'll ever find out now."

*

"No," Geoffrey said firmly. "Leila knew no more about it than you."

Redmond looked at his watch. They'd given it back to him this morning. It was now 6 p.m. He noticed that the tiny figure at the top of the dial had clicked round to '30'. So he'd been away for six days. He'd begun to lose all sense of time, cut off from the rest of the world. Today was his birthday and... he felt his muscles stiffen, his stomach tighten... the date Suzanne too had been born, *and murdered*.

"You must understand my motives," said Geoffrey. "I'm not interested in the gems or the money for myself. I am a patriot. I want revenge for Suzanne Burridge-Carnot's murder. I want no Germans, or Turks, or vicious characters like Vincent to derive the slightest reward from her work and sacrifice. That treasure belonged to her, and your grandfather was to have a share in the rewards. So you have been the lucky beneficiary."

Redmond turned to Geoffrey and asked if they had been hacking into his telephone conversations and computers.

"Oh no, that would be illegal. We would be in really hot water if we got caught doing that. Of course," he went on, "our contacts in the secret services do pass useful information on to us, but we don't ask how they obtain it. Never. Anonymity of sources and all that."

So, thought Redmond, they had probably been listening to conversations between him and Leila, reading emails and text messages, seeing everything on his computer. And, he suddenly realized, watching them at home, via the security cameras.

"You sods," he said.

Geoffrey smiled and said nothing.

"Look," said Redmond, "what if we *do* sleep together? What if we *don't*?" He paused, expecting some response. When none came, he seemed to calm down and added, slowly and deliberately, "Some people are obsessed with the question of whether a relationship between an older man and a younger woman is sexual or not. To us the companionship, the complicity, the partnership and understanding are what really count."

Geoffrey took no notice of what Redmond was saying, but came back to the Cabal.

"We were never short of cash to pay for air tickets, cars and armed escorts for you. The gems, you see. All those imperial jewels. And we had plenty of gold and silver. I told you we'd lost two metal boxes full of little bags with gems when that Indian plane crashed in the Alps in 1966. One of our chaps stayed for years in Chamonix, waiting every day for the boxes to emerge from the foot of the Bossons glacier. Rubies, sapphires and emeralds, worth about five hundred thousand pounds today. He never found anything. You know, we've had billions of pounds' worth, our rewards from both World Wars, especially the First. And there were the gold ingots that we lost when the *Malabar Princess* crashed in the Alps sixteen years earlier."

"Any more pink diamonds?" Redmond asked.

"No. Back in Suzy's time there were quite a few about, but they were worth nothing like as much as today. Their value has multiplied many times over since then, and multiplies again every year. They rarely come onto the market these days, and we couldn't afford them now."

"How come you couldn't get her treasure without our help?" he asked Geoffrey.

"Very simple. We didn't have the clues."

"Why didn't you steal them from us? With your resources, everything you've done, watching us, listening in, surely that wasn't beyond your capabilities?"

Geoffrey didn't respond. Redmond was now desperate to make contact with the outside world after being cut off for several days.

"Look," he said, trying to sound reasonable, "I think you could give me my mobile. I'd like to chat with a few friends, and reassure everyone that I'm still alive. Leila, and my children, they must be worried."

"No," said Geoffrey, "Jessica's at your house with Leila. Everything's fine."

A mobile rang. Geoffrey took a phone from his shirt pocket, said sharply "Cabal One," and listened. "When?" he asked. Redmond could hear a voice, but couldn't make out what it was saying. "Well find out quickly," Geoffrey snapped. He put his mobile back in his pocket, and hesitated.

"I'm afraid..." he began.

Redmond looked at him.

"It's Leila," said Geoffrey.

"What's happened? What's the matter?"

"She went out this morning, and hasn't come back. And Barbara Meyer has turned up at your house. She's been in there all day."

"Where is Leila?"

"We don't know yet, but we're on full alert and looking. They'll let me know as soon as they find anything."

"Please," said Redmond, "give me my mobile. I need to make some calls. You know her husband is out for revenge. He's been making all kinds of threats, and you know very well what he's capable of doing."

Geoffrey felt in his pocket, took out Redmond's phone, and handed it over. Redmond first looked for his messages, and saw that there were none.

"We've erased them all." Geoffrey had anticipated his question.

Redmond was worried, and very angry. They'd kidnapped him, taken his phone, and erased all his messages. Now Leila had disappeared in his absence, and Barbara Meyer was in the house with Jessica, who was not answering her phone.

He was trying to work out a plan of action, and showed no interest as Geoffrey insisted on taking him down to the wine cellar. Down the stairs, through a double door, into a long room with stone walls and a vaulted ceiling, through another door and into the cellar.

Redmond was suddenly alert as his eyes took time to adapt to the dim light. He made out a table with wine glasses, a corkscrew and a silver bucket. He kept his distance from Geoffrey, watching him carefully. It was the ideal place to launch a surprise attack. He had nothing hard in his pockets, but he stayed close to the corkscrew and silver bucket, then edged nearer to a pile of empty bottles, ready to defend himself.

Some of the wines had been down there in Burridge's time, others had been garnered over the years. Geoffrey asked what Redmond would recommend for dinner. They would be having oysters and a shoulder of lamb. But Redmond had lost interest in wine and food. He told Geoffrey to choose whatever bottles he wanted. He too seemed to show little interest in the wines. He quickly selected a Pouilly Fumé for the oysters and a Pauillac for the lamb. Redmond was relieved to get out of the cellar and, having insisted on carrying the two bottles, he walked behind Geoffrey back to the Senior Common Room. Geoffrey passed the wines on to the butler, saying they came from his own cellar.

'Geoffrey insisted on taking him down to the wine cellar... into a long room with stone walls and a vaulted ceiling, through another door...'

The three professors were waiting. Redmond and Geoffrey had settled into two deep armchairs when the butler appeared. He put the Pouilly in a bucket of ice, and left a tray of oysters on the table.

While they waited for the wine to cool, Redmond and Geoffrey started on the oysters. They looked at each other.

"How do you feel?" asked Geoffrey.

"Fine," said Redmond, "fine."

"Really?"

"No, not really, not at all. I'm worried. You know, when I look back, at my childhood, my marriage, my role as a father, my work, I think I've always pretended, ever since I was a small child. Pretended that everything was fine, when I knew that it wasn't. I live in a world of fiction. I don't know..."

He felt his mobile vibrating in his pocket. It began to ring. It was Leila!

"Hi, I'm in La-Roche-Guyon, about twenty miles west of Paris. I know where you are, you're in Oxford. The boys and Severina are at home with Jessica. They've got the Meyer woman with them. They've neutralized her, and Severina's going to put her out of harm's way. Guess what. I've uncovered clues to a new treasure, a hoard hidden by Rommel somewhere in his *château* here at La-Roche-Guyon. Actually," she laughed, "I've been with my husband. We followed Manfred Meyer, who was onto this. But, poor man, such a nice, friendly face." She laughed again. "They'll find his body at the foot of the tower. He followed us up a stairway, and... well, at the top, I hid, and he leaned out over the parapet to look for me. He leaned too far and, over he went. With a little help from Mourad. Very unfortunate. It'll look like an accident. Or suicide."

Redmond could imagine her grinning. He smiled, too, thinking that Mourad had finished what Leila had started when she spun the two Germans off the narrow road in the woods near Nestine. Then he thought "No, he's finished what Manfred's grandfather started when he shot Suzy eighty-one years ago today."

"Mourad and I have had a long talk," Leila added. "He was very interested in you, and us. He trapped me, but I managed to per-suade him to help me. He's got my share of the remnants of the gold bullion. There'll have to be some changes. I'll explain when we meet at home, tomorrow I guess. Take care. See you soon. *Very* soon."

She rang off. Redmond wondered how she knew where he was. She'd come to some kind of understanding with her husband. He it was—how ironical—who had got rid of the enemy of the Wright family, who had recovered what was left of the Nazi loot which he was now handing over to Leila, and who had, Redmond began to think, surely put an end to his own friendship with her.

He looked at Geoffrey. Perhaps Anastasia was right. "Harmless, just a bit eccentric... has his own agenda." He took a large mouthful of Pouilly, swilled it round, swallowed, and asked if Geoffrey was intending to keep the gems from the 'ruby' monastery.

EPILOGUE

1999

At 9 p.m. on 30th September the Thames Valley Police received a telephone call from the College. Four minutes later a patrol car drew up at the main gate and a distraught night watchman led the two police officers to the Senior Common Room. They were confronted by a scene of devastation the like of which they said they had never witnessed in their respectively eighteen and twenty-four years with the constabulary. Four professors were sitting in armchairs. They had been riddled with bullets. The carpet and walls were not so much spattered as splashed with deep red bloodstains.

Enquiries soon revealed that a Professor Redmond Wright had been present that evening. The butler, who had finished his service at 8.45, reported that Professor Wright had been a guest at dinner. He had left the room at around twenty minutes to nine, shortly after emptying his second glass of post-prandial port. Further questions led to the discovery that during the previous five days he had stayed at a nearby country manor house, where a return plane ticket to Paris and a suitcase of clothes were found. There were no clues as to the reasons for his visit, nor to his present whereabouts.

*

Redmond rapidly became number one on the list of suspects. All the more so since nothing was heard of him. He had simply vanished. The French police looked on his computer and scoured nine chapters recounting the history of his family and a succession of episodes in Berlin, Turkey, Rome, North Africa and the vineyards of France. Enquiries continued for three weeks before the British and French police suddenly reduced the resources devoted to tracing him from a team of sixteen, eight British and eight French, to one detective in Oxford and a small office in Paris where an examining magistrate and a young detective were allocated part-time to the case.

Contrary to Redmond's supposition, Leila did not go back to Mourad. He returned to Algeria. She stayed in the house in the suburbs north of Paris, waiting for any sort of signal from Redmond.

She believed he was alive, in hiding, and that he would contact her or his children and reappear as soon as he or they had been able to clear his name. She was convinced of his innocence, and was angry that the authorities on both sides of the Channel seemed to be making no effort to discover who had carried out the Oxford executions.

The press gave little coverage to the affair. Leila suspected that French and British intelligence services had given orders that there should be as little information as possible available to the general public.

Jessica moved in to her father's 'mansion', sharing her time between her prosecution of the corrupt former minister and working together with Leila trying to establish Redmond's innocence. Adam, Rebecca and Jordan worked on and off with them. But there was little any of them could do. They had no resources apart from Jessica's lawyers office and Adam's Foreign Ministry contacts, which had suddenly and mysteriously been restricted so much as to be virtually worthless. There was no response to their attempts to call Gino, Alessandra or Severina in Rome.

All they could do was wait for some manifestation of Redmond's existence. Either he was in hiding somewhere, or he had been kidnapped again. And murdered? This time there were no computer messages with hints. For two months after the assassinations of Sleepy, Dopey, Grumpy and Geoffrey in Oxford, there was not a single sign to suggest whether he was dead or alive.

*

One cold morning in December, a slightly dishevelled Redmond rang at the gate. All the locks and the security codes had been changed, and there he was, standing alone, as Jessica and Leila looked at the screen by the front door. Bonza was jumping up and barking, her tail stump wagging furiously.

"Top secret" was his only immediate response to their questions, along with an enigmatic smile that Geoffrey might have been proud of. Redmond said he was starving and wanted a large English breakfast. He would talk afterwards.

Jessica summoned her brothers to the house. They arrived with Rebecca, but after his breakfast Redmond declared he needed a nap. He in fact slept for eight hours and it was early evening before he could talk. He began by explaining that he'd hardly had any sleep the previous night. He had been put on a plane from RAF Northolt to Le Bourget, with a diplomatic passport that avoided any questions being asked on arrival. But he had undergone a long interrogation somewhere in central Paris, before being driven out to his house and dumped at the gate.

Back in Oxford two months earlier, after the meal and his second glass of port Redmond had left the dining room to go to the toilet. While there, he heard a bang and loud shouts, then a burst of what sounded like muffled automatic gunfire. He locked himself in the toilet, where he waited for ten minutes.

When he emerged he bumped into a middle-aged man who he later learnt was the deputy head of the Cabal. This was to be a fortunate turn of events for Redmond. Together they discovered the four corpses in the Common Room. Geoffrey's death meant the deputy was now the new head of the Cabal. He immediately took over with remarkable coolness.

"This looks bad for you," he had said, and led Redmond to his own private rooms in College before instructing the night watchman to call the police and prevent anyone from entering the Senior Common Room. Redmond stayed overnight and was thereafter kept hidden in the new head's quarters. A week or so after the shootings, he was introduced to seven remaining Cabal members. They had quickly carried out their own inquiry, and discovered that it was the professor whom Redmond had called 'Sleepy', a longstanding member of the Cabal, who had ordered the attack. He had always believed that he himself and not Geoffrey should have been nominated deputy and then head, and far from dozing off he had been wide awake and aware of Redmond's entry into the hidden rooms.

For him the revealing of the Cabal's secrets to an outsider was the last straw. That morning he had contacted a notorious local gang leader and promised £5,000 a head for the elimination of Geoffrey and Redmond. The details were not clear but the attack had been botched, for the gunmen had shot randomly at the four professors, so missing the temporarily absent Redmond but killing the man who had ordered the attack as well as one intended target and two innocent victims.

It was a complete fiasco that required the rapid spreading of false information. Two Cabal members who were MI5 agents used the usual sources to feed the press. Redmond was a convenient scapegoat allowing the blame to be laid outside the College. They invented a story about his resentment over a conspiracy to reject his application for a College Fellowship. The disproportion of the act of revenge was put down to overheated rivalries within the narrow confines of the academic world.

Redmond was told he would be declared responsible for the massacre, held for a while, and then released under a new identity. He refused. After two months he was officially declared innocent of the shootings, and the executions were left as an unsolved mystery. He was released under oath not to inform anyone. So his story really was 'top secret', though he had no intention of respecting his oath as far as his family was concerned, for he rightly considered that he had been tricked into the visit to Oxford and that he had done nothing wrong.

During his two-month confinement he had in fact played a role in the leadership of the Cabal. The eight recognized his experience in intelligence work, and made him a sort of 'honorary member' for the duration of his stay.

He took advantage of this position to ensure that Mourad returned to Algeria, courtesy of negotiations via a Cabal member who was an MI6 agent and the promise of immunity from prosecution for the murder of Manfred Meyer in La Roche-Guyon and the death of the man who had been killed by the explosion of Kamel's BMW in Algeria. Redmond also arranged that Severina and her team would, unknown to Leila and his children, keep a close watch over their security. He paid for this surveillance via one of his Geneva bank accounts.

So he was now freed and back home, having rather fortuitously escaped assassination thanks to a call of nature. But the consequences of his having been kidnapped, indeed of everything he had experienced since he had discovered his grandfather's First World War diary, were to take months and in some instances years to work themselves out.

2001

Barbara Meyer had a plan to get revenge at last for what she regarded as her many grievances. She had been arrested for the murder of Delcia Burridge-Carnot and held for over ten months in a prison just outside Paris. She was brought to trial but the proceedings collapsed for lack of evidence. There was only one witness as to her guilt, a museum employee who had been recruited by Anastasia. The 'Catacombs Murder', as the press labelled it, had been committed in the darkest corner of the cellars beneath the Louvre and the witness had failed either to give a clear description of Barbara, or to pick her out at the identity parade. The judge dismissed the case against the accused, pronounced an open verdict, and she was released.

She did not accept that her father's fall from the tower in La Roche-Guyon was either suicide or an accident. Whilst in captivity at Redmond's house, she had heard his children discussing Leila's account of Manfred's death, for which she knew Mourad and Leila herself had been responsible. Barbara had become increasingly angry that there had never been any inquiry into the circumstances of Gottlieb Meyer's death in a British prison camp all those years ago. Furthermore, the Meyers had recovered not a single item of Suzy's various treasures, most of which had been recovered by Redmond, nor any of Hans's gold bullion, the last of which had recently fallen into Leila's lap. Quite apart from the murders of her father and her great grandfather, she believed that the Wrights, Leila and her family in Algeria had profited handsomely from what should have come to the Meyers, of whom she was now the last survivor.

Manfred's Stasi network was by now reduced to half a dozen old stalwarts who regarded it as their duty to revenge the deaths of their leader and their comrades who had been killed during a car chase on a damp lane in northern France. Barbara had gathered them together and developed a plan that she believed would settle several scores with one single attack. They had for some weeks kept a watch on the movements of Redmond and his children. They soon discovered that the Wright family were making regular trips together in a Peugeot 5008, driving on Friday evenings from Paris to La Châtaigneraie in Picardy, returning the following Sunday afternoon. An accident could easily be organized on the dangerous two-lane main road that passed through the village, all the more so as there was now no Geoffrey, 'MI6' or Cabal to trace Barbara's movements and give warning of her scheme.

Very bitter and very determined, she believed she could in one swoop eliminate Redmond, his children and Leila, before taking care of Mourad. She was preparing plans to recover at least some of the rewards the Wrights had accumulated.

*

Delcia had been the sole survivor of the Burridge-Carnot family. Since her death and that of Maurice alias Vincent, the *château* and grounds at La Châtaigneraie and the six floors of luxury flats on the Boulevard Saint-German were left without legal ownership. No-one knew quite how a judge had decided within the record time of just over twelve months that these properties were to be auctioned off in separate lots. Apparently the imposter grandfather's claim to ownership had been declared invalid and the judge decided that the thirty-year 'no sale' rule had thus lapsed. The French State and the local councils were to be the beneficiaries.

There was great excitement on the day that one of the three famous Parisian auction houses held the sale. Despite telephone bids from abroad and a host of bidders from the floor, it was revealed two days later that every item of the estate had been purchased by a young man resident in Paris.

That young man was Jordan Wright. He had persuaded his sister to file a claim on his behalf, arguing that he and Delcia had been engaged to be married. His claim was quickly declared void, a verdict that Jessica herself had warned could be the only possible outcome. He had then set about implementing a scheme of quite unscrupulous dishonesty.

After Delcia's death he had left his job at the bank and seemed to be living a hippy sort of existence. He had a string of short-term girlfriends, took to drinking and soft drugs, and then suddenly acquired quite considerable means. His bank had been one of the four in Paris to hold Redmond's money and safe deposits. He had somehow gained access to his father's holdings. By quickly transferring his acquired funds through multiple accounts at different banks throughout the globe, and keeping hold of the gems he'd recovered from the vault, he had become a multi-millionaire overnight. Redmond believed that his son had been badly affected by Delcia's death. He had agreed that Jordan could keep the stolen wealth, on condition that he used his new resources to acquire all of the property that 'Vincent' had bequeathed to his now deceased grand-daughter.

Whilst strongly disapproving of Jordan's leaving the bank and adopting a lifestyle that promised to lead to self-destruction, Redmond had thus hoped to save his son by integrating him into an ambitious family enterprise to take over La Châtaigneraie and the Saint-Germain building. Redmond had plans for both. He persuaded Adam and Jessica to get over their indignation at their brother's behaviour and agree to his own ideas.

So it was that a regular ritual began as the Wright family hoped to at last profit securely from their considerable fortune, however dubiously acquired, and to relax safe from any threats and dangers from rivals and enemies. That ritual was the regular weekend trips to supervise the renovation and refurbishing of the buildings and grounds at La Châtaigneraie.

*

"I cooperated with him to find out where you were, get you released, and to get rid of Manfred."

Leila was explaining to Redmond what had happened when Mourad had forced her into his car and driven her to La Roche-Guyon. Her 'caïd' husband had built up an extensive network and his men were at the same time tracing the movements of both Manfred Meyer and Redmond. Mourad had had the latter followed by two henchmen to London where, they thought, he was to give a lecture. They witnessed his kidnapping and were unable to carry out their own plan to 'take care of him'. At the same time Mourad knew Manfred was on the track of Rommel's gold that had been taken to France.

It was the first time Mourad and Leila had met since she'd left him. They came to an agreement, a sort of uneasy truce. But Mourad had then met a much stronger force than his own, and been obliged to accept the arrangement whereby he removed his men from Europe and retreated to North Africa for his illegal operations. He had a pact with the British, French and Algerian intelligence agencies, in return for no action being taken over the murder of Manfred and the death of the man killed by the explosion of Kamel's BMW. It was actually Redmond who had dictated the terms of this agreement.

"Of course, he's completely unreliable, and could be a danger to us, to you, at any time. He will not respect any agreement if he believes it's not in his own interests," Leila had insisted.

Redmond replied that they were not without protection, and that they would see week by week, month by month, how the situation evolved. In fact he was more worried about the questions that might be asked concerning his own recently acquired wealth. He had after all accumulated a small fortune by solving Suzy's eighty-year-old riddles, finding and keeping her wines and gems, and converting the latter into millions of francs and pounds through a dishonest and almost certainly illegal arrangement with a crooked Italian diamond merchant. He was awaiting a demand for explanations. He expected to be questioned, taxed and perhaps find himself subject to the confiscation of much of his wealth and at least some of his new possessions.

Nothing happened. No-one intervened or asked questions. There were no records other than Gino's declaration of remuneration and taxation for work that in reality had not existed. So Redmond kept his house, his Ferrari and his wines, and prepared to transfer more gems to Rome.

Gino had lost interest in his business dealings after his wife's death. For a while his heart was no longer in making more money and protecting his affairs. But Alessandra recovered quickly from her injuries and she was soon encouraging him to keep going as before. They made enquiries about Margot's champagne business but decided it would not be a going concern. Gino bought a modest champagne house in Epernay for his daughter, and was soon his old self. He agreed to continue dealing for Redmond, and Severina's security team was strengthened.

Redmond had also feared that there would be inquiries and maybe prosecutions concerning all the deaths and murders he had recounted in his computer files. Jessica said that some of the cases would inevitably be reopened since her father's account of events had presented new lines of inquiry to the police. There was an ongoing investigation into the murder of Delcia, but no new evidence had been discovered since Barbara had been released. The arrangements allowing Mourad to return to North Africa without prosecution over the two deaths he had provoked had been implemented. Of the rest, those responsible for deaths or murder had themselves died or been killed and the cases closed. Information about the killing of Suzy and then Gottlieb had been passed on to the military authorities but there was little likelihood of anything being done eighty years on.

Five Islamists had been held for questioning over the van explosion at Charles-de-Gaulle airport. They had then been arrested and were now awaiting trial for conspiracy to mount a terrorist attack.

*

Mourad's connections with the Algerian underworld had led to the discovery of rumours of more bullion, hidden in La Roche-Guyon. But with Manfred's corpse at the foot of the tower, Mourad had had to postpone his search for possible traces of 'Rommel's gold'. Leila had said nothing about what she had learnt from her husband, hoping to follow up the rumour with Redmond and his children should he come home unscathed.

The castle at La Roche-Guyon, Rommel's headquarters in 1944 and the tower where Mourad finished what Gottlieb had started

After his return they went to La Roche-Guyon. The curator of the castle museum told them that the premises had been toothcombed many times since the war. No forgotten treasure had ever been found. But one of the guides who had overheard their conversation informed them that his grandmother had worked as a maid at the *château* when Rommel was in residence. She still lived locally, just down the road if they wanted to call on her. She turned out to be very talkative, recounting her memories of the time and showing them several old photos she'd kept in a box, where Redmond spotted a faded purple-blue carbon copy of some German documents. Yes, the lady's children and grandchildren had seen them but they didn't understand German and hadn't bothered any further. She said that in 1944 she'd seen the photos and documents in Rommel's bedroom, and when she heard he had been wounded in an allied air attack and had returned to Germany, she took them as souvenirs of her time as chamber maid to a famous general. Redmond asked if he could borrow the papers and she told him he could keep them.

They turned out to be more important than he had suspected. They included a list of packages that had been sent from La Roche-Guyon to Herrlingen, Rommel's home in Germany, between January and July 1944. Along with some personal items, the list included crates of wines from the castle cellar, half a dozen paintings, and ten gold ingots. At the bottom of the last page, dated July 2nd, was the handwritten statement that "Nothing must remain in France." So there was truth in the rumours, but no valuables had been left in La Roche-Guyon. Redmond decided there was no point in pursuing 'Rommel's gold' any further.

*

Jessica had triumphed in her prosecution of the former government minister. He was found guilty and condemned to eight years in prison. But he appealed against the verdict which was thus automatically annulled. The re-trial was to start some time in 2002. Jessica's name had appeared in the papers and she had been interviewed on radio and television, a common practice in France where lawyers in high profile court cases speak regularly to the media during trials. Her sudden fame had led to two of the main political parties pressing her to stand as a candidate in the parliamentary elections scheduled for the next year. There was even talk that she might become a junior minister in the Justice Department.

Adam continued to work long hours at the Foreign Ministry, and Rebecca played a leading role in two films that were on location abroad for several months. When they were able to spend time together they lived in her big house, with Hettie and Joshua. Ruth, on the other hand, seemed to alternate between angry outbursts against almost everyone except Rebecca, and withdrawal into the life of a semi-recluse at her house in Auvers. Hettie claimed that she was "slowly going crazy".

As Adam would later discover, Redmond himself became involved in more undercover intelligence work. Although he never spoke about it, he had some kind of brief that involved identifying and authenticating stolen artworks.

2022

By now, accidents and death had taken their toll on the Wright family.

Back in 2003, Barbara Meyer had put into operation her meticulously planned attempt to provoke a road accident. She had spent a long time studying the family's movements around La Châtaigneraie. At least one weekend per month, they travelled from Paris to supervise the renovation of the estate, driving back in Adam's Peugeot 5008 between five and six o'clock on the Sunday evening. Barbara studied carefully the local road network, in which several minor roads, including the one leading to the *château*, cut across the main road linking Paris to Boulogne and Calais. She noted that once on that main road, the Peugeot regularly drove well over the permitted ninety kilometres per hour speed limit.

She also noted that at one particular crossing two miles towards Paris, visibility was poor as a slight dip in the main road obscured vision of two side roads. Although there were horizontal white lines, a 70kms speed limit and a 'minor road crossing' sign, few cars slowed to below a hundred and ten kilometres, about sixty-five miles an hour.

The plan involved a complex set-up with Barbara herself parked in a lay-by and two vehicles driven by her ex-Stasi accomplices ready to cross the main road, one on each side, when she gave the signal. She insisted on being personally in charge of the operation, as she watched on a small screen the images transmitted from a bi-plane circling above the area. Her plan required split-second timing and a main road empty for a few seconds of other vehicles, so that at her signal one or both of the Stasi cars could suddenly pull out in front of the Wrights' Peugeot and cause it to swerve violently. Two

Stasi support teams waited in fields on either side of the road, ready to ensure that the Peugeot would burst into flames and that the driver and all five passengers would remain trapped inside their vehicle.

There were no doubt easier ways to eliminate the Wright family, but Barbara took especial pleasure in arranging this scenario. She and her Stasi team held rehearsals on three Sundays, and only on the fourth Sunday after that was the main road clear enough of other vehicles for the plan to be triggered.

'a slight dip in the main road obscured vision of two side roads'

The result was dramatic, but not quite as Barbara had hoped. Her plan was misconceived in that it relied on too many simultaneous possibilities being realized with perfect timing. Rebecca was driving the Peugeot, with Adam alongside her in the front passenger seat. When the Stasi car drove across the main road from the left, Rebecca swerved but not quite enough to miss it and spin off into the field. The front right of the 5008 struck the other Stasi car and pushed it along the road. The two vehicles skidded along the tarmac together for about fifty yards, and remained encased in each other.

The outcome was multiple injuries for Rebecca and Adam, one dead Stasi man and another gravely injured, but only a broken arm for Jessica, with scratches and bruises for Redmond, Jordan and Leila.

Barbara immediately left the scene and drove north, but she was arrested a week later in Germany and eventually spent five years in prison for her role in planning and executing this scheme for revenge. Whilst Adam recovered after two months in intensive care and many weeks of convalescence, Rebecca had suffered brain damage and severe injuries to her spine. The world-famous cinema star was to spend the rest of her life in a wheelchair, unable to talk coherently and with a mind that barely coped with the simplest of notions.

La Châtaigneraie was by now what Redmond had been planning as soon as he had learnt that his second son had purchased the property. It was an orphans home, financed by the rents from the flats in the Boulevard Saint-Germain building. Much of his wealth was also now devoted to paying for the home, and to extending it to neighbouring properties that were bought up one by one.

Adam and Rebecca had married two years before the accident. They had one child, a little girl called Sonia. Rebecca had continued acting, albeit with a reduced international schedule, until her multiple injuries put an end to any meaningful activity. Adam then gave up his job and lived with her and their daughter at La Châtaigneraie, along with twenty or so orphans and their carers. There was fortunately plenty of money to ensure full-time support for Rebecca. Adam devoted himself to looking after his wife and raising their daughter, who grew up to be a carbon copy of her mother, in looks at least. In 2022 she too embarked on an acting career.

*

Jordan had died of an overdose in October 2005. He had never got over Delcia's death and for six years had been increasingly 'off the rails'. Jessica and Adam had intervened to prevent their father trying to recover what his son had stolen, but Redmond had not made peace with him at the time of his death.

Redmond had been one of a small team at the head of a secret European agency responsible for tracing looted and stolen artworks and restoring them to their rightful owners. He was in fact the head of that agency. He retired at the age of seventy in 2014. He was now bald on top and close-shaven back and sides, which made him look quite tough despite the thinner face. He was still muscular as he continued his daily sessions at the gym. He and Leila stayed in the suburban 'mansion', celebrating from time to time anniversaries at Serre, Senlis, Chantilly, Reims and St Lié.

Leila had finally divorced Mourad, who wanted to marry a Moroccan princess. He was living in semi-retirement in an oasis palace, letting two underlings control his criminal operations that were now restricted to North Africa.

Redmond and Leila were about to marry in 2015, when he began to lose weight. He became visibly very thin, then suddenly stopped eating. He talked about his future plans for his granddaughter and for the orphanage, but he knew he was dying with a bone cancer that had been discovered too late. He was found in November 2015, at the age of seventy-one, lying in the garden beside what had been Bonza's little grave. Jessica obtained permission for her father to be buried in an adjacent plot.

Leila, now fifty-six, left France the next year and returned to Bordj-Bou-Arreridj.

Jessica had won the retrial of the ex-minister. He was imprisoned for ten years, a sentence more severe than in the first instance. She had been elected to Parliament in 2012, and was still being talked of as a future Minister of Justice. But she did not stand for re-election in 2017, keeping her own barrister's practice. In June 2017 she went off to Algeria and persuaded Leila to return to the suburban home north of Paris. There they stayed together, for the mutual fascination they had felt at that first meeting in September 1999 had survived and matured over eighteen years of ups and downs in the Wright family.

*

Gino too had died, leaving Alessandra with her champagne business which she soon expanded into other wine regions, Burgundy and Tuscany at first. She then married into a 'decent, dignified high-society' French family with a Bordeaux wine estate.

The Cabal, soon reduced to a membership of five, severed all links with MI5 and MI6. The secret rooms were opened, and in 2009 the organization was dissolved and all its assets, including a small bag of rubies and diamonds, were transferred to the College.

No-one had found the Burgundy & Champagne purses that 'Vincent' had hidden too well at La Châtaigneraie. Perhaps one day some orphans or their carers will find them under a slightly loose flagstone behind the confessional in the chapel at La Châtaigneraie.

Barbara Meyer, after serving her prison sentence, lived isolated in her Berlin flat which had become something of a shrine with photos of Gottlieb, Hans, and Manfred covering the walls of the smaller bedroom.

In 2013, a metal box with little bags full of emeralds, rubies and sapphires was found at the foot of the Bossons glacier in the French Alps. They were declared to be worth three hundred thousand euros. In the absence of claims from India, in December 2021 the proceeds were shared equally between the local council of Chamonix and the mountaineer who had found them.

One day a second metal box with little bags of gems from that same 1966 crash will be recovered, as might a small hoard of gold ingots from the 1950 *Malabar Princess* air crash. With global warming year by year speeding the retreat of the glaciers, they will surely have emerged before 2030.

APPENDIX

FRENCH & OTHER FOREIGN-LANGUAGE TERMS
The list includes all French and other foreign terms not translated
into English in the text.

à l'appareil: 'speaking' (on the telephone)
A la mémoire de mon oncle Vincent : In memory of my Uncle Vincent
Allée des Soupirs: Pathway of Sighs
asperges: asparagus
au bled: in (my) home village, or town
balcon: balcony
bâtard: bastard
Bibliothèque Nationale: National Library
bienvenue: welcome
bonjour: good day (morning, afternoon)
Bonnes-Mares: literally 'good ponds'
bonsoir: good evening
Bouzy rouge: red wine from the village of Bouzy in Champagne
brasserie: a cafe specializing in beer (literally a 'brewery'), but also serving a wide range of drinks and food; some *brasseries* in Paris and the big cities are well-known prestigious establishments
brut: bone dry
burnous: long woollen coat with a hood worn by Algerian men, especially Kabyles
butin: booty
cafés 2: two coffees
caïd: the local boss of a criminal gang
canapés: cocktail appetizers on bread or toast, usually savoury
chardonnay: white grape variety grown for champagne and good white Burgundy
châtaigneraie: chestnut grove
château: castle, stately home, large country mansion; in the Bordeaux region and the South-West, a wine estate
Chez Nathalie: Nathalie's (restaurant)

concierge: caretaker (in urban blocks of flats, usually an older woman whose room is on the ground floor by the entrance and who performs a wide variety of duties and services)

consommé de volailles: clear chicken soup

Côte: ridge or cliff, often refers to a hillside with vineyards, as in...

    Côte des Blancs: a hillside with exclusively white grapes grown for champagne

    Côte d'Or : a thirty-mile escarpment south of Dijon, home to Burgundy's most celebrated vineyards; it is sub-divided into the *Côte de Nuits* to the north, based on the town of Nuits-Saint-Georges, and the *Côte de Beaune* further south

côtes d'agneau: lamb chops

coup de coeur: a sudden falling in love, 'love at first sight'

cuisine: kitchen

danger de mort: risk/danger of death

déjeuner sur l'herbe: picnic lunch

demi-sec: literally 'medium dry', in fact quite sweet

doux: sweet (wine)

et le trône était environné d'un arc-en-ciel semblable à de l'émeraude: Revelation 4:3, "and there was a rainbow round about the throne, in sight like unto an emerald"

Exode: Exodus

FLN, Front de la Libération Nationale: movement set up in 1954 to fight for Algerian independence from France

Fräulein: (German) Miss, girl or unmarried woman

Frère: Brother

gendarmerie: police station, police force (the *gendarmes* are a branch of the military, sharing police duties with the national police force, especially in small-town and rural France)

gîte: bed & breakfast

glaces vanille: vanilla ices

grand cru: literally 'great growth', the top category of French wines

Guten Tag: (German) good morning/afternoon

haricots: beans

Herr: (German) Mr.

im Keller bei dem Fräulein: (German) in the cellar at the young lady's house

inch Allah: (Arabic) God willing

interdit au public: 'forbidden to the public', staff only

Jeu de Paume: literally 'real tennis'. The Jeu de Paume is a former real tennis court which is now a museum situated in the gardens of the Louvre

La Grande Rue: High Street, Main Street

Le Grand Cerf: The Big Stag

Les Deux Magots: a famous *brasserie* in the Saint-Germain-des-Prés district of Paris (the 'magots' are two Chinese figurines from a shop which used to occupy the premises)

mezeler: (Turkish) mixed appetizer dishes

mont: mount, mountain, hill

montagne: mountain

Orangerie: literally a winter garden or glass house with orange trees; the Orangerie in the Louvre gardens has been a museum since 1927

palazzo: (Italian) an imposing and luxurious town-house

petits fours: sweet cocktail confectionaries

pied-à-terre: small house or flat kept as secondary residence for occasional or regular short stays

pierre: stone

Pierre: Peter

pinot blanc: white grape variety

pinot gris: a grape variety

pinot meunier: a grape variety

pinot noir: red skinned grape with colourless juice, grown for champagne and red burgundy

plateau (de) fromages: cheese board

pommes rissolées: roast potatoes

premier cru: first growth (wine), a category below *grand cru*

Prière d'éviter les heures des repas: Please avoid meal times

Quai d'Orsay: short-hand for the French Foreign Office; river Seine embankment where the Foreign Ministry is situated

rakı: (Turkish) aniseed-flavoured alcoholic drink, taken neat or with ice-cold water, an aperitif similar to pastis (French) and ouzo (Greek).

roche: rock

rôti (de) boeuf bien cuit: roast beef, well done

Route des Grands Crus : literally, 'Road of the Top Growths'

Rue de la République: Republic Street

Salon des Refusés: exhibition of paintings rejected by the selection

committee of the official exhibition
salon: lounge
sec: dry
soles St-Germain: sole filets cooked in butter and coated with
breadcrumbs
Stasi: common acronym for the 'Staatssicherheit', former East German State Security espionage and political police
trattoria: (Italian) a modest inexpensive restaurant
U-Bahn: (German) the Berlin underground train network
un corps de rêve: a 'dream of a body', fantastic body
Unter den Linden: (German) Under the Limetrees, a famous Berlin
avenue
Via: (Italian) street
vigneron/viticulteur: wine maker, wine grower

IMAGE ACKNOWLEDGEMENTS

COVER : istockphoto, credit neverest.

p 4 : courtesy of Laurence & Philippe Renaux,
Mareuil-Caubert.

p 61 : © RMN-Grand Palais (musée d'Orsay),
credit Hervé Lewandowski.

pp 95 & 98 : courtesy of Jean-Pierre Boureux, Reims.

p 114 : istockphoto, credit Alessandro Giamello.

p 131 : istockphoto, credit Zakaria Roubache.

p 144 : istockphoto, credit MHJ Hoek Beheer BV.

p 168 : istockphoto, credit borisb17.

p 180 : courtesy of Lesley Heming.

p 216 : wikimedia commons, credit Jean-Christophe BENOIST.

All other images are the author's, or public domain.

Printed in Great Britain
by Amazon

82647335R00133